Praise for Amanda Sun's *Ink:*

"The descriptions of life in Japan…
create a strong sense of place, and set an exotic backdrop
for this intriguing series opener by a debut author."
—*Booklist*

"The unique setting and observing how Katie learns to live in…
foreign surroundings…make this story special."
—*VOYA*

"An enjoyable peek at a world very different from America,
yet inhabited by people whose hearts are utterly familiar."
—*Publishers Weekly*

"A harrowing and suspenseful tale set against the gorgeous
backdrop of modern Japan. Romance and danger ooze like
ink off the page, each stroke the work of a master storyteller."
—**Julie Kagawa, *New York Times* bestselling author
of The Iron Fey series**

"With smart, well-drawn characters, cool mythology,
and a fast-paced plot that keeps you on your toes,
Ink is a modern day fairytale that reminds us: Sometimes
you need to get a little lost in order to find your true self."
—**Amber Benson of TV's *Buffy the Vampire Slayer* and author
of the Calliope Reaper-Jones novels**

"Amanda Sun's *Ink* is a captivating story of love, passion,
and the choices people make to keep themselves safe.
The vivid portrayal of Japan kept me completely intrigued
and immersed. A beautiful story!"
—**Jodi Meadows, author of *Incarnate* and *Asunder***

"An imaginative and totally unique debut. Japanese gods,
mysterious magics, beautiful boys, and an exotic setting.
Ink is a fresh brushstroke."
—**Zoraida Córdova, author of *The Vicious Deep*
and *The Savage Blue***

"*Ink* is astonishing. Fresh, vibrant,
and impossible to put down. Amanda Sun is now on
my must-read list. Very highly recommended."
—**Julie E. Czerneda, author of *A Turn of Light***

A Junior Library Guild selection

A Summer 2013 Children's IndieNext Pick

A Chapters Indigo Top Teen Pick for 2013

A Bookish Young Adult Book for Summer 2013

A *USA TODAY* Young Adult Book for Summer 2013

Books by Amanda Sun

The Paper Gods series
(in reading order):

SHADOW (eNovella)
INK
RAIN

AMANDA SUN

RAIN

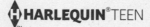

HARLEQUIN®TEEN

Recycling programs
for this product may
not exist in your area.

ISBN-13: 978-0-373-21111-1

RAIN

Printed in U.S.A.

HARLEQUIN®TEEN
www.HarlequinTEEN.com

For Mum and Dad, who always believed in me

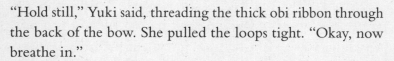

1

"Hold still," Yuki said, threading the thick obi ribbon through the back of the bow. She pulled the loops tight. "Okay, now breathe in."

I took a deep breath as Yuki shifted the bow to the center of my back, but didn't look up from my phone.

"How's that?"

No messages in my inbox. "Looks great."

"You didn't even look."

"Mmm-hmm." Yuki snatched the *keitai* out of my hands. "Hey!"

"Ano ne," she said, an expression which meant we needed to talk. That didn't surprise me. "You're starting to look obsessed. Yuu will call you; I'm sure of it. You don't want to be the needy girlfriend, right?"

I didn't say anything. How could I? Yuki didn't know that not being able to get ahold of Tomohiro could mean the Yakuza had him, or the Kami had kidnapped him, or that Tomo had drowned in an ocean of his own sketching. The Kami, descendants of the Shinto goddess Amaterasu, could make ink come alive on the page, although the power came with its own curse—a plague of nightmares and threats, scars carved by the claws and talons of their own feral drawings.

It had been two weeks since I'd almost left Japan, since the revelation that Tomo was one of the most dangerous Kami alive. Takahashi Jun, Tomo's kendo rival and the leader of the Kami in Shizuoka, said he hadn't seen anyone as powerful in a long time and wanted him as a weapon to help destroy the Yakuza. He also said that somehow, I was making it worse. I was making the ink in the sketches do strange and deadly things. Tomo lost control when I was around, his eyes vacant and his nightmares worse.

How? I couldn't be a Kami. I was blond…and more importantly, not Japanese. But whether Jun was right or not, after watching Tomo's sketched gun go off and put his best friend, Ishikawa, in the hospital, I knew the ink wasn't something to play around with.

It could've been Tomo in the hospital.

It could've been me.

Yuki grinned and sidestepped, pulling the sleeves of my *yukata* straight. "Now look," she commanded.

I looked.

The summer kimono made me look elegant, the soft yellow fabric draped around me like an origami dress. Pink cherry blossoms floated down the woven material, which Yuki had complemented by lending me her pink obi belt to tie around my waist.

"Dou?"

"It's beautiful," I said. "Thank you."

She grinned, smoothing her soft blue *yukata* with her hands. "Yuu is a jerk for not calling," she said. "But let's forget about that. It's Abekawa Hanabi festival, and you're still here with us. So let's go celebrate!"

Was he being a jerk? I hadn't been able to get ahold of him since deciding to stay. It didn't make sense, unless he was in trouble. Or avoiding me, in which case he'd clearly learned nothing from the first attempt to scare me away and I would pound him into tomorrow.

But it didn't matter if he was avoiding me. Sooner or later, I'd have to get in touch with him. Because as much as I'd wanted to stay in Japan to be with him, the real reason was that I wanted control of my life. I was connected to the ink, and I belonged here. If Jun was right, Tomohiro was a ticking time bomb, and I was the only one who could defuse him.

It was hard to believe Jun was a Kami, too, one of the many secret descendants of the goddess Amaterasu. Most weren't powerful enough to bring their sketches to life off the page, but Jun and Tomo could. I remembered how cold Jun's eyes had been as he'd talked about using Tomohiro as a weapon to wage war on the Yakuza, the Japanese gangsters who'd tried to force Tomo into their ranks. Jun had wanted Tomo to kill the Yakuza boss, Hanchi, and had talked about ruling the country the way the ancient *kami* once had. Did he really mean all that? He'd seemed so normal before—charming even—when we'd walked to school together. And he'd saved us from the Yakuza with his sketched army of snakes. Sometimes it was hard to know what lay beneath the surface of someone you thought you knew.

Which I guess was the case with Tomohiro, too.

My aunt Diane entered my room, carrying a tray of glasses filled with cold black-bean tea. The ice clinked against the sides as she set them down. A pink spray of flowers unfurled in a corner of the tray.

"Don't you girls look beautiful?" she said. "Katie, here. I picked this up for you on my way home." She lifted the spray of pink flowers off the tray, the little plastic buds swaying back and forth on pink strings. She tucked it into the twist of blond hair Yuki had helped me pin into place.

"Kawaii," Yuki grinned. "You look so cute!" I turned a little red. They were fussing too much.

"You, too," I said, trying to get the focus off me. I was the wrong shape for the *yukata*—too tall, too blonde, too awkward. Yuki looked stunning in hers. "We should get going."

"You should," Diane said. "I think Tanaka's starting to sweat a little out there."

Yuki took a gulp of tea and slid the door to my room open to find Tanaka waiting in shorts and a T-shirt.

"You guys are taking forever," he said. "Can we go now?"

"Let's go," I said, the long yellow sleeves tangling around my wrists as I slipped on flip-flops—no chance of finding *geta* sandals for my American-size feet—and shoved my phone into a drawstring bag.

"You look cute," Tanaka said.

"So do you," Yuki said, and she stuck her tongue out at him while he turned red. She grabbed my hand and we headed out the door.

"Itterasshai!" Diane called after us.

Go and come back safely.

The only word Tomo had written in the farewell note he'd pressed into my hands, the one with the moving ink rose that had sent me tripping over my own feet to catch Diane at the Narita Express platform before she left the airport. The goodbye that had made me stay in Japan.

Tanaka pushed the button for the elevator.

Jun had said we didn't know what Tomohiro was capable of. *We'll find out together,* Tomo had answered.

It didn't make sense. Why would he push me away again now, when I was so determined to help?

The light was fading outside as we stepped into the heat. It was the last week of summer holidays, before school started for the second semester, and the hot weather wasn't going to give up easily. We clattered down the street in our *geta* and flip-flops, hopping onto the local train for Abekawa Station.

"We're gonna be late," whined Tanaka.

"It's fine," Yuki said. "We'll still make good time for the fireworks."

The train lurched around the corner and I tried not to press into Tanaka's side.

"If the *takoyaki*'s all gone by the time we get there, I'll blame you."

"How would that even happen?" I said. "They won't run out."

"Right?" Yuki agreed. "Tan-kun, you and your stomach."

By the time the train pulled into Abekawa the sun had blinked off the horizon. We stumbled through the musty train air toward the music and sounds of crowds.

It felt like all of Shizuoka was here, the sidewalks packed with festivalgoers while dancers in *happi* coats paraded down the street. Lanterns swung from floats and street signs glowed, and over everything we could hear about three different songs competing for attention above the crowded roads. It was a little claustrophobic, sure, but filled with life.

"What should we do first?" Yuki shouted, but I could barely hear her. She grabbed my hand and we pressed through the thick crowd toward a *takoyaki* stand. Tanaka rubbed his hands together as the vendor doused the battered balls of octopus meat with mayonnaise.

"Anything's fine with me," I said. Translation: no idea.

"I'm good, too, now that I have my *takoyaki*," Tanaka said. "Want one?" The bonito flakes on the hot batter shriveled as if they were alive.

"Um, maybe later."

Yuki grabbed the spare toothpick from Tanaka's container and stabbed a *takoyaki*, taking a chewy bite. "We should try to get a good spot for fireworks soon, though," she said through the mouthful. "The bridge over Abe River would be best."

"We have lots of time, right?" She'd mentioned them about five times on the train, too. "What's the big deal about the fireworks?" I mean, I loved them as much as anyone, but now who was the one obsessing?

Yuki pulled me over, whispering in my ear. Her breath was hot and smelled of the fishy batter.

"Because," she breathed, "if you watch the fireworks with someone special, you're destined to be with them forever."

"Oh." Jeez, I could be so stupid. So this was some big scheme for her and Tanaka. "Do you want space or something?"

"No, no!" She waved her hand frantically. "Not like that. Let's stick together, okay?"

"Sure," I said. Like she'd tell me if that was the plan anyway. One thing I'd learned living in Japan was that sometimes it was hard to get a straightforward answer out of someone. They found it too direct, something that could make others feel uncomfortable. It was something I was trying to work on, another in my list of gazillions of daily cultural mistakes.

We rounded the corner to two rows of brightly lit tents.

All the thick, fatty smells of festival foods filled the air. Fried chicken, fried squid, steaming sweet-potato fries, roasted corn, strawberry and melon *kakigori* ice. My stomach rumbled and I moved forward, heading for the baked sweet potatoes. I handed over the yen and pocketed the change. Then I pulled back the aluminum foil to take a bite, the steam flooding my mouth. Beside me, kids dipped red plastic ladles into a water table while an old motor whirred little plastic toys round and round. The toys bobbed in and out of the ladles while the kids shrieked with excitement.

A flash of color caught my eye, and I turned. I strained to hear a sound above the music and chatter of the crowd, but I could hear it—faintly. The tinkle of the colorful *furin,* the delicate glass wind chimes that Tomohiro had sketched into the tree in Toro Iseki.

Across from me, the *furin* booth glowed with electric light, catching on the gleaming chimes as they twirled in the night breeze.

"Hello," the vendor greeted me in English, but it barely registered as I stepped into the tent. Almost a hundred chimes hung suspended around me in a rainbow of glittering colors, spinning above my head in neat rows. Tomo's had been black-and-white, like all his sketches, but they'd held the same magic, the same chorus that my ears could never forget. These sounded happier, though—his had been melancholy, the tones haunting and ominous, a sort of beautiful discord.

"You like the *furin?*" the vendor smiled. He had a kind, worn face and the early beginnings of a gray beard.

"They're beautiful."

"The sound of summer, *ne?* The sound of possibility."

I reached out, cradling a glass *furin* in my hand. Possibility.

"Yuki-chan, look—" I turned.

I'd lost her to the crowd.

Panic started to rise up in my throat. She wasn't one to abandon me on purpose. Even if she did want alone time with Tanaka, I knew she wouldn't leave me stranded.

It wasn't like I couldn't get home safely. Taking trains around Shizuoka wasn't a big deal for me anymore. Festivals just weren't as fun by yourself, and the loneliness stung a little. I clutched my fingers tighter around the *furin*.

"You looking for someone?" the man asked.

"I'm okay," I said, releasing the *furin* and stepping back into the darkness between the bright tents. I pulled out my *keitai*, ready to call Yuki, and then stopped with my finger on the button. Why was I so worried? I'd been in Japan long enough that being lost in a crowd didn't have to be a big deal. I could communicate and get around. Anyway, Yuki had wanted time alone with Tanaka, right? She'd always done so much for me, helping me with my Japanese and smoothing out my cultural blunders. I should do something for her, even something little like this.

I slipped my phone back into my bag and pulled the drawstring tight. I watched some plastic toys whir around the water table a little longer before I strolled down the row of tents.

I stared at the different festival games interspersed with food stalls. Eel scooping, pet bugs, *yoyo tsuri* balloons on strings floating in tiny blow-up kiddie pools. I finished my sweet potato, balling up the aluminum with a satisfying crunch. In the next tent a pool of goldfish darted around, slipping out of the way of the paper paddles dipped into the water to catch them. I watched the fish swim for a minute, their scales shining under the hot buzzing lamps of the tent. The paper paddles broke and kids shouted in dismay, while the vendor gave a good-natured laugh.

I shuffled closer to the tent as the group of kids left, a teen couple the only ones left trying to catch a fish. The girl trailed a goldfish slowly with the paddle, her movements deliberate and cautious, her giggle rising when the fish caught on and sped away. She crouched on the ground beside the pool, paddle in one hand and bowl in the other, her red-and-gold *yukata* crinkling around her *geta* sandals.

And then I realized I knew this girl.

The pregnant bump of her stomach under the light cotton of the *yukata*.

And the boy beside her. Tomohiro.

Not kidnapped. Not falling apart. Not dead.

Scooping goldfish with Shiori.

I stepped back. He hadn't noticed me yet, the two of them laughing as Shiori tried to maneuver another fish into her bowl.

I knew he was here with Shiori as a friend, supporting her. He wouldn't give up on us that fast, like we didn't matter at all. Maybe that was the attitude he portrayed at school, but I knew better. After a sketching accident had left his elementary-school friend Koji almost blind, he'd decided to keep his distance from everyone, except his childhood friend Shiori, and now me. Shiori had been abandoned to the cruel bullying that came with being pregnant at her prestigious school. Tomo knew what it was like to be alone. That's all this was.

But it still bothered me. I had to admit they made a cute pair. Seeing the closeness between them, seeing Tomohiro smile at another girl like that…I felt stupid suddenly, tall and ugly and awkward in my borrowed *yukata*.

Maybe Tomohiro wasn't as dangerous as Jun had led me to believe. He seemed normal enough squatting beside Shiori, his eyes following the goldfish, that smile on his face. He wore jeans and a dark T-shirt, the usual thick wristband around his right wrist. I could still imagine the ink stains streaking up his arms, the scars hidden on the inside curve of his skin, but in the evening darkness there was no trace of what had happened. He looked so...normal.

Maybe staying in Japan had been the wrong choice. What if staying away from Tomo really did give him the ability to rein in his powers? Maybe the Kami didn't need me—maybe he didn't need me.

"*Yatta!*" Shiori shouted. "I did it!" The fish had slipped from her paddle into the bowl. The vendor laughed and reached for a plastic bag to fill with water.

"*Yatta ne,*" Tomohiro grinned, reaching his fingers into the bowl to chase the fish.

I stepped back and my flip-flop scraped against the street. Tomohiro and Shiori looked up.

I stared at Tomohiro's dark eyes. They were unreadable, the smile slipping from his face as he stared back. They weren't cold like Jun's had been, not at all. They were warm, surprised, deep. I couldn't look away, like prey. I felt ridiculous.

Shiori stood up, a hand on her belly. "It couldn't be...Katie-chan? Is that right?" Tomohiro stayed crouched on the ground, unable to move.

I opened my mouth, but no sound came out. I didn't want her using *chan* with me, labeling me a friend. It was a closeness that felt stifling, that only made me aware I didn't really belong. Tomo had fallen seamlessly back into his life with her, as if I'd never existed.

"I thought you returned to America?" Shiori said.

"Canada," I said. My throat felt sticky and dry.

"Hai!" the vendor said, thrusting the newly bagged gold-fish at Shiori.

"Thank you," she smiled, reaching for the bag.

"Katie," Tomohiro said, his voice deep and beautiful and just how I'd waited to hear it. Everything shattered.

"Sorry," I whispered before turning to walk away. I pressed my way through the thick crowd, desperate to get away. I knew I was being stupid. I knew there was nothing between him and Shiori. But it stung, and I had to get away from them.

Behind me, even in the midst of all the festival noise, I was sure I heard Tomohiro call my name, but I kept walking. I wanted to see him, but not like this. I thought he'd been los-ing his mind to the ink—why did he seem just fine?

I should've left Japan after all. This was all a mistake.

I pushed past the *takoyaki* stand and the rows of roasted corn, turning down a darker street where some shrine-goers rang a bell and carried lanterns. I wove past them toward the big Abe River Bridge. It was late, probably about time for the fireworks. If I could just find Yuki and Tanaka, maybe I would be okay.

"Katie!"

I kept walking, but I could hear his footsteps, his black shoes clicking as he ran toward me. Suddenly his warm fin-gers wrapped around my wrist.

"Matte!" he said. *Wait,* like his ex-girlfriend Myu had said to him in the *genkan* when I'd first seen him.

I stood for a moment, staring at the swaying lanterns as the parade walked past. He held my wrist gently, and I knew I could shrug him away if I wanted to.

"Why?" he panted. "Why are you here? In Japan?"

"I called you," I said, but my voice wavered. I wanted to

be stronger—I did—but after two weeks of worrying, having him standing here unharmed was more than I could handle. "You've had your *keitai* off for two weeks! I tried calling the house but it never cut to voice mail. I sent you a text." Okay, more than one. "I even thought about visiting Ishikawa in the hospital to find out where you were, but I didn't want to get him involved in case…in case there was trouble. I thought you were taken by the Yakuza or the Kami or something!" I left out that I'd biked to his house, but chickened out about ringing the bell when I'd seen his dad's car parked outside. If Tomo was missing, he'd have reported it, right? I mean, it would've been on the news and everything.

"I didn't know you were here," he said. He ran a hand through his hair, the wristband snagging on the strands, pulling his bangs into little copper loops that sprung back into his eyes. *"Che!"* he swore. "You're worrying if I'm okay and I'm scooping goldfish at a festival. If I'd known…"

"I tried!"

"I was getting weird calls from the Yakuza. Threats to stay quiet about what happened to Sato. I barely deleted one on the home phone before Tousan heard it. My dad would've made me go to the police, so I turned off the voice mail and my *keitai*."

"Maybe you *should* go to the police," I said. I hadn't been far off the mark after all. The picture looked tranquil on the surface, but the tendrils of darkness spread beneath it. Nothing was normal after all—I'd been right.

"You know I can't," he said, his eyes searching mine. "They stopped last week, but then the Kami calls started. I wanted to phone you, to know you made it safely to Canada, but…I was scared they'd trace the call somehow. And now you're here."

"I decided to stay," I said. "I couldn't do it—I couldn't get on the plane."

Tomo's eyes turned dark. He crouched and buried his head in his hands, his fingers splaying through his hair.

"*Kuso!* What if something happens to you?"

I took a deep breath. "It's not your choice," I said as gently as I could. "I need to stay. I influence the ink, remember? There's got to be a way we can get this under control. Maybe somehow I can make it better instead of worse."

"What are you going to do if the Yakuza get involved again? Or the Kami?"

"Look, I thought about it, okay? But there are people I care about here, Tomo. Diane, Yuki…and you. Do you think I'll be safe even on the other side of the world if things blow up here? And how can I just live a normal life over there knowing the Yakuza and Kami are trying to recruit you? It's my choice."

"And what if that choice is selfish?" he said.

My eyes widened—that was a low blow. "You're calling me selfish for wanting to stay in Japan?"

He hesitated, staring at the procession of lanterns down the cross street. A shrill flute played a haunting melody in a minor key, some of the notes lost in the noise of the festival as it carried on without us.

"Not you," he said in a quiet voice. "Me. Choosing to be with you, no matter the consequences. What choice do I have? I'm a Kami. Anything I choose will hurt others. I have no choices."

This wasn't going at all how I'd envisioned. "That's not true," I said, my voice wavering. I was *not* going to cry in front of him, but already my sight was starting to blur. I held on with everything I could. "*Faito,* remember? Fight. You don't have to do this alone, Tomo."

He heard the tremble in my voice. He rose slowly to his feet, his eyes deep and lovely and melting everything else away.

"Katie-chan," he whispered. I stood with my arms folded, biting my lip to keep the tears from welling over.

And then his arms were around me, my face buried in the warmth of his shoulder. His heart beat rapidly under my cheek, his breath labored as he clung to me as if in a storm.

"*Hontou ka?*" he said. "You're really here?"

"I'm here," I whispered.

He stepped back, tilting my face up to his, and kissed me as though he thought I might break or disappear. Like I was a ghost, a dream. I closed my eyes, drifting on the moment. His warmth, his touch, the smell of his vanilla hair gel. Everything the same as I'd remembered.

"Tomo-kun!" shouted Shiori, and the moment ended. We stepped back as she walked toward us, her new goldfish swimming round and round the plastic bag as it swayed in her hand. I didn't like to hear her call him Tomo-kun, especially knowing Myu had never been allowed to call him such a close name. He'd held her at a distance and made her call him by his last name, Yuu. Was Shiori really only a friend?

But that's stupid of me, right?

"Shiori," Tomohiro said. "Katie's staying in Japan."

She slowed, a puzzled frown curling onto her lips. The frown vanished as soon as I noticed it, but I was sure it had been there. "You're not going back?" She smiled. "I'm glad! I was so sad to not even meet you after we talked on the phone that time." She squeezed my hand, and my insecurity evaporated. *She really means it,* I thought. *She is really clueless about the awkwardness between us.*

"You two talked on the phone?" Tomohiro asked.

"The time you decided to be an idiot," she laughed. Shiori pointed her finger at him, poking him in the chest. I didn't like it, but I pushed the feeling down. It was petty and dumb.

"Oi," he stuttered, annoyed.

Shiori smiled. "Katie, are you hungry? We could get some *yakitori* before the fireworks start."

"Oh, um…"

"Fried chicken," she said in English. "It's fried chicken." As if that's what had made me stumble over my words.

"Shiori," Tomohiro said. The seriousness of his voice made me shiver a little.

"Hmm, Tomo-kun?"

"She knows what *yakitori* is. And I've just discovered my girlfriend is staying in Shizuoka, permanently. Do you think maybe we could…you know, meet up in a bit?" The words hit me like a wall. Did he actually just ask that?

"Oh…oh, no problem. I'll get something to eat and meet you after, okay?"

"Are you sure?" Tomo said. "I just…" Shiori tried to smile and nod, but I could see the hurt on her face.

"Shiori," I said, reaching my hand out. "It's fine. You can stay with us."

She waved it away and shook her head. "No, no, it's okay." Her voice was way too cheerful. There was no way it was okay. "I'll catch up in a bit. This baby is always hungry." She circled her stomach with her fingers, smiling too widely. Then she turned, and she was gone.

Living in Japan meant reading between the lines, in this

case even more than when Yuki wanted time with Tanaka. No one ever said what they meant. I wasn't sure how mad Shiori was, but she definitely wasn't happy.

Tomo reached for my shoulders, wrapping his arms around them from behind, but I sidestepped his embrace.

"That was totally rude, Tomo."

"I know," he said. "I know. It was too much. I'll make it up to her. But I just want to be with you right now. I *need* to be with you." He leaned in, and this kiss wasn't fragile at all. His lips pressed against mine sent my heart racing and heat prickling up my arms. He pulled back, his eyes gleaming. "You look cute in that *yukata*."

I felt my cheeks go hot. "It's Yuki's."

"I didn't want to come here with Shiori, Katie. She showed up at my house the same time my dad came back from Kyoto. He pretty much ordered me to take her."

"Please, like you wouldn't have taken her anyway." He would've, too. He was that kind of friend. But I was glad he wanted to explain. Things were the same between us, and Shiori hadn't replaced me. "It's not like you looked bored catching goldfish," I joked.

He grinned, the happiness on his face so rare that I was flooded with the desire to always make him smile like that. "No one grows out of festivals."

"So you're childish, is what you're saying."

"*Oi*," he protested, but his eyes lit up with amusement. "Come on." He squeezed my hand. "Fireworks start soon, and I know a great spot." He took off running and dragged me along for a couple paces until my feet started working. I let him pull me around the side streets, Tomo laughing when we almost crashed into some serious-looking lantern carriers on their way to the shrine. It was a nice change—

running, but not for our lives. I hoped the Yakuza had given up if they'd stopped calling Tomo. I hoped things could be normal for us someday.

We rounded another corner, where a cast-iron bridge loomed over the Abe River. There wasn't much in the way of a river—even in the darkness I could see the large banks of gravel with pockets of water where it had once run deeply. The early moonlight gleamed off the pools like a trail of pale white lanterns. Tomohiro pushed his way through the crowds near the metal stairs down to the rocky beach and grabbed a spot against the railing.

"Well?"

"Beautiful," I breathed, looking out at the kaleidoscope of lights glinting around us. Lanterns in a rainbow of colors hung from the railings and rooftops, and the opposite shore gleamed with matching strands of lights. On the gravel banks, groups of kids lit small fireworks that sparked and fizzed with golden hues. The humidity of the air and the close-pressing crowds weren't so bad here by the freshness of the river—police had been stationed along the street to make sure things stayed orderly, though I doubted it would be a problem. And the sky was wrapped in clouds, waiting for the fireworks to light the darkness above us.

"Too muddy on the beach, but you'll get a great view up here. Do you want a drink?"

"I'm okay." I could just drink in the feeling of being there with him.

"You sure? There's a vending machine over there. Iced coffee? Milk tea? Melon soda?" With each suggestion he pressed his lips closer and closer to my neck until I laughed nervously.

"Okay, okay," I relented. "Milk tea."

"Got it." And then he was gone, and the humid air felt cooler.

I looked out at the lights across the river as I listened to the quiet lapping of water, nearly drowned out by the crowds. Everyone was chatting and laughing, waiting for the fireworks to start. I hoped Yuki and Tanaka had managed to get a good spot, too, and Shiori—she'd made me feel awkward, but I hadn't wished that on her. Watching the fireworks alone, feeling forgotten by the only friend she had. I know he hadn't really meant it. It wasn't even about her—it was about us. But that was selfish. Maybe it wasn't too late. Tomo could call her and—

"Katie?"

My name, deep and velvet on a familiar voice, except it wasn't Tomo's.

I clasped my hands tightly around the railing, clinging to the cool metal as I turned my head slowly. Black T-shirt, black jeans—he almost faded into the darkness. Blue lantern light glinted on his silver earring as he moved forward.

"Katie," he said again.

My whole body seized up with fear. I stepped backward, pressing against the railing. "Jun," I whispered. The Kami had found us. I looked up for Tomo, but didn't see him in the crowd. One of the policemen stood nearby. Maybe I should— But I couldn't, right? They couldn't know about the Kami. My mind reeled.

"It's okay," Jun said, lifting a hand to calm me. "I'm not going to hurt you, remember?" And then I saw his other hand, wrapped in a ghostly pale cast at his side—his broken wrist, the one Tomohiro had shattered with the ink *shinai*. I stared at it, trying to figure out if I should run. "I'm on your side," he said.

"Look, I don't want to be friends with you," I said. "I don't want anything to do with your little group."

He took a deep breath. "You're right. I didn't mean for everything to happen like that. When you called me from the truck, I wasn't sure what kind of showdown we'd have with the Yakuza. I just called a few friends in case we needed the help. I only wanted to be prepared, not to frighten you."

That gave me pause. I'd been so wrapped up in his weird Kami cult that I'd forgotten how he'd saved Tomo and me. That without his help, we might have been—

One of the blond streaks in his hair fell forward and swung against his cheek. He lifted his good hand to tuck the highlight behind his ear. The motion brought back the memory of him lifting the cherry-blossom petal from my hair. And then the way he'd protected me from Ishikawa on the bridge to Sunpu Park. I felt so confused. Jun was the enemy—right?

"I'm your friend," he said, as though he'd plucked the thought from my mind. I shivered—he could read me too well.

"Then don't stalk me," I said. "Stay away and give me space."

"Katie," he said, "I just want to help. You know as well as I do that Yuu is dangerous. But I'm not here looking for you, if that's what you mean. You make that choice—if you want help, I'm there."

"So why are you here?" I said. "Out of all the places in Shizuoka, why are you right here?"

Silence, and then he smiled.

"Because this is the best place to see the fireworks."

Oh.

"Katie?" Tomo arrived from the other side of the road, a

can of milk tea in each hand. When he saw Jun, his eyes narrowed. "Takahashi."

"Yuu," Jun grinned, his eyes gleaming. He lifted his arm so we could see his bandaged wrist clearly. "Want to sign my cast?"

Tomohiro pressed the milk tea into my hands, his eyes never leaving Jun. "If you don't get out of here, I'll give you another to match."

In the corner of my eye, I saw the policeman flinch. He'd heard Tomo, too, and had turned his attention to us. I had to get them to stop before things got worse.

Jun dropped his hands to his sides. "I'm just here to watch the fireworks, Yuu. I can go somewhere else if you want."

Tomo took a step toward him, his eyes gleaming. "Yeah. You can go to hell."

The policeman straightened, his fingers pressed against his radio as he listened. Things were escalating, and I felt powerless to stop it. So much for controlling my link to the Kami. I couldn't even handle two idiot guys tripped out on testosterone.

"Tomo—" I warned, moving toward him.

"No, it's okay," Jun said. "I'll leave."

And then *boom!*

I jumped a mile, terrified. Did Jun shoot him? Did the cop?

Another boom, and the sky flooded with light.

The fireworks. I breathed out shakily.

We all stared into the sky, the fight momentarily dropped, as bursts of color spread across the city. The crowd around us swelled, pressing the three of us close together against the railings. I became the barrier between Tomo and Jun, and it was not comfortable. Not at all.

And then I remembered Yuki's words, that whoever I watched the fireworks with would be there for me forever.

Could I really trust Jun? Even Tomohiro was unpredictable. He'd abandoned Shiori tonight. What if he did that to me—again? Who was really telling the truth here? I needed a better hand of cards to compete. I had to learn what it really meant to have ink trapped inside me, to be connected to the Kami.

Another burst of sound in the sky, but no color, just a brief oily shimmer as it splayed across the sky. And then suddenly everyone was screaming and scattering across the road.

Ink descended like a dark rain, warm as the drops splattered down my face and stained the sleeves of my *yukata*.

Another firework burst, all ink instead of color, raining down on the crowd with a faint sheen. The cop had forgotten us now, pressing his radio to his ear as he called for backup to get the area under control. A woman ran past, covering her head with her hands. She bumped me into the railing and I fell forward. I dropped the milk tea, trying to grab at the railing before I fell headfirst into the sharp gravel below. And then two sets of strong hands grabbed me, pulling me back.

Tomo. And Jun. Saving me together.

"Let's get out of here," Tomohiro shouted. I nodded and he grabbed my wrist, pushing his way through the crowd. I turned to look at Jun, who stood silently watching me leave, the ink dripping down his cast, running down his skin in trails of black. When I looked back again he was gone, lost in the frantic swarm of people.

I wound through the crowd, staying close to Tomo. "Was it you?" I shouted, but he didn't answer. I couldn't have heard him over the screams anyway. The inky rain splashed down as we ran for the train station, as we were soaked by the very truth of it.

Nothing was normal, and I'd known it, deep down. It wasn't something I could run from. The ink hadn't forgotten me.

My fate was raining down from the sky.

2

We burst into the train station and pushed our way along the platform, stopping near the lines for Shin-shizuoka Station. The travelers stared at us as we stood there drenched in ink, but their eyes fell from us as more and more ink-stained festival-goers flooded the station. It was already blaring on the news from the televisions perched above the platforms. They were calling it some sort of prank.

I wish.

Tomohiro swore under his breath and flipped his *keitai* open to turn it on.

"You need a new phone," I said, trying to keep things light. "If you had one with apps, you'd be too addicted to turn it off for two weeks." As the phone logged in, the several text messages I'd sent him all pinged in at the same time. I could feel my cheeks warm at the sound.

"I know," he said, pushing the buttons to scroll through them. "I'm an idiot. Turning off my phone doesn't ward off the Yakuza. But it's not like I knew you were going to stay in

Shizuoka. I'm going to text Shiori and make sure she's okay."
He punched a few more buttons and sent the note.

"I told you not to desert her," I said, and then I remem-
bered I hadn't come to the festival alone, either. "Oh crap.
Yuki and Tanaka!" I pulled out my phone and started texting
Yuki. This time Tomo raised an eyebrow at me and smirked.

"Shut up," I fumed, my face burning.

He answered me in a slow, singsong voice, emphasizing
every syllable. *"Na-ni-mo ha-na-shi-ne-zo."* Translation: *I didn't
say anything,* in tough-boy speak.

I smiled and smacked his arm, and a glob of ink fell from
his shirt to the ground. We stopped smiling.

Our phones chimed with replies about the same time.

"Shiori's fine," Tomo said. "She was under a tent when it
happened, and she's heading to the station now. She said to
go ahead."

"You sure?" I said. "We should wait."

"That's what I just wrote back. And…" *Ding.* "She insists.
And Watabe-san?"

The sound of Yuki's last name startled me a little bit. I kept
forgetting Yuki and Tomo didn't know each other very well,
so of course he'd refer to her more formally. "With Tanaka," I
said. "And they're fine. Drenched in ink, but fine. You know,
Shiori's probably embarrassed about how you brushed her off."

"I just wanted time with you, Katie, not to hurt her. I think
she'll understand."

"And if it comes back to haunt you?"

"It's worth it," he said. And my pulse drummed in my ears,
even though I didn't think I should be flattered by that. It always had to be complicated with him.

He headed toward the marked lines on the train platform
and I followed. The passengers around us spoke in quick, pan-

icked murmurs. They had no idea what sort of prank they'd just witnessed, but we did. We knew it wasn't a prank at all.

"Was it you?" I asked again, quietly, as we boarded the train.

"I don't think so. Maybe it was Takahashi. But who knows anymore? The ink does what it wants."

I leaned against the wall by the far doors of the train car. I couldn't exactly sit in the dripping *yukata*. The ink had stained all the embroidered cherry petals black.

"It's totally ruined," I said. "I hope Yuki won't be mad."

"It's not your fault. Well, it might be," he added with a grin.

"Not funny."

"Warui," he apologized, but he didn't wipe the grin off his face. He reached into his pocket and pulled out a blue handkerchief with a cute cartoon elephant on it. He gently wiped the ink off my face with it before pressing it into my hands. The elephant's adorable smile stared up at me.

Tomohiro, the kendo star of Suntaba School, the unreachable tough guy who sparked rumors and pretended to be bad-ass, carried around this adorable cartoon-elephant hanky. I couldn't help smiling a little as I mopped at the ink dripping down my arms. Poor Mr. Elephant turned pitch-black as the ink soaked into his smiling face.

The train car flooded with people, but more festivalgoers kept boarding, trying to escape the inky rain. We couldn't possibly all fit, could we? It was like a nightmare rush hour at Tokyo Station, the kind that needed professional people pushers to close the doors. The flustered crowd swelled around us, elbows and shoulders prodding into me, squishing me until I felt a claustrophobic panic attack coming on. It reminded me of Mom's funeral, the heat and sweat of all the bodies circling around me, too close.

"Here," Tomo said, pressing his hands against the wall on either side of me. The crowd continued to push toward us, but Tomohiro took the brunt of it, forced closer and closer toward me.

"Thanks," I said. He nodded once, bracing himself against the umbrellas and bags that jabbed into his arms and legs. We were pressed together like sardines; his breath was warm against my neck, and I could see the ribbons of badly healed scars trailing up his right arm. The biggest, where the painting of the kanji for *sword* had sliced him in elementary school, was mostly hidden under his soft wristband, but the edges of the scar trailed toward his palm and up his arm.

He hunched over me, trying not to press his body against mine, trying to give me some kind of modest space. This was the kind of guy he was, I reminded myself. Not the one who could lurk in dark alleys and call up people-eating dragons just by sketching them on paper.

But that was him, too.

The buzz of worried conversation hummed through the train car. No one would hear us, I thought. We were pressed so close together anyway.

"It was a warning, wasn't it?" I whispered, hoping everyone else would just think I was the foreigner who didn't really understand the Japanese she was using. "Those ink fireworks."

"A warning? Since when have there been warnings?"

"I don't know, it just feels like it. It's like when my doodles came at me that time. Or when the picture of Shiori looked at me." Like they were letting me know that they *saw* me, that they wanted to reach me.

"The doodles were an attack, not a warning," Tomo said. "And are you sure the message wasn't meant for me?"

"It knows I stayed in Japan. It's not going to stop, Tomo."

"You mean *I'm* not going to stop."

"Don't say that. It's creepy."

"Well, you talk about the ink like it has a life of its own." He looked around to make sure no one was listening, and lowered his face only a few inches from mine. "It's me, Katie. I'm the Kami. I'm the one drawing the pictures, not the other way around."

"Right, but the ink in you has its own agenda. If we can figure it out—if we can figure out how I fit into all this—we can stop it."

Tomo's voice was breathy and dark. "I think there's only one way to stop me."

I shivered.

The ink dripped off Tomohiro's bangs and curved down his cheeks. I reached up with the elephant towel and dabbed his face. *"Arigatou,"* he said quietly, and I wanted to kiss him right there on the train, to tell him everything would be okay.

"What about the other Kami?" The *k* came out so loudly. We shouldn't be talking on the train; it wasn't safe. I pressed my lips right to his ear. "What if one of them suddenly loses control? Although you're the only one I've seen that's so powerful, except for J—" *Oops.* "Um, I mean…"

If he was hurt by my comment, he hid it really well. "It's okay. Except for Takahashi. He's strong. I know it."

"But you can't be the only two. Has anything ever happened before? Some other you-know-what losing control?"

Tomo scrunched up his nose a little while he thought. The train curved around the Abe River and tilted us to the side. Someone behind Tomo stumbled, their bag smacking him hard in the leg. He buckled forward, stopping himself from falling over by pressing harder against the wall. He grimaced as they apologized, but all I could think about was how he was pressed up against me, the warmth of his body against mine.

He didn't seem to notice, still lost in thought. "I don't know.

Except for Takahashi and his groupies I don't know any others. Except my mom, and I can't ask her."

I thought about what Jun had said, about how the ink in me was pulled like a magnet to the ink in him and Tomo. If I was going to get anywhere, I needed to know more about how it all worked.

"Maybe Jun can..." I trailed off. The look on Tomo's face made me stop in my tracks.

"You can't trust him. He wanted to use us."

"I know," I said. But I wasn't sure. Maybe I'd overreacted. Sure, he was a little messed up in the head, but he'd done a lot more kind things for me than creepy. I mean, was it really such a bad thing that he wanted to take out gangsters and world crime? His methods were questionable, but his intentions?

The train ground to a stop and Tomo leaned into me as the doors sprang open beside us. We were pressed so close his cheek was against my ear, his bangs tickling my skin.

"We need to figure it out," I whispered, pretending that's what I was still thinking about. Only a few weeks apart, and I'd become this nervous around him again? *Must not think about his body pressed against mine. Must not think about how good he smells, like vanilla and miso.*

And then he pressed his lips against my neck, and my thoughts exploded.

"We can figure it out without Takahashi," he mumbled, his words tickling as they vibrated against my skin. "I've lived my whole life like this. Marked, stained, however you think of it. It's not going to go away. I'm not normal, Katie. I can never be normal."

You don't have to be normal, I thought. *You just have to be in control, so no one gets hurt. Especially us.* But the words never made it to my lips. I wished we weren't on the train, that we weren't surrounded by a hundred people pretending not to see him kissing my neck. I wished we could be alone in Toro Iseki, surrounded by *furin* and wagtail birds and a starlit sky. But we could never be there alone again, not with his drawings around us. Things would never be the same now that renovations at the site were done.

Shin-shizuoka was the next station and we stumbled out of the train, hands entwined. Tomo walked me the whole way to Diane's mansion—my mansion, I reminded myself. There was no time limit now. This was home, as long as I wanted it to be.

Tomohiro grasped both of my hands.

"I have to go," I said. "It's getting late."

"I know."

"It would be easier to leave if you let go of my hands."

"I know."

"Tomo."

"You're really here," he said, giving my hands a tug so I stumbled forward. "I have to protect you. I can't let anything happen to you."

"Me, too," I said. "I'm here to fix things, so don't worry, okay? I can take care of myself."

"Call me if the Kami or the Yakuza try to contact you. And I need to tell you something else."

"What?"

He looked away, his face pained. "I'm going to stop drawing."

"I thought you couldn't."

"I'm going to try," he said. "No more sketching. It'll eat me alive, but if you're going to be here, I can't risk it. Just notes at school."

His fingers felt so warm laced with mine. "But your drawings mean so much to you."

"Yeah, so much they bite and claw at me. Don't forget the gun that shot at me."

I shuddered. "Let's try to get the ink under control, okay?"

"Katie," he said, his mouth a grim line. "Do you think I set off the fireworks tonight?"

Yes.

"I don't know. But I do know that if I don't get in that door soon, Diane will sit me through a whole other set of fireworks and she may never let me come out again."

Tomohiro laughed. "*Wakatta.* I get it. Good night." He leaned over to kiss me, and the warmth of it threatened to knock me over. Suddenly meeting Diane's curfew didn't seem to matter at all.

Tomohiro's hands slid down my arms to my hips, pulling me closer. He made a gentle noise deep in his throat and every nerve in my body tingled with the sound of it. I clung to him as I kissed him, and his fingers threaded into my hair. This was the welcome home I'd waited for.

Something papery and sharp smacked into the back of my hand, and then again. Like sharp bugbites they pierced every patch of bare skin—my feet, my wrists, my ears. I pulled back from Tomo and stared. Cherry petals made of ink lifted off my *yukata,* leaving behind areas of pristine and unstained fabric. The shadowy cloud of flowers swarmed around us like black flies, whipping against us over and over like we were at the center of a dark hurricane.

"Ow!" One of them nicked my finger and a drop of blood oozed from the cut.

Tomohiro swatted the petals like bugs and they fell, shriveling on the ground around us until we were surrounded by a wreath of crumpled blackness. Slowly they melted into an oily sheen, clouds of golden dust catching the light like dim fireflies. The ink, lashing out at us like it always did.

38 • AMANDA SUN

"Sorry," he panted. "I... Maybe I should go home and clear my head. Damn hormones."

"Fine, but next time you want to make out, leave your swarming sakura petals at home."

He grinned and cupped my chin with his hand. "I can't think straight when I'm with you," he said.

He rocked back on his heels, hands shoved in his pockets, waiting until he was sure I was safely inside the lobby before turning to leave.

Like he wasn't one of the more dangerous things lurking in the darkness.

The elevator hummed as it pulled me upward. After the closeness of him, I felt acutely aware of how alone I was. I walked toward the pale green door of our mansion and pushed it open.

"Tadaima," I called out, kicking my flip-flops off in the *genkan.*

"Okaeri," Diane answered from somewhere in the living room. I checked that Yuki's *yukata* wasn't dripping before I stepped onto the raised hardwood floors. The cherry blossoms on it were spotless, but the rest of the fabric still had sprays of ink soaked into it.

Diane appeared in the foyer, still holding the TV remote, and stared. "What happened to you?"

"It's on the news," I said quickly. "Some sort of prank or something." She flipped the channel from the hallway, the voice of the newscaster blaring.

"Awful!" she said as she squinted at the screen. "Why would someone want to do that?"

"No idea," I said, studying the damage in the mirror. The spray of flowers in my hair was still mostly pink, and so was my face, wiped clean by Tomo's elephant towel. "Do you think the ink will come out?"

"I hope so. Poor Yuki. Her beautiful *yukata*."

I was a mess of blurred yellow and pink. Diane helped me un-loop the obi bow and untie the *koshi-himo* straps wrapped under-neath.

"Just terrible," Diane muttered. "I hope they catch the punks responsible."

When had my life become such a tangle of lies?

"Greene-san, could I see you for a minute?"

I stopped in my tracks. Suzuki-sensei waited with his arms folded across his chest, and I wondered if I'd done something wrong. It was only the first day back at school. I couldn't have messed up already, could I?

"I'll wait in the hallway," Yuki said.

"It's okay," I said. "I have to hurry to kendo after anyway." Yuki nodded and slipped out the door. *Lucky,* I thought. I walked toward my impending doom at the front of the class.

"Suzuki-sensei?"

He smiled, but it was a bureaucratic kind of smile, the kind that had the same warmth to it as a February morning. "Sit down, please." I sat in the nearest desk, while he sat on top of his. "We're glad to have you back," he said. "I'd heard from Headmaster Yoshinoma that you were heading to live with your grandparents in Canada for September."

"I changed my mind," I said.

"I see that. And I'm glad you can stay here with your friends." I was sure there was a *but...* in there somewhere.

"Shikashi..."

There it is.

"If you're going to stay in Japan permanently, you're going to have to give a lot of thought to your future. I know you have two more years before college, but you'll have to work harder than the others. This isn't an international school, Katie. You'll have to catch up your kanji and vocabulary quickly. I can't go easy on you."

Somehow I hadn't seen this coming. I'd thought things would stay the same. "I can keep up. I'm going to cram school, too."

"So are most of your classmates," he said. "Will you be able to take the entrance exams in two years? Can you even read a newspaper yet?"

I felt itchy. "Um, not yet."

"How many kanji are you comfortable with?"

"Er. Not enough?"

"I want you to think seriously about this, all right? I don't want to discourage you. You're bright, but you're taking on a lot. I won't be doing you a favor if I go easy on you, you understand?"

"I get it," I said. "I'll work hard."

He nodded. "I know. But think about it, because you still have time to transfer to an international school if the pressure's too much."

An international school, filled with English speakers like me. No Yuki, no Tanaka, no Tomohiro. Segregated somehow, separated from the reality of life in Japan. Another reminder that I could never really fit into the life I wanted to live here.

I'd just have to work harder.

"I don't want to transfer," I said. "I can do it."

"Okay. *Ganbarimashou ne?*"

"*Ganbarimasu,*" I said. *I'll do my best.*

So, figure out the ink and try not to flunk out of high school. Fine. I could do that.

Suzuki-sensei nodded and waved me out of the room. I rushed to the gym change room, hoping Coach Watanabe wouldn't skin me alive for being so late.

I slipped quickly into my *hakama* and peeked out the locker-room door to the gym—shoot, they'd already started the push-ups. The minute the coaches looked away, I sped toward an empty spot in line and launched myself at the floor. I listened, but no yelling. I'd gotten away with it. I grinned at the floorboards, feeling like a ninja as I bobbed up and down with the team. The victory vanished pretty quickly. I'd lost my edge over the summer; my arms wobbled and ached after we got to fifteen. At twenty-five, I pressed my fingers against the varnished wood and forced myself up. The cut from the dark sakura petal throbbed and stung, but I tried to ignore it.

When we were warmed up and sweating, Watanabe and Nakamura called us all to the front and told us to kneel in a semicircle. This wasn't normal. What was going on? I snuck a peek at Tomohiro, but he was looking down at the floor.

"I have some bad news," Watanabe-sensei said, and my nerves started to buzz. This couldn't be good. "Some of you have heard, but Ishikawa was injured over the summer." Watanabe cleared his throat. "He was shot."

Oh god. Murmurs ripped through the row of *kendouka*. Tomohiro kept staring at the floor. I hadn't thought about the consequences at all. I hadn't thought about the lies we might have to spin for me to stay in Japan safely.

"They don't know who did it," Watanabe said, trying to speak over the frantic students. "But the police are looking into it. Ishikawa is being less than cooperative, and so they're concerned that it was not a random attack. The police came by yesterday during our teacher prep to interview us."

"Is he still in the hospital?" asked one of the second-year girls.

Nakamura-sensei shook his head. "He'll be all right. Right now he's resting at home. His mother's let us know that he'll be strong enough to return to school in a few weeks. But unless the facts start looking more favorable, we may be forced to take disciplinary action against him."

Like what? Suspend him from school? Kick him off the kendo team? They had no idea what had really happened, and they couldn't. It was Tomohiro's sketch that had shot Ishikawa—a drawing of a gun. He'd saved Tomo's life by throwing himself in front of that bullet. How could we explain that, or why we'd been taken by the Yakuza, or anything related to that night? My heart twisted when I thought of Ishikawa in that stark white hospital room, being interrogated by the police and unable to say a word of truth. Just the idea of it gave me chills. How much trouble was he in?

"There's more bad news," Watanabe continued. "Takahashi Jun from Katakou School broke his wrist and will not be competing in the prefecture tournament."

"Ee?" One of the third-year boys, Kamenashi, called out in surprise. "So Ishikawa and Takahashi are out?"

"Lucky you, Yuu-san," grinned another, bumping Tomo with his elbow. "No competition left."

"Watch your back," laughed the second-year girl. "You might be next on the *kendouka* hit list."

Oh god. I hadn't thought of it like that. If you looked at it that way, it was a little suspicious. I rubbed my hands together, breathing slowly to calm down. It's not like the police knew about Jun's wrist, and there was no way they could link those events.

Watanabe raised his eyebrows as the *kendouka* laughed nervously over the joke. "Tomohiro?" he said. "Do you know something about these events?"

I glanced at Tomohiro, but his expression was stone as he shook his head. If he was worried, he was doing an amazing job of hiding it. It was hitting too close to the truth. My heart was racing as I tried not to look guilty. Tomo just looked pissed off, but anyone would expect him to look like that when his best friend was injured and his biggest rival was out of the competition.

But what if someone linked the injuries? Ishikawa was staying quiet out of loyalty to Tomo and to cover his own butt, but Jun? What if he spoke up about what had happened?

The lights overhead felt too bright as they glared down. Jun could destroy Tomohiro with a word. Maybe he already had.

"Let's not focus too much on the sadness," Nakamura-sensei chimed in. "We have to fight our best at the tournament for Ishikawa's sake. Let's believe in him, and let's lend all our strength to Yuu. He's our best hope in the championship now. *Ne,* Tomohiro?" He started clapping loudly and far too enthusiastically. The *kendouka* slowly joined in, until everyone was applauding.

"Yuu-kun, *ganbare!*" they shouted. "Tomo-senpai, you can do it!"

Everyone's attention was on Tomohiro. I could see his shoulders shaking, his eyes focused still on the floor. He was going to break under the pressure. He was going to confess everything. I watched, horrified.

He leaped to his feet, his hands in fists. And then he bowed to everyone with a smile, and they cheered, and Watanabe broke us up into groups for sparring.

I guess he'd had a lot of practice hiding secrets.

After kendo, Tomo and I walked to the bike racks in the courtyard of the school.

"You okay?" I said, grabbing the handlebars of Diane's bike.

He nodded, shifting his navy-and-white sports bag on his shoulder as he reached to unlock his wheel from the rack. "Fine," he said. "You?"

"Not totally fine," I said. He stood and grabbed the handle-bars, yanking the bike free.

"Thinking too much?"

I stifled a smile. "Maybe. Ishikawa's in a lot of trouble, Tomo."

"I know."

And you might be, too. But it seemed cruel to say. I couldn't imagine the guilt he was already feeling for putting his friend in the hospital with an unexplainable wound.

We walked alongside the bikes, both of us lost in thought. It wasn't safe to talk too much here, anyway.

"So...what's the plan today?" I tried.

Tomo attempted a smile as he broke from his thoughts. "I thought we could go somewhere. There's a place I've been wanting to show you."

"Like a date?" I said. He'd never used such an official term before. I swear his cheeks started to turn pink.

Then Tomo's phone chimed with a text. He leaned his bike against his leg as he reached into his pocket.

Tomo sounded puzzled as he looked at the screen. "Tou-san?"

"Your dad?" Tomo twisted the phone so I could see the message.

Come home right now. Important.

My mind fled to images of Kami and Yakuza. "Is he okay?"

"He's never home this early," Tomo said, which made me kind of sad. It was well past dinnertime already with kendo practice. Tomo had told me his dad worked long hours, that he almost lived alone in the silence of their empty house.

"What if the Yakuza called?" I blurted out.

Tomo stood still for a moment, staring at the screen. Then he shoved the phone into his pocket and took off running alongside his bike, lifting himself onto the seat as he sped toward Otamachi.

"Wait up!" I hopped on my bike and pedaled after him. Whatever he might have to confront, I wanted to be there.

We swerved around the streets surrounding Sunpu Park, coasting toward Tomo's house in the northeastern part of the city. A white scooter rested on the wall around Tomo's house, against the silver plaque that read The Yuu Family. Tomo dropped his bike to the ground and opened the metal gate, waiting to let me through before he clanged it shut behind us.

"Just a scooter," I said. "Is it a guest?"

"That's a police scooter," Tomo said as he opened the door, and my heart dropped. Tomo's dad had called the police?

"Tousan?" Tomo called out from the *genkan*. No answer at first and we kicked off our shoes, hurrying in. "Tousan!"

Then there was a shuffle of feet, and Tomo's dad appeared in the hallway. He was a somber and older version of Tomohiro, wearing a tight-fitting suit with a dark tie, his black hair slicked down neatly. He looked intimidating and somehow impressive at the same time.

Another man appeared behind him, this one in a light blue shirt with a navy vest over it. He had a balding spot on his head, and his thin black hair had been neatly combed around his ears. The policeman. He stepped forward, bowing to us.

"Hiro," Tomo's dad said, and it took me a minute to realize he was addressing his son. "You're late."

"I was at kendo practice," Tomo said, and I could feel the uneasy tension between the two.

"This is my son, Yuu Tomohiro," Tousan said, a fake smile plastered on his face. His eyes practically shot lasers at Tomo.

The officer nodded. "I'm Suzuki," he said. "I'd like to talk to you for a bit if that's okay."

Oh god. It's starting.

Tomo's dad looked me over, his eyes bulging a little in surprise. I guess Tomo hadn't told him he was dating a foreigner. "I'm sorry, but your friend will have to leave for now."

"I'm sure it won't take long," Tomo said. "Katie can wait upstairs in my room."

Tousan's eyes flashed. "Hiro, this is important."

Tomo squeezed his hand into a fist. "Wait upstairs," he said to me in English.

Well, this was an awkward first meeting with my boyfriend's dad. But I wanted to be here in case things fell apart. I wanted to know. And being on Tomo's side was more important right now then getting his dad to like me. I nodded and headed up the stairs toward his room. His father grunted, but didn't protest.

I stopped at Tomo's door, listening. They'd forgotten about me already and were moving into the living room to talk. I listened to the rapid Japanese flood the house. I still struggled with vocabulary. Tomo and my friends could communicate with me okay, and even school subjects I could get the hang of with Yuki's help, but listening to the formal talk with the police strained what language skills I had. I sat down with my back to the stair railing, squeezing my eyes shut to try to understand the conversation.

"Actually, Yuu, I'm sure you've heard by now about your friend Ishikawa Satoshi. We wanted to ask you some questions."

It wasn't fair that he had to face this alone. I'd seen just as much, but they'd never think to question me.

"Were you aware Ishikawa was getting involved in a gang

affiliated with the Yakuza?" I pieced together the question from the vocab I knew.

Tomo's steady voice answered, "No."

"But you're friends. You didn't notice anything strange?"

"We take kendo together. Otherwise I spend my time studying for exams."

"And what else?"

"That's it."

A pause. The policeman didn't believe him. The doubt dripped from every syllable.

"What about your girlfriend?" I took a shaky breath.

"Of course, we go for coffee sometimes, and we're in kendo together. But I don't have time for any other hobbies."

"I see." He asked a few questions I couldn't follow as I strained to listen in.

"Hiro and Satoshi have been friends since elementary school," Tomo's dad chimed in. "It's a shame if Satoshi has lost his way, but my son has not followed him down this path."

"I understand," Suzuki said. There was a pause, and I could hear the policeman scribbling down notes. Then he asked, "Tomohiro, do you know a Takahashi Jun?"

The silence pressed in around me as I waited for the response.

"Un," Tomo confirmed. "He's a *kendouka*. Sixth in the nationals last year, right? I sparred with him in the ward tournament."

"Were you aware he was admitted to Kenritsu Hospital the same night as Ishikawa?"

"No. But I heard he hurt his wrist. Our kendo coach told us today at practice."

"Hmm," Suzuki said. "Two of the three lead *kendouka* for the prefecture tournament out of commission in one night. Strange, isn't it?"

"What are you trying to say?" Tousan's voice rang out, and I shivered. It was a nightmare listening to all this at the top of the stairs, powerless to do anything at all.

"Only that some troublemakers have money riding on the outcome of the tournament," Suzuki said. "Gambling on kendo is becoming a problem, and we're concerned for Tomo's safety."

So they didn't suspect him. Yet.

"You think the two incidents are linked," Tousan said.

"Tomohiro, I think it's best if you keep from associating with Ishikawa for now. And if you receive any threats about the tournament, let us know. Someone may be trying to fix the outcome."

"But Takahashi only hurt his wrist," Tomo said. "How is that a crime?"

"The fracture pattern of the bone indicates an assault," Suzuki said. "And he arrived at the hospital only two hours after Ishikawa. We had police there when he arrived, and he was as unwilling to talk as Ishikawa was. We don't know for certain they're related. We're just trying to be thorough."

Assault charges. Gunshots and fractures. Could they track it to us? One confession from Jun or Ishikawa and they could get Tomohiro. And then what? He'd never admit I'd been there, but what about Jun's Kami groupies? The girl on the motorbike, Ikeda—she'd looked pretty pissed when we'd fought him. She'd talk for sure, and they'd arrest us both. They'd interrogate Tomo until the ink coursed down his arms, and then they'd stick him in a lab or an asylum or something. My mind raced with terror. I had no idea what might happen, but we were in danger in the worst way.

And if I was linked to it? Would they deport me? Suspend me? Send me to jail for assisted assault? Was that even a thing?

I'd been holding the *shinai* when Tomohiro had brought it down on Jun's wrist. I wasn't blameless.

The policeman spoke again. "You know Sunpu Castle, I assume."

"It's near my school," Tomo answered.

"Are you aware we found traces of blood there the morning after these incidents occurred? Takahashi's blood?"

Tomo sounded bored, but I knew it was an act. "So he hurt himself walking home?"

"We found something else, too." I heard the rustle of cloth while my heart beat in my ears. What had they found? "It said Yuu on the back. That's you, right?"

"My *tenugui*," Tomo said softly. I leaned my head back against the railing. One of his kendo headbands must have fallen out of his sports bag when I'd reached in for the *shinai*.

"With Takahashi's blood on it."

"Explain, Hiro," Tomo's dad said sharply.

"I don't know, Tousan," Tomo answered. "I bike home through that castle gate all the time. It must've fallen out of my sports bag."

"The boys face each other often in the kendo ring," his father added. "They even recently went on a kendo retreat together. It's very possible the source is from a sports encounter."

I heard a rustle of paper and the creak of the floorboards. "If it fell out of your bag, that's most unfortunate, Tomohiro-kun," the policeman said. "Tell me, did you attend Abekawa Hanabi this weekend?"

The memory of the policeman grabbing his radio flashed through my mind.

"One of our officers is an avid kendo fan and recognized Takahashi. And he overheard you threaten to break his other wrist."

Want to sign my cast?

If you don't get out of here, I'll give you another to match.

Tousan's voice rose. "Tomohiro!"

I waited, the silence thick as he hesitated. "It was just talk. We're kendo rivals. I didn't mean it."

Suzuki sighed. "Threatening someone must be taken seriously. And after talking to the teachers at your school yesterday, we know you have a history of getting into fights."

Oh god. The world around me stopped.

"That was after his mother died," Tousan broke in. "It was hard on him. He's come a long way since then. My boy isn't someone who would do this."

"We can't ignore this link, Yuu-san—we have to do our job, you understand." There was a creak that sounded like someone lifting himself off a couch, the click of something plastic. "Tomohiro-kun, if you remember any more details about Ishikawa or Takahashi, could you let us know? You can reach me at this number."

"Thank you for coming out of your way," Tomo's dad said.

There was another creak as Suzuki lowered himself into his shoes by the *genkan*.

The door snicked shut, and Tomo's dad grunted. "Stay away from those boys, got it? The last thing I need is you causing me more trouble."

He meant the accident with Koji, when Tomo's drawings had almost scratched out his classmate's eye and brought on a lawsuit.

Footsteps thumped against the stairs and I retreated into Tomo's room so I wouldn't look like I'd been eavesdropping.

"Hiro! Are you listening?"

"I'm listening!" Tomo shouted back. The door creaked open.

"Tomo," I said. "Are you okay?"

He slumped on the floor beside me, dropping his kanji-printed headband onto the hardwood. A faint trail of blood sprayed across the white cotton. Tomo combed a hand through his bangs and sighed. "How much did you understand?"

I stretched out my legs. "Enough."

"He thinks I had something to do with it," he said. "They found a spray of blood in Sunpu Castle. Takahashi's...on my *tenugui*. And they heard us at the festival this weekend."

"I know." I rested a hand on his arm.

"If it was just the Takahashi thing, I could've admitted to it. I could pass it off as a rivalry taken too far. Guys being stupid, right?" He leaned his head back against the frame of his bed.

"Except now they think Takahashi and Ishikawa are linked," I filled in.

"Takahashi's going to use this. If he talks, I'm done. I'll have to join his Kami cult."

"We'll find another way," I said. But everything was crumbling around us.

I had to talk to Jun. I didn't have a choice, even if Tomohiro wanted me to stay away from him. I had to get this under control fast, for both of us.

3

I waited almost an hour outside of Shizuoka Station for him. I checked my watch so many times I started to know what time it would be before I even glanced down. Tea Ceremony Club had made me later than usual, but I was pretty sure Jun still had the same cram-school schedule as the first term. I couldn't have missed him.

Every nerve in my body pulsed as I waited. Maybe my thoughts were running away with me, but the possibilities seemed endless and terrifying. Things had felt almost normal on my first day back to school—how had I not realized that the past would blow up in our faces?

A group of guys joked to each other and walked past me into the station. They wore the same Katakou School uniforms as Jun's—navy pants, white short-sleeved shirt, navy blazer and a striped blue-and-green tie. Almost identical to Suntaba's uniform except for the green stripes instead of red. The group of guys must have just gotten out of an after-school activity, so it was possible Jun could be arriving soon, too.

They probably had a ton of different clubs at school. I might have missed him.

Another ten minutes, and I was about ready to give up. I didn't want to face going home with all these questions in my head. How could I sleep knowing one word from Jun would get Tomohiro in trouble? Tomo could act all sly with the Yakuza, but what would he do once the police were involved? They didn't care if he made ink move—they cared if he shot one boy and hit another.

As I shifted my weight to leave, Jun rounded the corner toward the station. He had his leather book bag slung over his shoulder with his left hand, while his right hand swung awkwardly away from his side because of the bulky cast. The blond streaks in his hair clung to his face because he didn't have a free hand to tuck them back. A girl walked beside him, the two of them lost in conversation. Maybe she went to the same cram school, I thought. She had a green-and-navy pleated skirt, kind of like mine, and the handkerchief around her neck was green—also from Katakou School, then.

She turned as she laughed about something Jun said, and I hesitated.

I knew her. Ikeda, the girl on the motorbike.

Great. Two Kami to deal with. But I didn't have a choice. I needed to talk to him, whether she was there or not.

"Jun," I blurted out, approaching them. Jun stopped midsentence, startled. Ikeda's fingers wrapped quietly around Jun's arm. *Oh,* I thought. *She's either scared I'll hurt him again, or she didn't like me using his first name. Or both.*

"Katie," Jun said, lowering his book bag to his side. "Is everything all right?"

"Um." I stared at the two of them. A few weeks ago I would've been running from them, and now I was seeking them out? Jun tossed his head to try to get the black-and-blond hair out of his eyes. I sighed. I didn't have a choice, and anyway, he looked pretty harmless at the moment. Except for his eyes, which always looked too cold. "Can I—can I talk to you?"

Jun's mouth opened but he didn't say anything. Ikeda didn't look pleased.

"Oh," he said finally. "Of course. *Mochiron*. Here, or do you want to go somewhere?" He smiled pleasantly but my nerves buzzed louder. At least he looked more like the guy who'd gently plucked petals out of my hair than the guy who'd carved kanji into his own skin. I could see the corner of the scab where his blazer sleeve lifted up.

"Jun," Ikeda said, and her sharp voice startled me. "We'll be late."

"It's okay," he said.

"But—"

"Ikeda, this is important. Go without me."

Ikeda glared at me, and I felt itchy all over.

I blurted, "If you need to go…" What was I even saying? I needed to talk to him now.

"I don't," Jun said, his eyes gleaming. "Let's get coffee." He lifted his left arm slowly until the handles of his book bag slid up to his elbow. Then he stepped toward me and offered his open hand with a smile.

My face flushed. I still remembered the day he'd walked to school with me, the day my uniform had been totaled by the storm and I'd had to spend the night at Tomo's. Jun had given me his *keitai* number in case the Yakuza bothered me, and then he'd wrapped his warm fingers around mine. *I think you have someone you like,* he'd said. *But if things change, would you consider me? I'd really like to get to know you better.*

Did he still feel that way? Even after Tomo and I had bashed his wrist in with a *shinai?*

I didn't take his hand. How could he expect me to, after everything that had happened? And anyway, it didn't matter if he did feel that way. Tomo and I were together. Things hadn't changed. Instead, I squeezed the handles of my own bag with both hands and turned toward the coffee shop in the station. Jun followed close beside me.

I could feel Ikeda's eyes bore into me as we left.

"Is everything okay?" Jun asked as we walked.

"Not really."

"Is it Yuu? Did something happen to him?"

"It's not Tomohiro. I mean it's kind of him. But no."

We went into the *kissaten* and Jun ordered an iced coffee. I opted for melon soda and we sat in a corner where the leather booth nearly engulfed us.

"De?" Jun urged quietly, resting his good hand on the table. His eyes looked so earnest, even if they were cold. It was like his kendo matches—you could see him thinking out his every move. I guess if you were a Kami you'd have to have control over the situation all the time.

I decided to plunge right in. "Why didn't you tell me the police were questioning you?"

He said nothing for a minute, then reclined and took a sip of his coffee. "I haven't exactly seen you around lately. The festival seemed a poor place to bring it up. You were already scared of me."

I pressed my hands against the cool tabletop. "With good reason. You were being creepy. And your wrist—we were defending ourselves. What exactly did you tell the police? I thought you wanted Tomo to have a choice. Why are you pressuring him to join your Kami?"

"Whoa, *matte yo*," he said, lifting his left hand to tuck a blond highlight behind his ear. "I didn't press any charges. The police were at the hospital that night because of Ishikawa, and when I went in they recognized me. They wanted to know what had happened. But I swear I told them it was an accident, that I fell on my wrist and broke it."

"Well they don't believe you," I said. "They said the bone fracture showed it was an assault." I shuddered at the term. Is that what we'd done to him? But we'd had to fight back that night. Jun hadn't left us a choice. The bubbles in my melon soda swarmed my straw and it started to tilt over the side of my glass. I pressed it back down with a shaky hand. "And now because you and Ishikawa both went to Kenritsu Hospital the same night and wouldn't talk, they think the two incidents are related."

Jun leaned in, toying absentmindedly with his silver earring. "They are related."

"I know, but it has nothing to do with this whole gambling-on-kendo-results theory they have."

"Gambling?" Jun frowned. "Two of the prefecture's most promising *kendouka* injured and out of commission on the same night, a few weeks before the tournament." My straw made a second bubbly escape, but before I could reach for it, Jun grabbed for it and pressed it down. "Yeah, I guess that looks suspicious."

"I know. I hadn't even thought of that before, but it does. But that's not even close to what happened. It had nothing to do with the tournament." I rested my head on my arm. "And they...they think Tomo's involved. They found his *tenugui* at Sunpu Castle, and they overheard you two butting horns at the festival. You can't let us get pulled into this, Jun. It'll be bad for all of us. Please."

Jun frowned. "I can keep denying everything, but it's not like they're going to believe me when Ishikawa is being silent, too. It just makes it look gang related if we won't talk. I mean, what if they get video of us or something? We were all in the same places that night. *Che!* What a mess. If only I'd made it there before the Yakuza shot Ishikawa."

"They didn't," I said. "Wait, you didn't know that?"

"What do you mean they didn't?"

Crap. *Crap, crap, crap!* Of course Jun didn't know. He hadn't arrived until after the gun went off. Now I'd run off to the enemy and given him all our secrets. Now he had all kinds of info to blackmail us into joining his Kami cult. *Stupid!*

"Katie?" Jun asked gently. "Who shot Ishikawa?"

"Never mind."

"You can trust me," he said. "I'm not going to tell the police anything, and I'm not going to force Yuu to join me, either. Right now I just want to help you, but I can't unless you let me." My straw made another jump for the table and we caught it at the same time, our fingertips touching as they wrapped around the slippery plastic. His fingers were soft and warm, slender the way Tomohiro's were. I pulled my hand back but Jun didn't, holding the straw in place as he smiled at me. *"Ano saa,"* he said, "you really need to drink some of this before your straw leaps to its bubbly death."

In spite of everything, I felt a grin curl its way onto my lips. It seemed so ridiculous, the two conversations side by side. I took a huge sip of melon soda and the straw sank down.

I looked at Jun carefully. He seemed so normal sitting here. He sat forward, shrugging his blazer off in the booth. He looked a little flushed, his cheeks pink.

"It's hot in here," he laughed, but I wondered. Was it because of me? Did he— No, it didn't matter. Why did I keep thinking about it? He had way too many screws loose up there.

"Um," he said, "I have a problem."

"What?"

He grinned and rose to his feet, taking slow steps toward my side of the booth. His blazer was half off, half on, crumpled around his elbows like he was chained.

"The cast," he said, and I could see where the jacket had snagged on the thick white bandage. "Could you...?"

"Oh." I paled. "Um, sure." I lifted my hands to his sleeve, the weave of the fabric soft under my fingertips. I carefully unhooked the edge of the cuff from the cast, my fingers brushing over the hard bandaged shell as I worked the sleeve down.

My heart pulsed faster. *Shut up, shut up,* I told it. I wished I could shut off my shallow brain. Sure, Jun looked like a poster boy for the next TV drama series, but couldn't I look past that to the fact that he had some serious issues?

The sleeve slipped off his arm and I watched the jacket collapse into folds of fabric as it fell. Jun caught the blazer with his good hand, throwing it onto the bench beside him and sitting again.

"Thanks," he said, reaching for his iced coffee with his now-bare arm. I could see the welts of the snake kanji he'd carved into his skin, faint and scabbing.

"It's the least I could do," I said. "I guess the cast is kind of my fault."

His smile disappeared. "No, it's not. It's my fault—I came on too strong about the Kami. I should've given you more time to think about it. It's just—I've been alone with my secret for so long. None of the other Kami can do anything close to what Yuu can do. And when I realized there was ink in you, too—I was just so happy not to be alone. I got carried away. I'm sorry, Katie. I'm sorry for frightening you."

I didn't know what to say. He'd put his life in danger to rescue all of us. And the words he spoke now, they were genuine. He meant them.

"It was a sketch," I whispered. God, I hoped I was making the right choice.

"A sketch?"

"The gun," I said, my voice dry.

"A sketched gun?"

I nodded.

"Shit. Is that what they asked Yuu to do?"

"And money. Sketching money."

"Bastards." Jun's eyes shone like hard marbles. It frightened me, the way he looked. Maybe I shouldn't have told him after all. "They never learn."

"What do you mean?"

"Just old business. What matters is that the police don't suspect Yuu. I won't say a word, and if Ishikawa's any kind of friend he won't, either. It'll blow over soon enough."

My thoughts raced. This is why I'd met with him—to save us, and he was willing to do it. "Why are you protecting Tomo?" I said. "So the police don't learn about the Kami?"

"I'm sure the police know about the Kami, conspiracy-style," Jun smirked. "Some of them probably *are* Kami. But no, that's not why. First, I'm worried the stress of being arrested for assault would make Yuu more dangerous. Second, I'm not joking when I say I'm on your side. If Yuu can learn to control his power—if you can learn to control the ink—we'd be able to do anything."

"Like kill the Yakuza?" I said, rolling my eyes. I felt like I should be frightened, but sitting here in our school uniforms sipping soda and iced coffee somehow muted the terror.

"That's not fair," said Jun. "I don't really want to kill anyone, if I can help it. I just want to save the world from crime, poverty, famine—everything. Wouldn't you? There's so much these powers can be used for, but until Yuu knows how, he's just a mine in a field waiting to blow up the innocent. He's stronger than me, Katie. Two weeks ago he proved that. I can't do it alone—I need you two."

So the goal of the creepy goth cult was to save the world, feed the hungry, clothe the poor? That didn't sound so bad.

"That's it? You don't want to take over the world or something?"

Jun grinned. "Do I look like some crazy dictator?"

"Looks can be deceiving."

"Hey! That hurts." He spun his straw around his now-empty glass in slow circles. "I don't expect you to trust me. I know this Kami stuff is scary. But I hope you will. I want to help you."

"So we can help you."

"That's one of the reasons."

"The others?"

"Katie," he said, his voice velvet and smooth. He reached his left hand up to his earring, rubbing it gently as he looked at me. "There's only one other reason."

I turned all shades of red and stared down at my soda, my heart pounding.

Focus. You didn't come here to stare at his pretty eyes.

"I want to learn how to stop the ink," I said. "You said there's ink trapped in me, right? Why me? And what do I do?"

"Meet me again," Jun said. "It's too complicated a discussion for a café. To be honest, there's a lot I don't know, but I can give you somewhere to start. Plus, I do have to eventually get to cram school because we're having our mock exams today."

"Oh my god. I'm sorry!"

He grinned. "You wouldn't have talked to me if I'd told you." He stood and reached for his book bag, sliding it up his arm so he could grab his blazer. It was surreal to watch him struggle with the fracture Tomo and I had given him. How could I feel pleased and horrified at the same time?

"Text me when you can chat, or you can always meet me at Katakou and we'll walk to the train together." He started to leave and then turned to look at me. "I'm glad you came to meet me," he said. "We can help each other. And I know you can help Yuu see that."

As he walked away, I was a queasy mix of relief and utter guilt.

"Tadaima," I muttered, shutting the door behind me.

"Katie!" Diane said. "You won't believe it—look!" She swung Yuki's *yukata* in front of me, swaying on its special hanger. Too blurry, and my eyes glazed over until the summer kimono slowed down, and then I saw what she meant.

"Nice job," I said. "Not a spot of ink on it. What'd you use?"

"That's the weird thing," Diane said. "I went to get it from your room, and it was already clean. It's like it all just aired out or something. Maybe it wasn't ink."

"Um, yeah, that's totally weird." I hoped I was convincing.

"Well, if it was a prank like they're saying, I'm glad it wasn't permanent. They would've ruined a lot of expensive kimonos and *yukatas* with real ink. If they ever find who did it, he'll be in trouble."

"Definitely," I said. I grabbed the kimono from her and

went into my room to hang it in my closet until I could take it back to Yuki. A gleam caught my eye from the tatami floor.

A disintegrating pile of shimmering dust where the *yukata* had been left to dry. Kami ink powder, no doubt, like the firefly dust I'd seen glinting around Tomohiro's sketches. More evidence he was subconsciously behind the fireworks. Thank god he'd decided to stop drawing. Maybe things would finally take a turn for the better.

I lay down on my bed and stared at the ceiling for a while. When did all this ink stuff become my problem? Couldn't I have found a normal boy who didn't have these issues? But even more than that, Jun had reminded me of my own link to the Kami. It was the ink inside me that really bothered me. Why was it happening to me? How the heck did it get there?

I had to meet Jun again soon. I wanted to know exactly what role I played in this. In the meantime, there had to be a way to help myself.

I went to my desk and lifted the lid of my laptop. Searching for Kami just brought up the expected—Shinto gods, pictures of Amaterasu, a few mangas and animes. Apparently the internet didn't think Kami could possibly be real. Ancient myths, old stories. The Kami had done such a good job of hiding their tracks.

My *keitai* chimed suddenly from my book bag. I reached over and rifled through the bag's contents for it, flipping it open to a text from Tomohiro.

You okay? Didn't see you after school.

He'd probably freak out if I told him I'd met up with Jun. Probably better to mention it later and not over texts.

Fine, just worried about the Ishikawa thing, I typed back. Wasn't that kind of obvious?

Another chime, seconds later.

Thought so. Everything will be okay. You want me to swing by?

I wasn't sure what Diane thought of Tomohiro, but considering the look she'd given him when he'd shown up at the door last time, she'd probably want a little warning before he dropped in. There were enough reasons why being together was a bad idea—I didn't need Diane breathing down my neck, too.

Maybe next time, I wrote back. Just about to have dinner.

I like food. Invite me.

I rolled my eyes, sure he was joking.

Do you also like being grilled by family members?

I closed the phone and put it on the table beside me.

How did I affect the ink? There were other Kami around, but Tomo hadn't lost control because of them. He'd never lost control like he had since I'd arrived in Japan. Well, maybe when the dog drawing had attacked his friend Koji, and also when the *sword* painting had sliced his wrist open—but both of those he'd sketched on the page. The demon face he'd created when Ishikawa had threatened him with the Yakuza, and the black wings that had unfurled on his back—he hadn't drawn those. I'd made those happen, some kind of reaction between my ink and his.

Maybe it was emotional. Maybe he was just serious about me. I flushed a little at that one.

So if it wasn't that—then what?

"Am I a Kami?" I whispered. I twirled my hair between my fingers—no, that had been pretty much ruled out. There's no way my absentee dad could be Japanese, not with blond hair like this.

What other options were there?

My phone chimed again.

Meet you at Shizuoka Eki tomorrow, it said. And don't skip kendo—you need all the practice you can get.

Baka, I wrote back. *Stupid.*

"Katie!" Diane called, and I tossed the phone onto my bed.

I had no clue how I could have ink in me. There was no choice—I had to depend on Jun.

I headed for the table and pulled out a chair as Diane scooped the *nikujaga* into my bowl.

"So?" she said. "Things back to normal again?"

"Yeah," I said, spearing a potato with my fork. I had to think of school-related things to talk about so I'd stay away from the Kami problems. "Suzuki-sensei threatened me with international school. I'm not using enough kanji in my schoolwork."

"You'll be fine," Diane said. "I wouldn't have enrolled you at Suntaba if I didn't think you could handle it."

"I know."

"Have you talked to that boy yet?"

I cringed. "What boy?"

"If you don't know who I mean, why did you wince just now?"

My fork clanked against the side of the bowl. "There are just so many boys after me. It's hard to keep track."

"Katie," she warned, but her face looked a shade paler under her plum lipstick. "You know who I mean. The punk I *thought* was Tanaka before when he showed up here with those ripped jeans and that smirk. What was his name? Yoshida? Yu-something… Oh, what was it?"

"Yuu Tomohiro."

"Right, Yuu. He in your class?"

"Not exactly," I said. She looked worried enough—no need to stress that he was a senior. "He's in kendo, remember?"

"Oh yeah. I thought he looked violent."

I moaned. "Diane."

"Kidding, kidding. Well, bring him around sometime so I can get to know him."

"You mean scrutinize him and pick him apart."

"Exactly."

I rolled my eyes.

"There's something a little off about him," she added.

"You mean his fully tattooed torso that links him to every gang-related crime in Shizuoka Prefecture?"

"Funny," Diane said, pointing her fork at me, "but no. I meant his eyes. Is he nearsighted?"

"Um. That's weird. Do I look like an optometrist?"

Diane sipped her cold oolong tea. "Well, never mind, Miss Snarky. I just thought his pupils went pretty large for a minute there."

I nearly dropped my fork.

"Just wondered if everything was okay with his eyes, that's all," she mumbled. "Your bowl's empty. Want more?"

"Please," I managed, my voice barely a whisper.

I swear my hand was shaking when I passed her the bowl.

4

I waited outside the station, leaning against the wall beside a buzzing vending machine. The summer heat was lingering into September, but I'd pulled on a light sweater just in case. Tomohiro had rescheduled our mystery date, and I couldn't be sure where we were going. *Just trust me,* he'd said, to which I'd reminded him about the last "date," which had been an elaborate plan to push me away before the Yakuza had hunted him down. He'd laughed, which hadn't left me feeling reassured.

A moment later he sailed around the corner on his bike, heading way too fast toward the racks. At the last minute he leaped off his bike and the wheel crashed against the bar with a loud echo.

I grinned. "Is that display of manliness necessary?"

"Very," he said, stooping to lock the wheel to the rack. "Life is boring if you only do necessary things." He stepped toward me, brushing his hands off on his jeans, a dark satchel hanging from his shoulder to his hip. "Sorry I made you wait."

"It's okay, I only got here a minute ago."

"Then let's go." He took my hand in his for a minute, letting my fingers slip through his before heading toward the station doors.

"Where are we going exactly?" I said, following him up the steps and toward the train platforms. "You kind of left that detail out."

"Ah, so remember when we were trying to find a new place that was just ours?"

"Yeah?" When Toro Iseki had been under renovations, Tomohiro could draw in peace, but not so much now.

"It turns out Antarctica is a hell of a commute," he said. "So I've found the next best thing."

"Wait," I said. "I thought you said you were going to stop drawing."

"I am," he said, reaching for his wallet. "I have." He pulled out his train pass and scanned it on the platform barrier. The gateway buzzed and the little metal doors flung open.

"So then why do you need a new place?" I said, scanning my own train pass and following him through. He turned to the east platform, and we sat on a bench to wait.

"Because," he said, speaking quietly in the busy station, "first, I don't know how long I can go without drawing. Remember how I said I'd have the nightmares and wake up with ink on the floor? Or the ink during the kendo match and maybe even those fireworks? Trying not to draw might be a way to contain the ink, but if it falls through, my only other choice is trying to control the drawings. And for that, I need a safe place to sketch. And second, I need a place to be alone with my girlfriend where others can't snoop."

"And Antarctica is just too far," I smirked.

"I hear the penguins are cute, though."

"So in non-penguin news, I've decided I'm going to learn how to control whatever it is inside me," I said, watching

Tomo's eyes carefully. I wanted him to know he wasn't alone, that we'd figure it out together.

He looked surprised, and worried. "Katie, we don't even know if that's true. Just because Yuki's brother said that to you...you're not a Kami okay?"

"I know that, but there's something going on, right? Even Jun thought that—" I stopped. When Jun had told me I manipulated the ink, that there was ink inside me, Tomohiro had been writhing on the ground haunted by shadows. He hadn't heard a word of it.

"Jun?" Tomohiro echoed. He looked at me with concern. "Takahashi is dangerous, Katie. He's not bothering you again, is he?"

"No," I said, looking away. I felt like the truth was written all over my face. "I just feel like—don't you think he might at least know some things we don't? I mean, there's got to be a reason the ink reacts to me."

"There is," Tomohiro said, tucking my hair back over my shoulder. He leaned in and his lips grazed the top of my ear. "We're linked, Katie, and we can fight this together. We don't need anyone else's help."

I nodded.

"Katie...can I ask you something?" His breath was hot against my ear and I shivered.

"What?"

"Can you—I mean..." He leaned back and sighed. "I know you're still learning Japanese. So you won't take offense, right?"

"Oh jeez," I said, the heat of the embarrassment coursing through me. "What did I do?"

He paused, looking troubled. "It's—it's Takahashi. When

you call him by his first name, it's...not really comfortable for me."

"Oh," I said, staring at him. Of course. Calling someone by their first name in Japan was personal. Intimate. "You're jealous!" I laughed.

"It's not funny," he said quietly, and it wiped the grin right off my face. I hadn't thought about it before, but it was probably humiliating for him that I called another guy by his first name.

"I'm sorry."

"It's not just for me," he said. "It'll sound bad if you call him that in front of anyone. Especially since he's older than you. It sounds like—it sounds like you're more than friends. A lot more."

I'd heard another girl call him Jun, and he'd never seemed to mind, so I'd gone along with it. *Takahashi* sounded strange and distant to me, but I remembered Ikeda's response when I'd called out his first name. Maybe it really *was* a mistake to use it.

"Got it," I said. "My bad."

Tomohiro smiled. "It's okay."

The train whirred into the station, its brakes squealing as the arrival announcement chimed on the loudspeaker. The stale station air whisked around our faces.

And then I heard a familiar voice calling over the sound of the train.

"Tomo-kun!"

He looked up, hands in his pockets and expression frozen, like he was completely confused.

"Shiori?"

I glanced at him for a minute. Wasn't he calling another

girl by her first name? That was the same thing he'd just been upset about. But wait—she was younger than him. I'd have to ask Yuki. Names were way too complicated.

Shiori ran toward us, waving a hand. She wore her school uniform, a tartan red-and-blue skirt with her pregnant belly ballooning under her white blouse. Her white socks were pulled neatly up to her knees, her black loafers clunking against the ground. She swung her black book bag in her other hand.

"Dame yo," Tomo warned as she approached. He shook his head disapprovingly. "You shouldn't be running."

"Heiki, heiki," Shiori said, swishing her hand back and forth. "You worry too much, Tomo-kun. Hi, Katie."

"Hi," I said, trying to smile. I knew her life was hard right now, but I didn't like the way she was leaning into Tomo. She knew we were dating, right?

Tomo stepped back, as if he was thinking the same thing. He ducked into the train and we followed.

"Are you on your way home?" I asked.

Shiori shook her head. "I take this train to my doctor's office."

"Oh." I felt my cheeks flush. "How...how's it going?"

"Good," she smiled. "The baby's very healthy." The train was crowded, but Tomo spotted a narrow spot for two beside a salaryman on the red leather bench. He sat, his back pressed against the window, and looked up at me. I took a step forward, but Shiori brushed past me and sat down next to him, resting her bag on her lap. *Guess I'm standing.* It was fine, though. Shiori probably needed the spot anyway. I wrapped my fingers around the metal pole, trying to take it in stride.

"Katie, sit down," Tomo said, starting to lift himself up.

"It's okay," I said. "Shiori needs to sit."

She beamed, a little too proud of herself. We were both trying to be thoughtful, but I worried she was reading into it too much. I took a breath as the train lurched into motion. She didn't have anyone but Tomo looking out for her. I had to trust him to let her know if things went too far.

Tomo rose out of his seat. "Sit," he said. His eyes searched mine, apologetic. I felt awkward to sit next to Shiori, but standing would make the situation worse, like I was being difficult. I sat down beside her; neither of us looked happy.

"So, Tomo-kun," Shiori tried. "I have three more weeks of school and then that's it."

He nodded. "Not long now, *ne?*"

"That's exciting," I attempted. Shiori smiled, but it was forced. I could see that.

"Thanks," she said. "So why are you headed this way, Tomo-kun? You couldn't be going to Myu's house…?" Tomo winced at the mention of his ex-girlfriend. Obviously he wasn't going there. Why was she messing with him?

"We're going to some mystery place," I said, trying to lighten the tension. "My guess is possibly the zoo, but he won't tell me."

"Oh, I love the zoo!" Shiori said. "Tomo's taken me many times."

Tomo looked as uncomfortable as I felt. I knew she was like a sister to him—why was she trying to make it sound like more? But then I looked at her face and the look in her eyes. *Oh. She wants it to be more, doesn't she?* He protected her, stood up for her through all the bullying. He was her knight in shining armor, and I was in the way.

"We like watching the lemurs, right, Tomo-kun?"

Tomo folded his arms, leaning the back of his head against

the metal pole. The beams of light from the window lit his hair like a flame. "It's the red pandas I like."

Shiori's voice was quiet. "Right," she said. "The red pandas. I forgot."

"Lemurs are cute, though," he added, trying to soften what he'd said. "Anyway, Katie and I aren't going to the zoo, but we are going on a date." The words startled me, since he'd been too indirect to say it like that before. Then I realized— he was trying to get the message across. He was trapped, but he didn't want to embarrass either one of us.

Shiori's face fell. "Oh."

This whole thing was stupid. Couldn't we just come out and say how we felt? Tomo and I were together, but I didn't want to hurt Shiori.

"You can come with us," I blurted out. Tomo raised an eyebrow, but said nothing. "It's more fun that way anyway, right?"

"Oh, I'm too busy," Shiori said. "I have that appointment, and then I need to stop for a couple things we need for dinner." The train was slowing, pulling into the next stop, and the motion sent an elderly man's bag skidding across the floor. Tomo dashed after it, returning it to the bowing, grateful man. Shiori leaned into me while he was gone, her voice low. "It's a shame you don't know how to cook Japanese food, Katie. How will you ever keep a Japanese man happy?"

Did she actually just say that? "Sorry?"

Shiori sighed. "It's pathetic, you know, trying to steal Tomo from me."

My mouth opened, but I had to force words out. "Steal him?"

"Tomo-kun and I have been inseparable since we were little. You think you're going to change that?"

My stomach twisted; I'd never heard Shiori sound like this. "I'm not trying to get between you.".

"I don't need your pity invites to everything you do. Anyway, do you even know the first thing about dating a Japanese guy? Poor Tomo-kun. Japanese guys have totally different expectations than Americans, you know. I could never date a foreigner. I mean, for a bit of meaningless fun, maybe, but not long-term. You know your relationship with Tomo isn't going to go anywhere serious, right? Wait…did you know?" She looked at the bright red plastered on my cheeks. *"Ara,* you did! Never mind. Enjoy your date. It's nice to be exotic, even if it's short-lived, right?" She rose to her feet as the train doors opened, waving her hand at Tomo with a big smile as she went out the door. I stared at her like a blowfish, my mouth open in a big O as the train pulled away.

Tomo collapsed into the seat beside me, the motion making the seat jump a little. *"Daijoubu?"* he asked. "You look pale."

"I'm not okay," I said. "Not at all. Did you hear what she said?"

He leaned forward. "What?"

But I couldn't say it. It was hurtful, but it was true, wasn't it? I was stumbling over every cultural difference, like Jun's name. What kind of expectations did Tomo have? Was I supposed to cook lunches for him like in animes? Women working in the offices brought tea for their male coworkers at break time, and Diane had told me about a teacher who'd quit working because she'd gotten married. Did Tomo expect me to do that, too? Were we really too different to have a future?

"Nothing," I said. I was scared Tomo would agree with what she'd said. He'd already acted pretty jealous about the Jun thing.

"Forget her," Tomo said. "It's probably baby hormones talking. Today it's just you and me, *ii?*" He ruffled my hair with his slender fingers, a grin carving its way onto his lips. I smiled back, confidence slowly flooding back into me. Tomo liked to cook, for one thing. Yuki had told me that was pretty unconventional for a Japanese guy. Maybe he wasn't typical in any way.

Shiori had reminded me that I was different, that I didn't fit in. But the way Tomo looked at me right now, I didn't feel different at all.

"Up a mountainside?"

Tomohiro grinned. We'd been riding the bus for fifteen minutes, scaling closer and closer to the summit on the narrow roads that tunneled through the trees.

"This isn't exactly the most convenient spot for everyday meetings," I said.

"Okay, fine, maybe it's a bit far for every day," Tomo said, slouching into the bus seat. "But it's worth it."

I stared out the window as the bus pulled up to a platform. Forests surrounded us in a blanket of leaves, more lush green than I'd seen in one place since moving to Shizuoka. Above the trees, a thick wire ran up the hill.

"What is this place?"

The bus shuddered to a stop, and we hopped off the front, dropping our yen into the plastic box beside the steering wheel.

"Nihondaira," Tomo said, and the moment we stepped out of the bus, the fresh, sweet mountain air gusted around us.

The chirps of wagtails and Japanese bush warblers echoed from every corner of the forests. It was as though Toro Iseki had burst through its boundaries and transformed into an overgrown secret garden.

The crows cawed incessantly, the only familiar sound that we were still in Shizuoka.

"Look," he said and stretched out his arm. It was hard to see, but there was something in the distance across the bay, a looming shape with a cap of white at the top. "The air's muggy, but you can kind of make it out."

Mount Fuji towered over the landscape, reaching into the sky like a giant. I'd never seen a mountain that huge in my entire life.

"It's beautiful," I breathed. "This whole area is."

"And remote," he said. "Well, except the tourists." Most of the ground around us was paved into a huge parking lot for the tour buses. But on the edges of that platform, the rolling mountains teemed with life and sound. I turned—behind us stood a variety of radio towers in striped red and white. To the right of us was a touristy-looking building about half the height of the towers.

"Gift shop?" I wondered.

"This is where a lot of the Shizuoka tea is made," Tomo said. "They sell some of it in there."

"Oh," I said. "So these are the rolling lands of your dad's tea empire." I poked him sharply just above his hip and he jumped a mile.

"*Oi!*" he snapped. He reached for me and I raced toward the tea shop. The sound of grinding gears and wire scraping against itself stopped me in my tracks. Tomo crashed into me, grabbing me around my waist and lifting me off the ground.

"Hey!" I shouted as he laughed. A few of the Japanese tourists looked over and then quickly away. I was a foreigner, so they made it their business to politely ignore the shenanigans I was causing.

My feet touched the ground again and Tomo broke off his hold on me.

"That's the ropeway," he said, following my gaze.

Little cable cars bounced up and down on the wires as they whirred slowly through the air, rolling along the thick cord toward a distant mountain peak.

"Is that where we're going?"

"Not exactly, but we can take a detour. There's a shrine up there, so there'll be more tourists. But on the edges of the shrine are forests, and no fence."

"Got it," I grinned. "Let's ride the ropeway. I want to be surrounded by forest."

He grinned. *"Ikuzo." Let's go.*

We'd lost something important without Toro Iseki. We needed to be alone among the trees and the birds, somewhere horses could come to life if we wanted them to.

The thought was sobering. No, we couldn't bring anything like that to life again. No horses, no butterflies, not even any *furin* chimes in the trees. They'd been dangerous, sinister, but they'd been beautiful, too. It made me sad to think I would never see those things again.

I noticed a weird frame covered in brass squares while we waited to enter the cable car. A large metal frame held a dozen rows of silver pipes, and along these pipes hung hundreds of brass padlocks like on vintage high-school lockers or construction-site fences.

"What's this about?" I said.

Tomohiro rested his hand on the locks, giving them a shove so they swayed back and forth. Now that I looked closer, kanji names had been written down the sides of the locks in black pen.

"Lovers' locks," he said. "Lock your heart here so your relationship lasts forever."

I felt too warm then, looking at the rows of locks. Were these couples all still together? Every lock had a keyhole at the bottom, but no keys in sight. The locks weren't going anywhere.

Tomo spoke beside me, his breath warm on my ear. "They threw the keys away," he said. "Guess they're stuck together until the end. Maybe I should get a lock for us, too."

"You sure you want to be stuck with each other that long?" I was joking, but what Shiori had said still stung, leaving an uneasy hole at the edge of my confidence where it seeped away into the shadows.

Tomo took a deep breath as the cable car arrived, a lady opening the door and announcing it was time to board. "It's not that long until the end for me," he said, and I shivered.

We crowded into the cable car with the tourists and lifted into the air.

"So we can fly after all," Tomohiro said, but his voice was sad. He'd thought once he could fly safely on a dragon, but that didn't end well. Now here we were, suspended by a cord, bouncing over every pole along the ropeway.

"At least this mode of transportation won't try to eat you," I said. "Although it is kind of rickety."

"Well, it's run fine for the past fifty years," Tomo said, his eyes gleaming. "I guess it's due to break down and throw us to our untimely deaths."

"You better grow feathers fast if that happens."

He tucked his bangs behind his ears—where they stayed for a few seconds before tumbling back—and closed his eyes. I knew he was pretending we weren't surrounded by tourists.

At the end of the ropeway, we followed the crowd as they

curved around the platform and toward a staircase of what looked like a hundred giant stone steps. They rose sharply from the cable-car platform, and I gasped when I saw the *roumon* gateway at the top.

It looked like the entrance to an ancient castle, a fortified gate of deep crimson and white. The roof tilted up like a bird raising its wings, the black rounded tiles stubbed with crests of shining gold. A thick rope wound around the gate, little thunderbolts made of white cloth hanging down from it and swaying in the breeze.

"Kunozan Toshogu Shrine," Tomohiro said. "That's just the entrance."

We walked up the steps slowly. "A shrine? So it's Shinto, then, not Buddhist."

"Yeah," said Tomohiro. "Dedicated to the most famous Kami of Shizuoka, Tokugawa Ieyasu."

"That sounds like a person's name, not a mythical *kami*," I smirked.

Tomohiro stopped climbing the stairs to look at me. "It is," he said. "He built Shizuoka Castle. And when he died, after months of sickness and nightmares, he was buried here."

I felt the blood drain from my face.

"When?" I whispered.

"Sixteen-hundred-something," Tomohiro said, and he kept climbing. I followed him. "Don't worry. I'm sure the ghost is long gone."

"And you think he was really...?"

"A Kami?" Tomohiro stopped to catch his breath and then continued up the stone steps. "Well, let's see. He was kidnapped during an uprising when he was six. The abductors demanded Tokugawa's father break ties with their enemy clan or they'd kill his son. And his father said, 'Go ahead.'"

I raised my hand to my mouth, my eyes wide.

"Yeah," Tomo said. "And after three years of the boy suffering in their hands, his captors suddenly dropped dead. So did his father. So did half the Japanese in the area."

Shit.

"Tomo," I said, my throat dry. "How do you know all this?"

"I'm just looking for answers," he said. "It used to be Taira no Kiyomori in my nightmares. Now it's Tokugawa. And I want to understand why."

"I thought we were looking for a new place to be alone."

"We are," Tomohiro said. "But you wanted to come here, and I felt the pull, too. I feel like I'm supposed to be here. He led a lot of successful battles in his time. Maybe he knew something I don't about controlling the ink."

We'd reached the gateway now and could see the shrine before us. It was a flurry of bright rainbow colors. I'd never seen any shrine or temple like it in Japan. The posts and foundation of the house were painted bright red, but the walls were a deep black and covered in bright images of dogs and birds. Every surface shone with elaborate whorls of intricate gold. The painted dogs curled around the building had blue and white spots, with tails and manes like lions. Once-brass lanterns, now turned green and scaly with time, hung from thick chains in the roof. Just under the ceiling beams wove an elaborate pattern of blue, red, white and green flowers and shapes. Everything gleamed like it was alive.

"Tomo," I said, stepping forward. My breath caught in my throat.

That was when I heard the gasp, like air being wrenched from his lungs.

The painted dog's lip curled back with the sound of wood snapping and grinding, a growl echoing from his mouth of sharply drawn teeth.

    I turned just as Tomohiro collapsed in the gateway, his head cracking against the stone. Ink pooled around his skull like blood.

5

"Tomo!" I shouted, racing back to the gateway where he fell. The ink spread in a shimmering pool on the stone as tourists clustered around him. I collapsed onto my knees beside him, putting my hands on his shoulders. His eyes were closed and it didn't look like he was breathing.

Behind me I could hear the groan of ancient wood bending and snapping as the painted dog snarled, but I didn't have time to worry about it. I shook Tomohiro by the shoulders gently, but nothing happened.

Above us, in the shadow of the gateway, I heard strange groans and whispers. Something was really wrong. Adrenaline coursed through my veins. We needed to get away from here, fast.

"Someone call for help!" one of the tourists shouted. Several had already reached into their bags for their *keitais*.

"No," I shouted, and they hesitated. I knew what Tomohiro would say. Don't draw attention. But how could I help it? He'd passed out in a pool of ink.

I hooked my arms under Tomo's shoulders and started dragging him away from the gateway, toward the top of the stone stairs where I could look at him in the light. The ink left a bloodlike trail as I pulled him forward to see what the emergency might be.

The moment he was out of the shadow of the *roumon,* he gasped as if he were drowning, like he was breathing in life itself.

"Tomo!" I smoothed his hair out of his face. The ink had soaked into his copper spikes and they stuck together in matted tangles.

He opened his eyes and looked at me. His pupils were huge, alien, glistening black.

No! Like the times he'd lost control while drawing. The Kami in him had taken over.

He kept gasping for air, his voice frantic as he groaned.

"It's okay," I said, my eyes filling with tears. "It's okay." My hands dripped with ink as I stroked his damp hair.

A woman stepped over and offered her water bottle. I nodded my head in thanks and opened it, the ink slicking over the cap and trickling down the sides.

"I'm going to call an ambulance," another tourist said.

"No!" I said. We couldn't risk getting the hospital involved. What if it drew the police or something? "It's okay. He's okay now, see?"

Tomo closed his eyes, and when they opened again, they were their normal dark brown. I pressed a hand against his heart.

Please calm down. Please.

"Katie," he managed.

"Pull it together, Tomo," I said quietly. "Everyone's worried."

He got the message, and his breathing slowed.

"But he's bleeding!" shouted a tourist.

"It's ink," I said. "See?" I splayed my fingers, showing the black liquid to the crowd. It was strange, showing off the one thing I wanted to hide. Their faces crumpled with confusion and I had to fix it, fast.

I reached into Tomo's satchel, hoping for a pen, anything I could lay the blame on. My fingers brushed against glass, and I pulled the item out.

A bottle of ink, sealed shut, but the ink on my hands muddied up the container so the crowd couldn't tell.

"It leaked," I said, my body shaking. "He's in *Shoudo* Club. It's for his calligraphy projects. He's okay. Come on, Tomo, sit up."

He took hold of my arm and pulled himself upright. His body was shaking, his heartbeat erratic.

"I'm okay," he managed, bowing his head to the crowd. "I'm sorry for the commotion. I…I got too hot."

"He just needs some water," I said, passing him the bottle. He drank deeply, the water spilling over his lips, dripping onto his shirt and the satchel strap.

"Well, if…if you're sure," said the tourist.

Tomohiro ran a hand through his ink-caked hair. He curled his legs underneath him and stood slowly. I kept a hand on his arm just in case.

"I'm all right," he said again. "No need to call for help. Thank you, everyone." And he bowed deeply to the crowd, his eyes cast to the ground. He stayed like that, and I just stared at him. But then I realized that the whole occurrence would have been considered troublesome for the tourists. Japanese courtesy called for us to apologize. I bent over in a deep bow, too, until Tomo reached for my wrist and led me down the steps.

We couldn't make it into the woods to be alone. There

were too many eyes on us. So we got on the ropeway, making our way back to the platform.

I squeezed Tomohiro's hand, but he pulled it away from me. "Are you okay?" I said quietly. "Really?"

"My head's killing me," he said. "That stone was hard."

"It's stone."

He grinned, rubbing the back of his head. "I'll live," he said. But that wasn't what I'd meant.

On the other side of the ropeway, Tomohiro walked silently down the winding road past the red-and-white radio towers.

"Are you really okay?" I said, but he wandered like he was dreaming. After a few minutes, the Nihondaira Hotel came into view, which he circled past. A vast green field stretched out behind it, edged by forest and hidden mountain slopes. In the center of the field, two pools of deep blue water gleamed in the sunlight, separated by a tiny wooden bridge that barely looked safe to walk across. A sprawling tree with deep green leaves reached high above the pool like a ginormous bonsai tree. In the distance I could see the looming shape of Mount Fuji through the haze.

"It's...wow," I said as we sat at the base of the tree.

"This is what I wanted to show you," he said. "Somewhere we can be alone. And a new place to draw, if it comes to that."

I looked around. It was far enough from the ropeway that there were no crowds.

"It's not exactly private," Tomo said. "But most days it's quiet. Especially at night."

"Wait, you've been coming here at night?"

"In theory," he smirked.

"You have, haven't you? To draw?"

"I told you, I'm not drawing."

I figured the fact we were having a coherent conversation

meant he was okay from his hit against the stone. "So if you're not drawing, why did you have a bottle of ink in your bag?"

He rolled his head back to look up at the tree. A crow near the top cawed at us. "To get us out of situations like collapsing at shrines?" He laughed and shook his head, the ink loosening from his hair like fine golden dust.

I didn't believe him. Without a word, I reached into the satchel on his lap, my fingers grazing the curve of his hip bone through the fabric.

"*Oi,*" he protested, his eyes gleaming with mischief. "If you're going to violate me, I'd appreciate if you wait till I'm naked."

Heat raced up the back of my neck at the thought of it. "You definitely hit your head too hard," I stammered, but he saw how flustered I was and grinned. And then my finger sliced alongside the edge of a paper. I winced at the cut and pulled the black notebook from the satchel. "Explain this," I said, letting the notebook drop on the ground.

Tomohiro grabbed it and shoved it back in the bag. "If Yakuza and Kami were after you, would you go out unarmed?"

It was a pretty good point, really.

"So what the hell happened back there?" I brushed the golden ink dust off his shoulders.

"It was like the nightmares," he said, lying back in the grass. The giant bonsai tree made splotchy patterns of sunlight down his body. *Damn it.* I was still thinking about what he'd said, about him being naked. I remembered the feel of his skin when we'd been alone in his house that night, the way he made my fingertips pulse with heat.

Still working on those priorities, Greene.

He sighed. "I couldn't pass through the *roumon.*"

"Why, though? Why couldn't you go through the gate?"

He shook his head. "Because I'm Kami, I guess," he said. "Because I'm evil. The shrine probably protects Tokugawa from others who might've harmed him. Like me."

I stared at him. "You're not evil," I said quietly. "And I thought you said Tokugawa had his own issues. He killed them all when his powers showed up, right?"

Tomohiro snorted. "Yeah, but most who died either kidnapped or betrayed him. Isn't that kind of justice? I mean, back then it would've been. But it still doesn't make sense. I've never had a problem entering a shrine before."

"Maybe this one was booby-trapped or something? Being abducted would've made him paranoid."

"Or maybe I'm losing myself," Tomo said, sitting up and gazing across the bay to Mount Fuji. "Maybe I'm more demon than human now."

My throat was dry. "That's not true." But I thought about what Jun had said, that the ink in Tomo was taking over. That the ink in me would make it happen faster. I shook my head. "I mean, I made it through the gate, but I saw the painted dog on the shrine move. So it must not take much Kami power to make it happen, right? Or something."

"Wait, you saw the *inugami* move?" He looked at me, his eyes wide.

"*Inugami?*" It was a Japanese word I didn't know.

"Dog demons," he said. "Bigger than dogs, sloping ears, demonic eyes. Tokugawa had *inugami* painted on the shrine wall. And one moved?"

"Well, it didn't move, exactly," I said. "But he did open his mouth to growl. It was kind of like when the painting moved at Itsukushima Shrine."

Tomohiro rested his head in his hands. "It was a mistake to come here. I never should have brought you to the shrine."

"It's fine," I said, rocking onto my knees to be closer to him. "You're okay now, and that's what matters."

"It's worse than I thought. Moving sketches is one thing, but the *inugami*..."

"Like I said," I tried again. "It was probably just some kind of alarm system Tokugawa had." I rested a hand on Tomo's shoulder.

He shook it off and I moved my hand back, surprised.

"Yeah," he snapped, "and why do you think the alarm went off? Me, Katie. The *inugami* fear *me*. This is all wrong. Just like I thought—you shouldn't have stayed in Japan." He rose to his feet, storming toward the bus stop.

I followed behind, feeling like I'd been stung. "Jeez, what's your problem? What was all that before about solving this ourselves, huh? About not needing anyone else?"

He stopped in his tracks, his hand clenched into a fist. He looked down at the ground, his copper spiked hair gusting in the wind.

"I was wrong," he said. "An *inugami* is what got Koji, you know? You saw me back there. I lost control."

"And together we got out of it," I said. "I want to help."

Tomo turned slowly, his eyes glistening with the tears he held back.

"We'll beat this," I said.

He pulled me toward him and held me tightly.

We didn't speak much on the bus. Everything was unraveling.

I sat at a deserted table, tracing kanji strokes with my pencil. No one ate lunch in the school library when the weather was this nice outside. Most of the kids were out in the court-yard or up on the fenced-in roof. But then, most kids weren't going to fail because they couldn't read and write Japanese.

One more stroke and then another. I leaned back to study my handiwork.

"Only fourteen-hundred kanji to go." I moaned, flipping the page of my cram-school textbook. It wasn't just learning the characters that was tough. They all had multiple ways of being read depending on which kanji they were paired with, or on the word origin, or other inconsistent reasons that just added up to me being illiterate.

I couldn't go to international school. My life was here, at Suntaba. If Tomohiro had really stopped drawing, maybe we could enjoy a normal school life without having to worry about exploding pens for once.

I smiled. When had school in Japan become normal? But it was, and I wanted to belong. I had Yuki and Tanaka, and a million kanji to learn so I wouldn't flunk out. That wasn't the only problem I wanted to deal with. I was ready to con-quer this Kami thing. I hoped Jun—Takahashi, I corrected myself—could give me some answers after school.

The library door creaked and I looked up.

"There you are," said Yuki, and she turned, motioning into the hallway. Tanaka followed her in, both of them carrying *furoshiki*—wrapped *bentou* boxes. They put them down on the desk with a clatter and pulled up two squeaky chairs to join me. "How come you weren't on the roof?"

"Ugh," I said, pressing my forehead onto the desk. "Be-cause I'm going to flunk out of Suntaba?"

"Extra kanji practice, huh?" said Tanaka.

I mumbled into the paper, "Any wisdom you'd like to im-part?"

"Let me see," Yuki said, pulling the book toward her.

"Hey," Tanaka said, pointing at the character I'd just drawn. "I learned that one in third grade."

"Seriously, Tan-kun, you're not helping," I said.

Yuki smiled. "You'll get it, Katie."

"There are just too many," I said. I reached across the notebook for my chopsticks and yanked off a piece of the cold sweet egg Diane had rolled in the corner of my lunchbox.

Tanaka shook his head as he untied his blue *furoshiki* cloth. He lifted the lid off his *bentou* and shoved half a strawberry-cream sandwich into his mouth. "You'll get it," he said, his mouth full. *"Faito, ne?"*

"Exactly," Yuki said. "Keep fighting, Katie. We won't let them send you to another school. Let me look at this page, and then we'll quiz you."

I looked gratefully at them—Tanaka with his mouthful of cream and his glasses sliding down his nose, and Yuki with her nails painted in pink sparkles as she pulled my textbook toward her.

I couldn't leave them for some other school. I belonged here.

"Thanks," I said. "Thanks so much."

Yuki smiled. *"Atarimae jan,"* she droned. "Of course we'd help you. We're best friends." She raised her hand in front of herself and clenched it into a fist. "Okay, Tan-kun, this is our new lunch spot. Every day we'll help Katie until she can read kanji better than you."

There are friendships you know will last for the rest of your life. It was like Yuki and Tanaka and my life in Japan had always been waiting for me, like I was always meant to come here. Even if Tomohiro might regret me coming back, I didn't.

I loved my life here. And I would do anything to protect it from the ink.

★ ★ ★

Yuki and I stayed behind after class to wipe down the chalk-boards. I dipped my cloth in a bucket of water and wrung it out, the drips trailing up my wrists as I cleaned.

"Yuki," I said. It was just the two of us left, a chance to talk alone.

"Hmm?" She swished her rag around the other side of the board as we each got closer to the middle.

"Do Japanese girls usually cook for their boyfriends?" I felt stupid bringing it up, but I couldn't stop thinking about what Shiori had said. Maybe dating a guy from another culture had its own set of problems.

"Are you thinking of cooking for Yuu?" she said. "I bet he'd like cookies or maybe a jelly roll. No...that doesn't sound right. Maybe something more traditional?" She clapped her hands together. "*Wagashi!* Japanese sweets."

"I'm just wondering," I said, leaning against Suzuki's desk. "What kind of...expectations do Japanese guys have?"

Yuki scrunched her face up as she thought, twisting from side to side. "Well...I don't think being able to cook is so important. Yuu cooks anyway, right? I think the main thing is not to hurt his pride."

"His pride?"

"Yeah." She squeezed out her cloth with her sparkly fingernails. "Guys care a lot about their pride. Dumb stuff like wanting to be taller than their girlfriends and stronger, too, and they care about their fashion and hair color because they want to look cool, right?"

"Tomo asked me to call Jun by his last name. That's a pride thing, right?"

Yuki raised an eyebrow. "Yeah, that would be bad. I bet he was jealous. But, Katie, Yuu's already kind of different. Some

Japanese guys are too shy to date a foreigner for very long. They get nervous about their English, or they want a wife who will stay home. It's confusing with a foreigner because you don't know what to expect."

She was listing all the things Shiori had said. Long-term, Tomo and I would have problems.

Yuki saw my expression and patted me on the shoulder. "Don't worry, okay? You and Yuu have something special. I can see it. Just go day by day and you'll be okay. Not all Japanese guys are the same, *ne?*"

"Thanks, Yuki."

Yuki smiled. "Just be the strong woman you are, like me. If the guys can't handle us, it's their problem." She was right, of course. I didn't have to overthink this. And yet, everything Shiori had said echoed in my ears. Tomo and I had both lost our mothers; that and the ink bound us together. I thought he understood me better than anyone, but maybe we didn't really know each other at all.

I pushed the thought to the back of my mind. Right now I had to focus on what had happened at Tokugawa's shrine. I had to figure out what had happened, and for that, I needed someone who knew more than Tomo and I did.

After waving goodbye to Yuki, I headed toward Katakou School. I hadn't exactly told Jun I was coming, but I hoped he was still on the same cram-school schedule as me. And since I was free, I crossed my fingers he would be, too.

I avoided the shortcut through Sunpu Castle. I was just too creeped out to go there, knowing the Kami met up there, adorned in their all-black outfits. Instead I took the street, walking along the other side of the Sunpu Park moat teeming with dark koi that lurched through the sluggish waters. Jun's—Takahashi's school was east of mine, but I'd had to map it to make sure I was going in the right direction. It also helped to make my way upstream of the mass of green-and-navy-uniformed students.

I slowed as I reached the iron gates of the school.

"Holy crap," I said. The school was seven stories high, no lie, taller than the bare sakura trees in the courtyard. This school had money, no question about it. I mean, Suntaba was well-off, too, but this was a more impressive school than our students gave it credit for. A thick wall ran around the school boundary, and there was a brass plaque secured to the smooth white tiles. It read, 片刃高等学校.

Okay, Katie. Let's see how well you've studied, I thought. This had to be Katakou, but I didn't want to barge in without being sure. The last two kanji I knew from way back in my Japanese class in Albany, the one I took after Mom died. They read *school. Well, that narrows it down.* The first four I couldn't read.

Damn! Why couldn't I be fluent already? It was so frustrating.

A girl passed by in a navy blazer. She saw me staring at the sign and paused.

"Can I help you?" she asked in English.

I stared at her for a minute. Hearing English felt so foreign, and my tongue tripped over the once-familiar sounds. It was amazing how quickly you could forget who you used to be.

"I'm looking for Katakou School," I answered in English. "Only I'm having kanji issues."

The girl smiled. "This is Katakou," she said, running her finger along the raised kanji on the brass sign. "*Kataba Koutou Gakkou.* Or Katakou for short."

"Thanks," I said. I'd heard the full name of the school before, in the change room at Kendo Club. The word *kataba* meant the edge of a sword, something strong and focused, dangerous when applied. But the first kanji alone, *kata,* meant fragment, broken, imperfect. Suntaba students liked to use it to poke fun at their kendo rivals. But I knew Katakou students commonly used another kanji for *kata*—strength. It was their response to all the jeering from schools like ours. They wrote it differently on the banners they brought into the kendo tournaments.

"No problem," she smiled, hoisting her book bag over her shoulder. "I used to be an exchange student in California."

"Oh," I said. "That's great."

She nodded. "Are you having a good time on your exchange?"

I felt itchy around the neck. Having blond hair meant explaining myself constantly. I was always a foreigner first, no matter what. "Actually, I'm not on exchange. I moved here."

"Oh! That's great! Well, it's nice to meet you." She bobbed her head in a nod and turned on her way.

"Wait!" I said, and she paused. "Um…can I go in? To Katakou?" The gate seemed ominous somehow, and I wondered if I could get in trouble for going on another school's property.

"Are you looking for someone in particular?" she asked. A cluster of interested students were hanging around us now, trying not to look obvious as they eavesdropped on our English.

"Takahashi Jun," I said.

She smiled. "Of course. Our most famous student. Sixth in the national kendo championship last year. You're a fan?"

"Oh, no, I'm a friend," I answered, and then I realized what I'd said. Well, it wasn't like Tomohiro was here, and anyway, I doubted the girl would let me through if I said I was anything less.

"He's in the music room," she said. "I can lead you if you want."

"Music room?" But then I remembered him asking me my favorite composer, saying music was his other passion. "Could you show me? I'd appreciate it. I mean, if you're not busy."

"Sure, it's right this way," she said, grinning. She looked really pleased at the attention she was getting from the other students for her English skills, but maybe she was just happy to be speaking her second language again. I knew how great it felt when people understood my Japanese. "My name's Hana," she said as we walked into the *genkan* of the school. "Do you mind taking your shoes off?"

"Sure," I said, pulling my shoes off. I didn't have slippers here, but the floors were spotless anyway.

"You're from America?" she asked as we curved down the corridor.

I nodded as I followed her. "Albany," I said. "New York."

"Ee...?" she mused to herself. It was a typical answer here— she was just processing what I said and expressing polite interest.

I grasped for something to say. "Your school is really big." *Really, Katie?*

"The teachers have an elevator," Hana said. "But we don't get to use it. My homeroom is on the sixth floor, you know? It sucks on days when you're late."

It was the longest conversation I'd had in English with someone for over eight months, except for Diane and some broken dialogue with Yuki. It felt so strange to be able to express myself completely. I guess I'd always taken it for granted.

"Okay, music room's in here," she said, stopping in front of a wide sliding door. "Sometimes he practices in the concert hall, which is at the end of the hall right there." She pointed to the next set of doors. "But it sounds like he's practicing in here today." We could hear the muffled sound of a piano inside the music room.

"Thanks so much, Hana."

She smiled. "No problem. It's nice to have a chance to speak English. I miss California. I have to go to *juku* now, but see you later, okay?"

"Thanks," I said. "Have fun at cram school."

She rolled her eyes. "Yeah right," she smiled, and then she was gone, winding back down the hallway to the entrance of the school.

I listened to the piano start and stop, followed by muffled conversation. I pressed my hand to the cool handle of the door, ready to slide it open. I felt nervous, like I was intruding. But he'd said to come by anytime, right? And if he was busy with a Music Club practice, I could wait in the hallway until he was finished. I just needed to let him know I was here.

The piano started up again, followed by the rich sound of a cello. And then it stopped, a few bars in, followed by more conversation.

Seeing my chance to enter with the least amount of interruption, I slid the door open with barely a sound. But as I stepped into the room, the piano started again.

I stopped, startled by the sight in front of me.

There was Jun, sitting on a dark chair with a cello resting against him, his fingers poised on the strings and on the bow, ready to draw it across. He wore that black bracelet with silver spikes on his wrist. No sign of his cast.

And at the piano, Ikeda, her fingers dancing across the keys.

6

They didn't see me at first. Jun's eyes were closed, waiting for his cue to join the piano melody. And Ikeda focused on the keys of the piano as she played, swaying her body slightly to the music.

I'd never thought of how they might know each other. It was way too weird to see them being so...so normal.

Ikeda played a long, slow intro, and it was like time stopped. Jun sat completely still, his fingers barely touching the strings. Then Ikeda played a loud chord and Jun's bow moved, spanning the instrument slowly, the rich sound resonating. And then more waiting and more piano.

Eventually he joined in, and the two played. It was a slow piece, gentle and beautiful, everything I'd thought to be the opposite of the Kami. How could they create such stirring music and yet stalk around Shizuoka at night hoping to build an army to kill Yakuza? It was like some kind of sick joke.

Jun's arm arced with the bow, his whole body swaying gently as he played. I was more of a dancer than a musician, at least back in New York, but even I could tell he had an incredible connection to the instrument. It was beautiful to watch him play.

The piece swelled, more pronounced, the chords almost angry in their expression. It was then that Ikeda noticed me, when she glanced up from the piano to look at Jun and saw me standing in the doorway. The silence in the music room felt thick and uncomfortable. Jun opened his eyes to see why Ikeda had stopped.

She glared at me. "You."

"Katie," Jun said. He smiled, lifting his hand with the bow to tuck his blond highlight behind his silver earring.

"Your cast," I said, suddenly self-conscious.

"Came off this weekend," he said. "But I'm not allowed to do anything strenuous for another few weeks. So no tournament, I'm afraid."

"What are you doing here?" snapped Ikeda. "You're not supposed to be on school grounds if you're not a student."

"Hana showed me the way," I said, as if that gave me some kind of authority. Maybe they didn't even know who she was. It was a pretty common name.

"Has something happened?" Jun asked. He bent away from the cello to rest his bow inside an open instrument case.

I looked at Ikeda. What was her problem? So she was possessive of Jun—well, fine. Didn't she know I was with Tomohiro? I wasn't some kind of threat. I really didn't like her looking at me like that.

"I just want to talk," I lied. No point telling Ikeda what was happening. What if she put Jun up to pestering Tomohiro again?

"You'll have to come back later," Ikeda said sharply. "We're in the middle of practice."

"It's okay," Jun said, gently lowering the cello. "My wrist's starting to give me trouble anyway." He lifted his bow back out of the case and unscrewed the bottom to loosen the horse-hairs.

"*Naruhodo,*" Ikeda muttered to herself. *Yeah, right.* She didn't believe him, which was fine. I didn't, either.

"*Jaa,*" he said. "See you later."

She closed the fall board of the piano over the keys and grabbed her book bag, walking past me without looking up.

"Jeez, what's her problem?" I said to myself. But Jun heard me and laughed.

"I think her problem is that you broke my wrist," he said.

"Valid, I guess."

"Uh-huh." He snapped the cello case shut and crouched down to push the heavy container near a wall of instrument cases.

"So you said you played an instrument, but I didn't real-ize you meant a cello." I guess I'd expected something more typical like guitar or piano.

"It's the deep tone of it," he said, hunched over the case. He rose and turned to look at me. The blond highlights had tipped from behind his ears and now clung to his face until he tucked them back. His bangs had grown so long over the summer that I could barely see through them to his left eye. "When the bow moves against the strings, I can feel the vi-bration of it in my heart."

"You're really good," I said. And then, feeling awkward, I added, "You and Ikeda, I mean."

He smiled, and the room felt too warm. He'd always been striking, but why couldn't I get over it by now? I was with Tomo, and Jun had issues.

"We're practicing for the school festival. It was Beethoven, you know. Sonata no. 2 in G Minor. I chose the piece."

"Nice," I said. He was passionate about it, I could see that. How could this Jun be so different from the one who'd asked Tomohiro to kill someone? A criminal, but still.

"So," he said. "You wanted to talk?"

"If you have time."

He pressed his hands into his pockets and twisted his body from side to side, like he was stretching. He gave me another sweet smile. "I always have time for you."

Despite all my willpower, I started turning as red as those *daruma* dolls they sold in the tourist shops. The only thing that helped me regain my normal pulse was how cold his eyes were, like he was always thinking deeper thoughts that he wasn't sharing. Like I was a kendo opponent he was sizing up. *How will she move? How can I counter?* It was unnerving.

"Let's go to the art studio," he said. "I've been doing a lot of thinking, and I have something to show you."

I put my hands up in front of me. "You're not going to draw, are you? I mean, it wouldn't be safe to draw here." But he didn't stop; he just kept walking toward the door. I followed him into the corridor and slid the music-room door shut.

A group of students passed us in the hallway, staring at my different uniform. I wondered what they must be thinking.

"*Oi,* Taka-senpai!" they shouted. He waved and they cheered to themselves. "*Kakko ii!*" they flailed, discussing how cool he was as they wandered down the corridor.

I'd forgotten he was some kind of kendo celebrity.

And then I caught the eye of one of the students. I knew him—he was one of the Kami from that night. I froze.

Jun saw me looking. "He's harmless. His drawings move, but they don't come off the page."

"Oh." So Jun's Kami friends weren't even dangerous after all.

"The Kami were there for support that night," he said. "In

case there was a fallout with the Yakuza or if Yuu had questions."

He led me up the stairs, endless stairs, until we reached the sixth floor.

"Your school is…really tall," I puffed.

He whispered conspiratorially, exaggerating his expression. "Sometimes I sneak a ride in the elevator."

"Daring."

"I'm a rebel," he said. "Leading a revolution."

He'd meant at as a joke, but the comment was kind of true in a creepy way.

He pulled open the door to the art studio. The white tables in the room formed an open square, with a smaller table in the center, probably to put reference objects while sketching or painting. Along the back of the classroom ran cupboards full of supplies, and one wall of the studio was floor-to-ceiling windows. The sun would set soon, and already the light streaming in was golden and diffused. I stepped toward the window, admiring the view from six floors up. The tennis court outside looked tiny and deserted.

I heard the click of the door and looked to see Jun's hand on the lock.

"So we're not interrupted," he said. "We don't need any more ink sightings in Shizuoka after that dragon Yuu drew."

"I don't get it," I said. "If there are so many Kami in Japan, why are you underground? Why are you hiding?"

He headed toward the supply cabinets and started raiding them, piling rainbows' worth of paints on the white counters.

"A few reasons," he said. "One, because most Kami are not as powerful as Yuu and me. Usually it's just enough to weird someone out—bad nightmares, drawings that flicker. It's not the kind of thing you want to draw attention to. Kids who do mention it usually get put on meds because they're 'hallucinating.' Two, because we have a long tradition of hiding to survive."

"Tomohiro told me the Kami went underground at the end of World War II," I said.

Jun tilted his head. "That's only half-true. The Samurai Kami went into hiding long before the emperor denied lineage to Amaterasu during the war. That was a message to those who *knew*. It went over everyone else's heads. No, hiding began with the Kami from samurai families. If you seemed like a threat to the royal family, you were eliminated, so samurai stopped mentioning it. You only hear about the Imperial Kami being descended from Amaterasu, right? Everyone thinks that's myth now, and they've forgotten there are others. And that leads to the third reason we keep quiet. We know the abilities we have would cause mass panic in Japan and the world. People don't believe in that kind of stuff anymore." He looked over his shoulder, a paint bottle in each hand. "When the time is right, when the people are assured of the Kami's right to rule, then we'll reveal our power again."

"You mean it'll be easier to take over Japan when no one is looking?" I said, rolling my eyes.

He grinned. "Something like that. But it's for their own peace of mind. I mean, how did *you* react when you first saw the ink move?"

Not very well. There was truth to what he was saying. The Kami would probably be rounded up and sent to labs or something to be poked and prodded. They definitely wouldn't be left to roam free.

If anyone knew what Tomohiro was capable of... I shuddered. He would've been considered a threat by the royal family back then.

Jun grabbed an armful of the paints and paper and brought them to the square of white tables, putting them down with a thud.

"What do you mean by Imperial and Samurai Kami?" I asked. He took an empty glass and carried it to the sink at the back of the room. "Are they different?"

"The Imperial Kami are the direct connection to Amate-rasu." He pushed a knob on the tap and water rushed into the cup. "The emperors have always claimed descent and the right to rule. The problem is that history is never straightforward, because people aren't, either." He slammed the knob off and carried the water back to where I was waiting. "Kami children started showing up in the samurai families. Sometimes it was infidelity, but other times emperors and their family members married into the samurai families to show loyalty. But as the different clans fought for power, both sides became paranoid." He put the glass down and pulled out a chair, motioning for me to do the same.

"Like a Kami war?"

He nodded, tucking his blond highlight behind his ear so he could see me better. "The emperors worried the Samurai Kami would try to overthrow them. It sparked a lot of battles, assassinations and even suicide requests."

I gaped. "The emperors asked the samurai to kill themselves?"

"Hara-kiri," Jun said. "You've heard of it, right? The emperors could claim it was because of their dishonor, and the real reason could be covered up. But the samurai families caught on. And suddenly there were no Kami children being born anymore. Strangest thing, huh?"

"They hid their abilities to survive."

"Some parents tried to make matches that would dilute the

Kami blood so the powers would decrease through the family line. Others wanted to retain the power, but had to send their children away so their talent would go unnoticed. And the ink doesn't awaken in everyone, so it's hard to determine who's descended from a Kami and who isn't. Which is why now Kami often don't know how to control their powers. They aren't taught. It's a dirty secret, one many families don't even remember."

"I know there are a lot of people in Japan," I said, "but if the ink goes back that far, there must be a ton of Kami now."

Jun shook his head as he unscrewed a bottle of red paint. The room filled with the chemical smell of the acrylic. "It's sort of like a recessive trait, you know? It shows up the strongest in the imperial family and descendants of the samurai families, where the chances of the trait are strong. But once the bloodline between the elite clans and the common people intermixed, the ink started to go dormant. More human than Kami, you know?"

That's what he'd said to Tomohiro that night. *Stop thinking you're human.*

"How do you know all this?"

Jun grimaced. "I'm from a family that believed in retaining the Kami bloodline. When I started showing signs, it was required learning."

"So the reason you and Tomohiro are stronger than, say, Ikeda, is because you're from samurai families?" I asked. It was lame, but I felt smug for slipping in a passive-aggressive jab at Ikeda.

Jun grinned. "Or imperial," he said. He squirted the red paint into the glass of water. It spread its tendrils, tinting the water a deep crimson.

"What are you doing?" I said. He didn't answer, but grabbed

the blue paint and squirted some into the glass. He grabbed yellow and then green, giving them each a squeeze into the glass. They swirled into a disgusting brown. "Okay, whatever art project this is, you're totally getting an F. That's just gross."

He slapped the lid on the last of the colors and pushed the glass toward me.

"Drink this."

I stared at him. "Have you lost your mind?" Maybe he really was crazy.

"Drink," he said, tilting the glass from side to side.

Ew. "No way. Do you know how sick I'd get? Believe me, it wouldn't be pretty."

"Exactly," he said, putting the glass down and leaning back, his arms folded.

"I don't follow."

"If you drank this, you'd get sick," he said. "Your stomach would hate you."

"Yes. We've all learned something today. So…?"

"Okay," he said, twisting the spiky bracelet around his wrist. "So say you did drink it. You'd get really sick, but after that, would you be okay?"

"Depends. Is it nontoxic?"

He laughed. "Yes."

"Then yes, I'd be okay."

He pushed the murky paint water away and grabbed a sheet of paper. He reached for a pen and began sketching. I leaned as far back as I could in my chair.

"It's not…it's not going to attack, is it?"

Jun looked up at me, frowning. *"Kowai ka?"* he said. "Are you scared? Man, how bad is Yuu's control?"

Damn. Even without meaning to, I was giving him way too much information about Tomo.

"His control is fine," I lied. "It's you I'm worried about. Those snakes you called up against the Yakuza were pretty vicious."

He smiled. "But none attacked you." He was right.

He sketched and I peered over his left arm, curled casually around the drawing. He was bolder in his drawings than Tomohiro was. Tomohiro's strokes were more delicate somehow, more thoughtful and hesitant. Jun's were determined, steady, practiced.

He drew a glass of water, and before he'd even finished, the water sloshed around with each stroke, dripping down the side of the glass like beads of ink.

When he was finished, he lifted the paper upright and touched the surface gently with his hand. The blur of the image against his skin made me feel sick, and I had to look away. It was the same kind of motion sickness I had watching Tomo draw. There was something about that moment when the drawing stopped being a drawing and started being something else. Something alive.

When I looked up again, the glass of water still sloshed on the page, but Jun held a copy of it in his hand. The edges of the glass looked uneven and scratched and the water inside swirled with veins of black, like the ink had dropped into the clear water, spreading out in tendrils. The water didn't muddy with color like the paint water had.

"Thirsty?" Jun asked.

I stared at him with disbelief. Knowing what I knew about the ink, a drink like that could kill someone.

He could probably tell what I was thinking from the pale look on my face. He lifted his free hand and waved it back and forth.

"I drew water, not poison," he said. "It would probably make you really sick. But at the end of it, you'd be all right."

Hesitant, I touched the glass. If Tomohiro had drawn it, I would've gotten a sharp cut. I knew I would've. But Jun's glass was smooth to the touch, and except for the sprawling ink in the water, it looked almost normal. Why did I feel guilty thinking that?

"The thing is," he said, "if you drink something that makes you sick, there's a good chance you'll come out of it okay. But what if it's not just you? What if, say, the person who drank this was pregnant?"

My eyes widened, and I lifted my hand to my mouth. I got it. I got what he was saying. My voice wavered. "You think my mom ingested ink when she was pregnant with me."

"If someone drinks the ink, they don't acquire the abilities of a Kami," Jun said. "Not even by blood transfusion. But if that ink got trapped somehow, got pumped into you as you were forming…your body might think it was natural."

"Oh god."

Jun's voice was gentle, quiet. "Katie, when you were about ten or eleven…is that when you noticed the ink reacting?"

"No," I said. "I didn't notice anything until…" My voice dropped away. "Until I came to Japan. When I first arrived, I felt like something was coursing around inside me. The plane—there was this turbulence, and I could've sworn it moved in time to my pulse. It happened again when I started at Suntaba, and then I started seeing Tomo's drawings move."

"That makes sense," he said. "It was probably dormant until it returned here. Until it could sense the other Kami around. Not that it's alive, but…it's the power given by Amaterasu. And that power will seek its own like a magnet. It's like how people are driven to a certain calling in life. The Kami are driven to protect Japan."

"But how did the ink get to my mom in the first place?" It was horrifying to think about. I was shaking now, and I rested my arms on the table to steady them.

"What about your aunt?" Jun said. "Did she send any *omiyage* gifts from Japan?"

I shook my head. "She didn't move to Japan until I was eight. And Mom's never been. Diane could never convince her to visit, and I doubt she would've gone before I was born, either. She doesn't like traveling outside the country." *Didn't like,* I meant. I still couldn't think of Mom in the past tense.

Jun looked away. "What about your dad?" he said, reaching to fiddle with his silver earring. I was starting to notice he did that when he was anxious.

"My dad wasn't in the picture," I said. "He left Mom before I was born."

"*Sasuga,*" he said. *As expected.*

"What?"

"Nothing," he said. "Just...my dad was a deadbeat, too."

"He ditched you guys?"

"Sort of. He's dead now."

"I'm sorry," I said. "My mom's dead, too."

It was news to him, which just reminded me that we really didn't know each other. So why did I feel like we did?

"I'm sorry," he said.

"It was a heart attack, a year ago now. What happened to your dad?"

Jun's eyes were dark and cold, more than usual. He lowered his hand from his earring and tightened it into a fist. He didn't say anything.

I knew that look, that pain. I wanted to reach out to him,

like Tomo had reached out to me. The death might have happened a while ago, but Jun's wound was fresh. He hadn't dealt with it.

I rested my hand on his wrist and he looked at me, surprised. "I want to help if I can. I've been through the same thing, you know?"

He'd always looked so controlled—I'd never seen him look shaken like this. "Yakuza," he said. "It was the Yakuza."

Oh my god. No wonder he wanted to take them all down. I remembered now, what he'd said when Ishikawa's henchman had threatened me. Jun had wrestled the knife from the thug and stopped him. *I don't like gangsters,* he'd said. *I've had run-ins with them before.*

"My dad was a Kami," he said. "He used to work for Hanchi."

My eyes went huge. "Hanchi's the one who tried to get Tomo to work for him."

He nodded. "They asked me, too. But there was no way in hell I'd work for them. They destroyed our life. Mom and I had to move back in with her parents. We lost our house, our car, everything."

"After your dad died?" I said. He nodded, closing his eyes. His skin was hot beneath my fingers. I wanted to hug him, but it felt awkward. What if he got the wrong idea? So I just clung to his wrist while he sat there, still, silent.

"Those bastards," he said, his voice dark and unforgiving. "That's why I'll use the ink to get rid of them. So they can't hurt anyone else."

I understood his suffering and his longing for justice. I couldn't agree with the way he wanted to achieve his goals, but at least it was something...at least he was coming from somewhere.

"Anyway, never mind," he said, looking up. He looked composed again, in control. "What's important is I think we've figured out how you're connected to the ink. Next is how to control it."

"Control it?" I said. "I'm not a Kami, though."

"You are, in a way. You're like a manufactured Kami."

"That's creepy," I said, and he laughed.

"Sorry," he said. "I thought it was cool. Your drawings don't move, but you can manipulate the ink."

The art studio was getting darker, lit by the dim glow of the sunset.

I glanced at my watch. "Yikes. Diane will wonder where I am. I was supposed to be home for dinner half an hour ago."

"Ah, *gomen!*" he apologized. "Let me drive you."

"No, it's okay," I stammered. I didn't really want him to know where I lived.

"At least to the station," he said. "Until we know the Yakuza will leave you alone, it's dangerous for you to wander Shizuoka in the dark, don't you think?"

He had a point. Anyway, he seemed less intimidating than before. I didn't feel like he was out to get us. He had his own agenda, and it was a little twisted, sure. But his heart seemed in the right place.

"Thanks," I said. I helped carry the paint bottles back to the cabinets as he scratched out the water-glass sketch. The paint made a murky black swirl in the sink as we poured it out.

"Mazui," he said, grossed out. He looked away, sticking his tongue out as he made a face.

I laughed. I couldn't help it. "Thirsty?" I said, imitating his deep voice.

"I knew you wouldn't actually drink it," he said, "or I wouldn't have asked."

We stopped by his locker in the *genkan* to get an extra helmet and our shoes. "Sometimes I drive Ikeda home after music practice when she doesn't bring her motorbike," he explained. I couldn't figure out their relationship—he called her by her last name, she used his first—but I guess it was none of my business anyway. His sleek black motorcycle was parked beside the bike racks. The sun was setting fast, and the air was crisp. I guess fall was on its way after all.

I straddled the bike behind him, resting my hands on his waist. It was awkward, holding him like that. It was a closeness that was embarrassing and thrilling at the same time. *Get over it,* I said to myself. *Yes, he's pretty. But you're taken. So forget it.* It was stupid to feel this way. I was just holding on to him so I wouldn't fall off the bike. He knew that, and I knew that.

Jun revved the bike to life and we took off down the street. Thank god I was sitting behind him, because the wind held a sharper bite as we sped through it. The road led past Sunpu Castle and I stared at it, its towering white walls lit up by strategic spotlights on the bridge. Then past the police station, the perfect cover for the Kami against the Yakuza.

I couldn't forget how Tomohiro and I had brought that *shinai* down on Jun's wrist, the sound of the bone as it snapped.

What the hell am I doing? I thought. But with Jun's help, maybe Tomo and I stood a chance of getting the ink under control.

I didn't have a choice.

And telling myself that helped ease the guilt that sloshed around in my stomach.

I got off the bike the minute Jun pulled into the station. The air felt cool against my fingertips as I lifted them from the warmth of his waist. It was like he'd left an impression of warmth on me, and now it felt bare.

"Are you sure you'll be okay the rest of the way home?" he said, lifting the visor on his helmet. I could barely hear him over the engine of the bike, revving with life.

I nodded. "Thanks again."

"I mean it, Katie. I'm not the enemy. I'm worried about Yuu and you. Come by Katakou anytime, okay? And you have my *keitai* number."

I nodded.

"Good night, Takahashi," I said. It sounded weird and awkward, and I wasn't the only one who noticed.

"Takahashi?" he repeated. He smiled unsteadily, the word warm in his throat. "I'm Takahashi now?"

"It's not that," I said, turning beet-red. "I just… Isn't it kind of…not right to call you Jun?"

"Is it bothering you?" Jun said. "Or is it bothering him?"

My whole body shivered. I felt so stupid.

"Katie…you don't have to feel weird about it. Ikeda calls me Jun. Almost everyone in the school calls me Jun."

Ikeda probably wasn't the best example he could come up with. And Hana and the junior students hadn't called him Jun at all.

"Listen," he said, "it was awesome when I placed so high in the nationals last year. But Takahashi…I feel like he's the *kendouka,* you know? All the reporters, the newspaper articles, the fame and the scrutiny. I felt like I kind of lost part of myself, like people forgot I was just me. That's why Takahashi feels distant to me now. It's not really me." He smiled, his eyes gleaming. "That's why I like to be called Jun. I get to just be me, you know?"

"I get it," I said, relieved. He wasn't taking it in the way Tomo thought at all, then.

"Exactly. You don't have to feel strange about it. I ask everyone to use it. I prefer it."

"Okay," I nodded. Thank god that's all it was.

Jun revved the handle of his bike, reaching a hand up to tuck a stray blond highlight back into his helmet. He hesitated a moment and then leaned in toward me.

He smiled. "If it bothers him, it can be our secret."

My stomach flipped over, my confidence fading away. His eyes shone as he looked at me. I pushed the feeling down, the thrill of having a secret together. No, the guilt.

He winked and flipped the visor of his helmet down, speeding away from the station.

7

The walk back from Shin-shizuoka was lonely and a little cold. I wondered if I should've let Jun drive me the whole way, but it just felt too weird. Sure, he was acting nice now, but I couldn't turn my back on what had happened. And anyway, I felt off-balance about the "secret" we were sharing. Where exactly was the boundary with him?

I felt my *keitai* buzz in my book bag, so I pulled it out and checked. Two missed texts and a missed call from Tomohiro. I hit Redial right away, like I had something to prove, like I hadn't been sneaking around doing the opposite of what he'd asked me to.

The tinny ring echoed in my ear for a minute before Tomo picked up.

"*Moshi moooosh,*" he answered with a drone.

"Hey, goofball," I said in English.

"Huh?"

"Never mind," I said, switching to Japanese. "What's up?"

"So…you know how I'm a jerk and an idiot all the time?"

I smiled. "Yep."

"*Oi,*" he said. "You could at least *pretend* to refute it."

"Sorry. I meant, you're never a jerk."

He gave an awkward laugh. "Okay, the thing is, I screwed up again. What I said at Nihondaira… I'm glad you stayed in Japan. I'm just…"

"Scared?" I suggested. He didn't answer, but I wasn't surprised. He wouldn't want to admit it. Pride, like Yuki had said. "I'm scared, too, Tomo. When you collapsed at Nihondaira, when I saw that look in your eyes again… I just don't want to see you lose yourself to the Kami, you know?"

"I know. I have to stay in control."

"Right. So if you ever need me to back off, fine. It's better than turning into some kind of unleashed monster, right?"

Silence.

Shit. I'd overdone it.

"Tomo, I didn't mean it like—"

"It's okay," he said. "I am a monster, Katie. But I'm tired of running."

"Well, maybe soon you won't have to," I said. He started to answer, but his voice cut out. "What happened?"

He sighed. "Shiori's calling me on the other line."

The jealousy twinged in me. I couldn't help it. "It's fine. Just answer her."

"No," he said. "I want to talk to you, Katie."

I smiled. I felt guilty for being happy about it, but I was. I couldn't lie. "It's just that…what if she's in trouble?"

By now I'd reached my mansion, so I walked through the automatic doors into the warm lobby. "I gotta go anyway. I'm late for dinner. Just answer it."

"You sure?"

I couldn't let Shiori rattle me. I couldn't trust her, but I could trust Tomo. I knew that. "Sure."

"Okay," he said. "I'll see you at kendo practice tomorrow." The phone went silent, and I tried to think about other things.

I rode the elevator up, thinking how much control Jun had had over his sketch. Tomohiro could have that, too. I knew it. And I could help him.

I stared at my hands, flipping them back and forth. There was ink running in my veins. There always had been.

"Tadaima," I called out, opening our front door. I tapped my school shoes off and stepped up onto the raised floor of the hallway.

"Katie," Diane shouted from the kitchen. "You're late."

"Sorry," I said. "Stayed after school to hang out." I could hear something frying, my nose flooding with the delicious smell of rice and egg as I walked toward the stove.

"Lucky for you I left school late, too," she said, a spatula in hand. "Dinner's just ready." There was a pot of fried rice mixed with enoki mushrooms and chicken, all glistening in a tomato sauce, and an omelet sizzled in the frying pan.

"Omurice?" I said.

Diane grinned. "Your favorite, right?"

"Thanks," I said. I was so glad I could keep living with Diane. She always noticed the little things that mattered. I watched her spoon the rice into the center of the omelet, wrapping the sides of the egg around the filling.

I opened the cupboard and grabbed a plate for her.

"Since you're home just in time, you get the first one," she said, taking the plate from me. In a quick motion she flipped the filled omelet upside down and onto the plate. It came out only slightly unshaped, so I grabbed a napkin and pinched the ends together.

"When did you suddenly become interested in cooking?"

Diane joked, watching my handiwork. She cracked another egg into the empty frying pan.

"Tomohiro cooks," I said. And I didn't want to let him down as his girlfriend, but I felt silly saying it out loud.

"You're pretty serious, huh?"

"I don't know," I shrugged. It still felt awkward to talk to her about it, but I was trying to be a little more honest. There was so much of my life I couldn't share with her—the Kami, the Yakuza, the ink—it made me want to share what I could.

The ink.

"Diane," I said suddenly.

She looked at me, noticing the urgency in my voice. "Everything okay?"

Tone it down, Katie. Casual is what we're going for.

"Fine," I said, taking my plate to the table and pulling out a chair. I grabbed the ketchup bottle and started writing kanji on my *omurice.* Why stop practicing?

Diane flipped her filled omelet and sat across from me, taking the ketchup bottle and drawing a smiley face on top of hers.

"We're doing a unit in biology," I said, feeling guilty for lying yet again. "About, you know, how foods affect the body and all that."

"Oh, a nutrition unit?" She dug a hole in her omelet and the steaming rice spilled onto the plate.

"Kind of," I said. "Like, how if you're pregnant, you shouldn't eat soft cheeses, stuff like that."

"Mmm-hmm."

"So," I said, poking the *omurice* with my spoon, "I guess I was wondering if Mom did that kind of stuff with me. I mean, avoiding dangerous foods and all that."

"I guess," said Diane. "I don't really know about that stuff much, Katie. I never had kids, you know."

"Yeah," I said. *Shoot.* I had to find another way to get at the question. "So I guess Mom's pregnancy with me was pretty typical, huh?"

Diane's face went pale. Her spoon stopped digging into the omelet. I'd hit on something.

"What is it?"

"Well...truth be told, Katie, she almost lost you."

"What?" I thought Jun had said the ink wasn't dangerous to ingest. Had it been that bad?

"She got really ill about four months in. She was in the hospital, hooked up to machines and IVs... It was awful. They were monitoring your heartbeat constantly."

"Holy crap," I said. "Why didn't anyone ever tell me this?"

"She didn't like to talk about it," Diane said. "She never told you?"

I shook my head.

"She couldn't keep food down for almost two weeks. We thought she was fading. But she pulled through, and that was that."

"Wow," I said. "That's scary."

Diane gave me a sad smile. "But you both came through it badly beat up. The doctors said there'd be side effects. Um... you know, birth defects."

"Defects?"

"They said you'd have brain damage, that you'd never be able to walk. That you might not be able to see or communicate." I could barely hear her; my world had stopped. Diane reached across the table and squeezed my hand. "But don't worry about any of that now," she said. "When you were born, you came out just fine. You were young enough at four months that your brain just kept growing, and here you are, just fine."

Not completely, I thought. *I'm not fine at all.*

"It's why your mom was always clinging to you," Diane said. "Why she never wanted you to leave her side."

"Because I almost left her before I was born," I said. The tears welled up in my eyes. I hadn't even known I'd fought for my life. The ink had tried to kill me long before any of this. "I always thought it was because Dad left...that she was worried I'd leave, too."

One look at Diane, and I knew. I just knew. My heart thudded in my ears.

"Oh god," I whispered. "Dad left her because of that, didn't he? Because there was something wrong with me?"

Diane's eyes filled with tears. "He was a sorry excuse for a man," she said, her voice wavering. "You're better off without him, Katie. We always loved you just the same, no matter what."

The *omurice* turned in my stomach. Everything made sense, as horrible as it was. Everything except one detail.

"How did Mom get sick?" I asked.

Diane frowned. "We were never sure where she got the food poisoning," she said. "We think it was the fruit your dad brought back from a business trip to Tokyo."

Oh shit. "He went to Tokyo?" I whispered.

"He brought back these wrapped dragon fruits. You've probably seen them at the *supa* when we go shopping. Pink and green on the outside, but inside white with these little black seeds. The one she ate was really dark purple on the outside. Must have gone bad. The lab tested the other fruit and they came back fine, though, so we don't know for certain."

Black-and-white fruit. *Oh god. Mom ate a dragon fruit sketched by a Kami.* Who knew how it had got into the box. Maybe a worker had sketched the fruit because he'd swiped one to eat. Maybe…maybe Dad had poisoned her on purpose. But that was dumb. I was pissed he would leave her because something was wrong with me. What the hell? But still, something twisted in my stomach. In a way it was all my fault—Mom's fear of losing me, all the overly careful parenting she'd done. All the loneliness she'd endured.

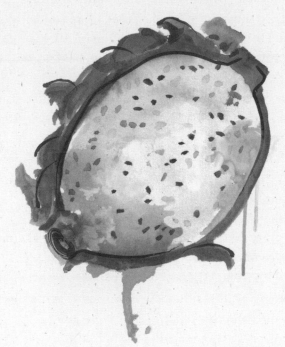

It was Dad's fault, but now I felt responsible, too, even though I hadn't asked for any of it to happen.

"Oh, Katie," Diane said. "Did I tell you too much?"

"No," I said. "No, I wanted to know." I'd needed to know. "Thank you. For being honest with me."

"That all happened a long time ago," Diane said. "So never

mind, okay? Look how strong and healthy you turned out. Nothing's going to hold you back now."

She was wrong. I was still suffering from the ink. I was still marked like I had been before I was born.

I was always destined for this. And like Tomohiro, the ink in me had been bringing sadness to those around me before I'd even known.

Yuki met me in the library at lunchtime the next day to go over my latest list of kanji. Tanaka had suddenly decided he needed to try out for the baseball team after watching the Giants game on TV the night before, so he'd gone to beg the club to take him halfway through the year.

"Okay, and this one?" Yuki said, pointing at the kanji from yesterday's study session.

I racked my brain. "Um…guilt?"

She shook her head. "*That* one is guilt." She pointed. "This one is to—"

"To put down," I blurted out. "I remember."

"Are we going too fast?"

I sliced my stewed egg in half with my chopsticks and shoveled a piece into my mouth. The salty soy sauce melted on my tongue. "I have to," I said. "I don't have time to learn these slowly. Anyway, that's the only one I didn't remember. Well, and this one, and this one…"

"Katie," Yuki said, reaching for her salmon *onigiri,* "you're really distracted today. Is everything okay with you and Tomohiro?"

I flushed red. "What? Why?"

Yuki grinned. "Because you're not spilling the details, and if there's drama going on, I need to know."

"It's not about Tomo," I said, taking another bite of the egg.

"It's something I learned about my mom. She was really sick when she had me, Yuki-chan. I almost died."

"Uso," Yuki said in disbelief. "You're kidding. But I'm glad you're here, Katie, that you're in Japan with me."

"Me, too," I smiled. And then I wondered if maybe I wasn't supposed to die from that ink. Maybe I was supposed to survive, to move to Japan. Maybe there was actually purpose behind it all.

"So everything's okay with Tomo, then?"

"It's great," I said. Except the whole me-lying-to-meet-up-with-another-guy thing, but obviously it wasn't how it sounded.

"Good," Yuki said. "Then let's keep working on kanji so you can stay. Let's work on *myoji.* Can you write my name?"

In phonetic hiragana I could. But *myoji,* the kanji for names…

I concentrated and wrote. 渡部雪。

"That's it!" Yuki squealed. She erased one of my strokes and fixed it up a little. "This one needs to be longer than this one," she said, and I nodded. "Okay. Write another name."

勇智宏。*Yuu Tomohiro.*

"Oh please," Yuki said, jabbing me with her elbow. "Spare me. You guys are sappy beyond belief."

I missed our time in Toro Iseki. I wished things didn't feel like they were slipping between my fingers.

I only had to put the chairs on the desks for cleanup, so I arrived early to the gym for Kendo Club. Today was the last practice before the prefecture tournament over the weekend. I headed into the change room and pulled on my *hakama* skirt. Today's practice was all about Tomohiro, really. With Ishikawa out and only a couple of our junior *kendouka* participating, he was the only one who had the skill to advance for Suntaba at the tournament. It would be such a relief to have it behind us. I wondered if the police were still hounding Ishikawa and Jun. I'd have to ask Jun the next time we met up.

The next time. How many times would we meet up? But the control he'd had drawing that glass of water—I wanted that for Tomohiro. Jun could live a normal life. Maybe Tomo could, too.

We started the class with the usual push-ups and laps around the gym. Many in the class hadn't bothered to suit up in full *bogu* armor, but Nakamura-sensei and Watanabe-sensei didn't notice, or at least didn't care. They hounded Tomohiro, shouting at him to go faster as he did his laps.

"Pick up your feet!" they shouted during his *kiri-kaeshi* movements. "You're stuck to the floor, Yuu. Lighter!" It was brutal, like they were hazing him.

"Ossu!" Tomohiro shouted to show he was listening, conforming.

"Swing harder. Focus! Better aim. Again!"

"Ossu!" he yelled back. The sweat was dripping off the ends of his *tenugui* headband onto the floor.

"Not good enough! More!" What the hell were they talking about? He was in peak form. It was almost cruel. They were pushing him to his limits, screaming at him, and he took it, time after time.

I realized I was staring, so I went back to my exercises.

"I've never seen them work him so hard," I whispered to my partner.

She nodded behind the mesh screen of her *men* helmet. "The competition is going to be really tough."

"Okay, together!" Nakamura-sensei shouted, and all the *kendouka* gathered. We sat in a circle except for Tomohiro, who stood in the center, his body shaking with every breath. "Kamenashi, you're up," Coach said, and the *kendouka* stood to spar with Tomohiro. But Kamenashi was beaten down easily, even though he was high level.

Nakamura called another *kendouka* and then another. These two were a difficult match, and I started to realize what he was doing. Each team member he called had a different strength. Kamenashi was quick on his feet; Matsumoto had incredible defense; Hasegawa was aggressive and powerful. In this way, the coaches were training each aspect of Tomohiro's abilities and looking for weaknesses.

"One more, and then we're done for the day," Watanabe-sensei said. "Katie, you're up."

What? I was still a junior *kendouka.* Tomo could beat me easily, way more easily than he'd beaten each of the partners I'd watched. Even with his body swaying, exhausted, the copper spikes sticking out from under his headband flattened with sweat, it wouldn't be a challenge to him.

He looked at me through the bars of the *men,* his soft eyes looking into mine. And I realized why we'd been paired.

He'd trained on speed, defense, offense, power, aggression. There was one thing left. How would he fare when the battle was emotional? Pit him against his girlfriend—would he make mistakes, let down his guard? Smart thinking from the coaches, but did it ever suck for us.

"Get into *seiza.* Ready?"

I pulled myself from the circle, feeling numb. I crouched into *seiza* stance, my *shinai* gripped tightly in my hands.

"*Hai, staato,*" yelled Watanabe, and Tomo and I started circling. My thoughts were racing. Tomohiro looked collected and calm, but I hadn't had his training. I yelled a loud *kiai* to steady myself, but it was hard to focus. He looked ready to collapse, and even then he was dangerous.

He swung, totally unexpected, and I barely dodged it by leaping back.

"Faster footwork, Tomohiro," said Nakamura-sensei.

Tomo screamed, *"Ossu!"* His voice was strained. What were they trying to do, make him collapse?

I lunged at Tomohiro, but he blocked my *shinai* with his own. The crack of wood on wood echoed to the rafters of the gym, and the vibration shook in my hands. I barely recovered in time to dodge his next attack.

But I didn't make it, and the *shinai* tapped into my *dou.*

"Point!" shouted Watanabe.

One more hit and we could stop this. One more point and he could rest. I wanted to just give in, to let him win. But it would be too obvious and he was the one who'd get in trouble. So I kept fighting.

He swiped at me and I backed up, almost into the circle of *kendouka.* I had to get back into the center of the arena or I'd end up out of bounds. I circled away, avoiding him. The shouts and encouragement of our classmates around us were disorienting paired with the stifling heat of the armor.

I circled Tomohiro, watching him carefully. And then he lunged, yelling his *kiai* as he approached.

Only that didn't sound like his voice at all. It sounded strange, warped, like many people shouting at once. The same kind of shout I'd heard when we'd fought Jun at Sunpu Castle.

He hit his *shinai* so hard against mine that I collapsed onto the ground, my *shinai* skidding across the sleek floor. My whole back was out of bounds of the circle. He'd basically won.

But he didn't stop. He raised his *shinai* high above his head as he screamed.

Why isn't he stopping? Attacking me now was like beating

someone with a broomstick. I would get injured for sure, with my spine against the hard floor like this.

"*Yamero!*" ordered Watanabe sharply as he and Nakamura approached Tomohiro. "Stop!"

They weren't going to make it in time. The *shinai* was going to hit first.

I looked up at Tomohiro, my hands instinctively up to protect myself. His eyes shone dark and angry behind the *men*.

Dark angry pools of ink, vacant, lost.

He'd lost himself. And he was going to attack me.

He cried out, swinging the *shinai* down.

I cringed, waiting for impact. I could try to roll away, but I knew I wouldn't be fast enough.

"Yuuto!" came a loud shout from the side of the gym.

Tomo stopped, the *shinai* a foot above my hip as I rolled out of the way. The *shinai* clattered against the floor as Tomohiro grabbed his helmet to steady himself.

I could see a shock of white hair from the doorway. Ishikawa. It had to be.

"What the hell were you thinking?" snapped Nakamura. Tomohiro was lifting the helmet off his head, his eyes normal and completely disoriented.

"You could've seriously hurt her!" said Watanabe. He reached up and smacked Tomohiro hard on the back of the head. I stared, terrified.

Tomohiro dropped to his knees, his armor clattering against the ground.

"*Sumanakatta!*" he shouted, a pretty serious apology. His shaking fingers clawed at the floor as he bent over, bowing low to the coaches and me. But it was a cover, I could see that. He'd collapsed to his knees from exhaustion and was turning it into the most serious apology he could make.

"Greene, you okay?" Ishikawa was beside me now, offering a hand to help me up. It was so weird to have Tomohiro as the danger and Ishikawa as the one to help, but I was too shaken to protest. I took his hand and got to my feet, lifting the *men* off my head.

The *kendouka* circle was silent, horrified.

"Dismissed!" said Nakamura, and they scattered to the change rooms. "To attack a *kendouka* like that is unacceptable, Yuu. What the hell is wrong with you?"

"Look at him," Ishikawa said. "He's exhausted, Coach. He's as slick as a fish with all that sweat. He was probably delirious or something."

"You," said Watanabe, narrowing his eyes, and he pointed at Ishikawa. "You're not even supposed to be here. You're suspended from kendo until the police investigation is complete."

Ishikawa was silent. It was a huge risk for him to come.

"I just wanted to cheer Yuuto on," he said quietly.

"Go home," Nakamura said. "We have enough trouble to deal with right now."

"He's right, though," Watanabe added. "Yuu's exhausted; he has better discipline than that. Katie, are you okay?"

"I'm fine," I tried to say, but it came out shaky.

Tomohiro heaved the breath into his lungs, looking at me with what looked like tears in his eyes. He looked terrified as he reached a hand up to pull the headband from his hair.

"*Sumanakatta,*" he said again quietly.

I couldn't believe it. I didn't want to believe it. He was losing to the ink, and it had tried to hurt me.

The Kami in him was taking over.

8

Tomo and Ishikawa were chatting by the change-room door when I came back out.

"Katie," Tomohiro said, rushing up to me and resting his hands on my arms. "Are you okay?"

"Fine," I said, "but I'd really prefer you didn't try to pound me into a pancake."

"Greene," Ishikawa said, running a hand through his white hair, "close one." So suddenly he cared what happened to me? Between him and Jun, the lines of friends and enemies were blurring way too much for me to understand.

"Aren't you supposed to be at home on bed rest?" I said.

"Yeah, I am." Ishikawa started unbuttoning his shirt, and I threw a hand up like a visor over my eyes.

"Okay, I don't need to see that."

"No, stupid. The wound." He pulled the side of his shirt back to reveal a mass of bandages. "Still hurts like crap, but they managed to dig the bullet out, so I guess I won't be setting off any metal detectors."

Tomo tucked a strand of hair behind my ear and Ishikawa

looked away, I guess because we both felt awkward. "So you're really okay?" I knew Tomohiro hadn't been himself when he attacked me, but still—I needed time to digest what had happened.

"What gives?" I said. "You've lost control before, but never toward me. I mean, the drawings, sure, but not...you."

Ishikawa piped up. "I'm thinking this isn't the best place for a discussion. And I'm hungry for something that isn't *konnyaku* soup."

"Oh no, *konnyaku*," I said, rolling my eyes. "The tortures of being shot."

"How about *okonomiyaki?*" Tomohiro said.

"Fine, let's go," I said, and we twisted down the hallways toward the *genkan* to get our shoes. I couldn't believe I was going for lunch with Ishikawa.

But he had saved me just now. Maybe he was a changed person or something.

In the *genkan,* Tomo and Ishikawa headed over to the third-year shoe cubbies. I watched, feeling like I didn't fit in with the two of them. Ishikawa's occasional attempts at tolerating me were only because of his friendship with Tomohiro, anyway.

We headed toward the *okonomiyaki* place and sat across from each other, a giant black square griddle between us. I grabbed the menu, staring at the kanji for each item. A lot of the ingredients were in katakana, the Japanese system used for foreign words. *Hamu. Cheesu. Bekon.* I was tempted to order a ham, cheese and bacon version just to show them I was literate.

I stared at the ingredients I wasn't so sure about. But before I could decipher everything, the waitress had arrived, and Ishikawa was rattling away our order.

Damn. Literacy was still out of reach.

Ishikawa leaned back, his arms folded across his chest. "So what the hell happened back there, Yuuto?"

"I blanked out," Tomohiro said, looking at me. "I couldn't focus. It was like being in a dream, where you can't really control what you're doing or thinking. You know something's wrong, but you can't fix it."

The waitress came back with the ingredients in a large bowl. Ever the chef, Tomo grabbed the bowl and started stirring.

"Well, it has to stop," I said. "First the *roumon* and now in kendo practice. Why do you think you're losing control so much lately?"

"Wait, this has happened before?" Ishikawa said.

"Yeah, including when your goons tried to grab him, Ishikawa." I sighed. "Remember the giant demon head and the ink wings and the way his eyes got huge when he drew that gun? And since when are you in on this discussion anyway?"

"*Mou!*" Ishikawa said, lifting his hands toward me. "That's enough! Jeez. Of course I remember those, but I didn't know they were all linked to the weird eye thing and losing control. Yuuto never tells me anything."

"Which turns out to be a good decision on my part," Tomo said. "You sold me out, Sato."

"And I'm sorry, okay?" Ishikawa said. He grabbed the bowl from Tomo and poured the contents onto the griddle, where they sizzled and steamed. "I thought the Yakuza could offer you a good life. Make you rich, protect you, you know. I mean, you were already helping me with my jobs anyway."

"Not helping," Tomo said. "Just making sure you didn't get your face bashed in."

"Which is helping."

"Helping *you*, not the Yakuza, okay? I don't want that kind of life, Sato."

I grabbed one of the metal paddles on the side of the table and started flattening the ingredients as they fried. I breathed in the smells of cabbage, bacon and noodles.

"I know, okay?" Ishikawa said. "I just thought— Never mind."

I had no idea what he'd thought. The idea was so twisted. Had he been jealous of Tomo? There was no way he really thought life would be better with the Yakuza, was there?

"How did you possibly think that was a good idea?" I said.

"Look, the Yakuza aren't all bad, Greene." Ishikawa grabbed the other metal spatula and pounded on the side of the *okonomiyaki*. He winced at the motion and rubbed his shoulder. "Do you remember that huge earthquake in Kobe? And the tsunami? They helped out, you know. Hell, they sent helicopters and volunteers before the government did!"

"Okay, none of this is the point," I said. "The point is that Tomo is out of control and that, thanks to you, the police think someone went after you and Takahashi because of the kendo competition."

"*Uso*," Ishikawa said in disbelief, his eyes wide. "Is that true, Yuuto?"

Tomohiro gently took the metal spatula from me and the other from Ishikawa. He slid them under the pancake and flipped it over, the smell of the golden-brown batter making my mouth water.

"There's only one major contender left in the prefecture, Ishikawa," I said. "And you're looking at him."

"Well, shit," Ishikawa said. "Don't worry, Yuuto. I haven't

told the cops a word. I can't for the life of me remember how I got this gunshot wound." He grinned.

"Can you take this seriously?" I said. "You think it's some joke. What do you think would happen to Tomohiro if they took him into custody for assault, huh? You want him to go to some mental institution?" I regretted the words as soon as they came out. "Oh god, I'm sorry."

"It's okay," Tomohiro said. He focused on the *okonomiyaki,* his eyes unreadable.

"Look, I didn't mean you're crazy or anything. I just—"

"Smooth, Greene."

"Shut up, Ishikawa."

"Guys, seriously," Tomo said, slicing the pancake into pieces with the spatula. I reached for the sauce and poured it on while Ishikawa zigzagged mayonnaise over the top. "Off topic. The question is, why am I losing control? And I think I know the answer."

Me. It's me. I knew he would say it. We all knew it was true. He lifted a piece of the *okonomiyaki* onto my plate and I tore a piece off with my chopsticks. The salty noodles and bacon flooded my mouth.

"It's that I haven't been drawing," Tomohiro said.

"What?" I said. "Are you sure?"

He nodded. "The nightmares are worse, too. Think of it like a river. Flowing along, no big deal, right? Now plug the river with a dam. You get a buildup, and it's strong. And finally it's so strong that *don!* The dam washes away."

"So things are going to get worse if you don't draw," I said. Tomo's eyes locked with mine, and I knew he'd only spoken half the problem aloud. The other was us, together. The ink would get worse as long as I was around.

"What do you mean by 'get worse'?" Ishikawa asked. "Demon faces, dragons, guns, and now acting all spaced-out and attacking Greene. How can it get worse?"

Tomo didn't even know what I knew, that Jun had said he was like a bomb waiting to go off. That the Kami blood could eventually take over, that he could black out permanently.

"Takahashi wants to use me," Tomo said. "Like the Yakuza did, but on a bigger scale. He's building some kind of Kami army and he wants me as a weapon."

"Are you fucking kidding me?" Ishikawa said, his eyes wide. "You're in this much trouble, and you've never told me? What the hell kind of best friend are you, Yuuto?"

Tomohiro looked away.

"Ishikawa," I sighed. "Tomo was protecting you, like he was protecting me. He didn't want us to drown in the aftermath of the dam breaking. He's the best damn friend you could have, so shut up."

Ishikawa closed his mouth and picked at his food. I guess it had finally hit him.

"You better start drawing again, Tomo," I said.

He nodded. "I'm sorry my stupid experiment put you in danger."

"Well, at least we know now. Not sketching really isn't an option."

We finished our dinner and paid at the counter, stepping outside into the chill of the early evening.

"Gotta head home before my mom freaks out," Ishikawa said. "She punches harder than Hanchi." He laughed, but I shuddered at the name of the Yakuza boss. I didn't want to meet him again, ever.

"Catch you later," Tomo said. Ishikawa lifted a hand to

wave, walking slowly away from us. Tomo's phone beeped and he reached for it.

"Shiori?" I guessed. Who else?

"Yeah," he said. "She wants to hang out. Just give me a sec while I tell her I'm busy." He started answering her text and I stepped away to give him space.

I looked up at Ishikawa, walking away. He hunched slightly, his arm hanging funny on the side where he'd been shot. I felt a surge of gratitude to him, seeing him limp like that. He'd saved Tomo's life that night, and maybe mine, too. And he'd been there for me at kendo practice to stop me from having a limp of my own.

I hurried toward Ishikawa and touched his arm. He hesitated, tilting his head in an unasked question.

"Hey," I said. "Thanks. You know, for saving me in the gym."

He snorted. "I didn't do it for *you*, Greene." He looked across the road to where Tomo was hunched over his phone, his bangs covering his eyes as he rapidly pressed the buttons. Ishikawa's eyes shone, and his voice was soft. "I did it for him."

My hand slipped from his arm and I stared at him for a minute, watching him watch Tomo. Then he snapped out of it, giving me a lopsided grin and a light smack on the shoulder as he walked away.

I watched him go. The look he'd given Tomo... I'd looked at Tomo like that before, too.

"Katie-chan," Tomo said, and I turned, pushing the thoughts aside. He wiggled the phone at me. "I'm finished. Let's go."

I nodded, and we turned toward the station. "Shiori okay?"

Tomo sighed. "I'm starting to wonder if she exaggerated

the bullying. The last few times I went to help her she was just lonely."

"I'm sure it's stressful being pregnant and alone," I said. The sun was setting, the streets golden around us. "Heading home, then? Or possibly somewhere else?"

"I have entrance-exam homework," Tomohiro said.

"Ah."

"Which I plan to blow off. I have more important things to do, like making it up to you for almost braining you in kendo." He grinned, his bangs scattered in front of his eyes.

I raised an eyebrow, trying to hide the shiver that ran through me. "Are you going to be okay for the entrance exams?"

"Are you going to be okay with your kanji?"

"How did you know about that?"

"The way you studied the menu," he said. "Just guessing."

"Suzuki-sensei threatened me with international school."

He looked concerned, brushing his fingertips against mine before he took my hand. His fingers were warm and soft, and I loved how mine curled inside his.

"Do you want some help? I could study with you."

"Yuki and Tanaka are helping me at lunch every day," I said. "But I could always use some extra help."

"Of course. But…I need a favor from you, too." He took a slow breath, his eyes distant. "I have to start sketching again. I don't want to put you in danger but—"

"But you need someone there in case you lose yourself," I said. "Are you sure I can pull you out of it? I couldn't today at kendo practice."

"But you did at the *roumon* gate. And if you're there, I know I'll fight harder to be in control. I'm sure of it."

I nodded. "Okay. But no ink bottles, okay? And no dragons."

He grinned and nodded in agreement. "Let's go."

★ ★ ★

This time we took the bus directly from the station, which was a shorter trip and made Nihondaira a feasible new choice over Toro Iseki. We crept toward the clearing behind the hotel, near the gigantic bonsai-looking tree and the two ponds.

Tomohiro sat down under the tree and I followed. By now the stars were coming out, and the view from the mountain was spectacular. Fuji was just a shadow in the distance, and we could see Suruga Bay, the little lights from ships blinking on and off, and the lanterns strung along the shore by the strawberry farms.

"It's beautiful at night," I whispered.

"Like I said." He grinned. "I'm glad you got to see it."

I texted Diane that I'd be late at school studying kanji with Yuki. I felt guilty lying again, but there's no way she'd let me be out with Tomohiro this late at night in a place this remote. Her aunt-turned-mom senses would be flaring.

Tomohiro reached into his bag for his notebook. Despite the danger we were in, the frightening way he was losing control, my heart still jumped to see the black cover of the notebook. Maybe there was a dangerous Kami lurking in Tomohiro, but there was beauty living in him, too. His sketches left me breathless sometimes. That dark cloud of butterflies for one, the wagtails and plum blossoms, and the *furin* chimes. I would never forget the sound of the *furin* in the sweet early-summer breeze.

Tomohiro opened the cover of his notebook and a stack of loose pages fell out. He gathered them up, shoving them into his bag.

"What are those?" I asked.

"Just stupid drawings."

I frowned; why did his voice sound off? "Let me see."

"They're all scratched out anyway," he said. "I'll draw something new. I think my sketches will be more powerful after the hiatus."

"Should I stand back?"

"I'll just draw something contained. Something harmless," he said. He reached for the pen clipped over the notebooks pages, pulling the cap off with a snick.

"Harmless?" Everything he drew managed to be harmful. Flowers had thorns; glass wind chimes had glass edges you could cut yourself on. But he was already drawing.

It was harder to see the dark lines as they swept across the page in the dark. But then suddenly I could see a little better, and everything was brighter.

Specks of silver light blinked into existence around me as Tomohiro drew. They sparked everywhere in the darkness, like disconnected fireworks, hovering in the air, blinking in and out of view. Some of them burst into being like tiny explosions.

"Fireflies," I said, standing. There was a cloud of them, woven through the tree branches like strings of lights, flashing in strange rhythms as they lit up and died out. The whole tree was aglow, Tomohiro's page flickering with their light as he drew more. "Won't the people in the hotel see?" I breathed.

Tomohiro smiled. "Tourist season is over," he said. "Hotel's closed."

So that's why it was so quiet here.

I stepped into the clearing, the fireflies thick in the air around me. If I reached out my arms, I wondered if I could touch them. They fluttered, blinking in and out, always in a new spot when they lit again.

"Beautiful," I said, "but hardly contained."

He laughed. "They can't do much damage," he said. "But they're for light. I figured a candle might burn down the whole mountain. At least from my notebook."

He was right. Drawing fire was way too risky. But fireflies—it was magic, the only way to describe it. Their wings rasped like paper as they hummed in the air around me, and their lights were silver instead of gold or green, but walking through them with my arms outstretched felt like walking through a fairyland. They cast moving shadows everywhere, so that the whole world seemed to light like a carnival.

Tomo gasped, and I turned quickly. "Are you okay?"

"Katie," he said, reaching his arm out for me. I moved toward him, taking his hand as I knelt in the grass.

"What is it?" I said. I looked at his face as it flickered in and out of the shadowy light. Beads of sweat rolled down from his forehead; his eyes looked strange.

"The voices," he breathed. He shuddered now, and I tilted my head to listen. I could hear the wind, swelling with sound. "I can't."

I squeezed his hand. "You can, Tomo. It's only because the ink is flowing again. You're in control, okay?" His eyes held mine as he gasped. The fireflies swarmed into a tornado around us, spinning with an unnatural frenzy. "Do you need to cross them out?"

He shook his head. "Just…just stay with me." I nodded. A moment passed, our eyes locked as he searched mine for strength. "It's like swimming in a current," he gasped. "It's… wonderful, but…too much."

"You're strong," I said. "I'm here with you."

He squeezed my hands tightly, and another moment went

by. I tried not to think about the part where he'd said it was wonderful. I loved the beauty of his drawings, too, but it was scary to think he took any pleasure in losing control. He must not have meant it that way, I decided. His grip loosened, and he stopped shaking. The fireflies stopped swarming, spreading across the clearing again as if they were real.

"Better?"

He nodded.

"*Yatta,*" I said, and he let out a short laugh.

"That's hardly celebration-worthy," he said.

"How do you feel?"

"Better...and I want to draw something else." He let go of my hands and took the pen.

"Are you sure?"

"It feels right," he said, and his pen scratched across the paper. But I worried...was it his own idea or the Kami's?

Something lit up in the pool.

"What are you drawing now?"

"Go see," he said, and I could hear the smile in his tired voice.

I stepped forward slowly, cautiously. What if he was drawing something that yanked me into the water? But the silver glow in the water was no bigger than my hand and almost as wide. The shape started circling in fluid patterns.

It was a papery white koi, his eyes jet-black, ink tendrils swirling on his fins. He glowed with an unnatural light, his fins flapping against his sides as he glided through the sleek, dark waters. His black and silver scales gleamed in the firefly light. Beside him, another area of the pond lit up, like a light-bulb gradually brightening, and then there were two koi, circling. Then a third, and soon the whole pond gleamed with fish, making their own firework patterns in the water.

I barely heard Tomohiro as he approached from behind me. His breath fell softly upon my neck as he wrapped his arms around me, peering over my shoulder to watch the koi.

"Dou?" Tomohiro said quietly, his voice at my ear. "What do you think?"

I turned in his arms to face him and saw him looking at me with his deep eyes. The fireflies clung to the spikes in his hair, casting moving light and darkness across his face. He looked like a prince; he looked like a demon. The glow and shadow flickered like candlelight, and I wasn't sure which he belonged to.

But I knew I wanted him to belong to me.

I raised myself up on the balls of my feet, pressing my lips against his. His arms tightened around me, drawing me closer as he kissed me back. My head filled with sweetness. Every movement of his fingers, everywhere his skin grazed mine, felt like a spark.

The fireflies alighted on his arms, his legs, the waistband of his jeans. They flashed out of sync, like they were broken.

They tangled in my hair, too, and on my clothes. I could feel them clinging, their papery wings fluttering against my skin.

Tomo and I were draped in stars, floating among a thousand iridescent wings.

A loud splash startled me out of the moment. We both hesitated, clutching each other as we turned to look.

The ghostly white koi thrashed in the water as if they were on dry land, desperate and frantic. They were all swimming in one area of the pond, as if they were attached to each other.

Crimson blood swirled through the water, thick and black in the moonlight.

I raised my hand to my mouth. "They're killing each other."

Tomohiro dashed to his notebook, grabbing the pen and flipping the pages. He scribbled over the fish, slicing lines of ink through their necks and fins. One by one, the paper fish floated belly-up in the water, until it was nothing but a graveyard of drifting koi lanterns.

They melted into pools of black, swirling around the inky blood as they disintegrated into nothing. The ink caught on the wind and lifted like dull gold, glimmering among the silver firefly light.

"*Kuse-yo,*" Tomo swore in a hiss behind me. "Can't anything ever go right?"

That's when I felt the first bite.

"Ouch," I said, swiping at my neck. My fingers crumpled the firefly's wings and he tumbled into the grass below, his light dim as he struggled to flicker.

Another bite. "Ow!" Tomohiro still didn't look up. "What the hell?" I snapped, and then he looked.

"*Doushita?*" he asked. *What's wrong?*

That's when I realized, yet again, the language gap held me

back, even from getting help. *Ow* and *ouch* wouldn't cut it in Japanese—he had no idea what they meant.

"Itai!" I said, swiping at the fireflies on my leg. Tomo looked at me with panic in his eyes.

The fireflies began to gather again, a massive silvery cloud hanging above us. They swarmed like a plague, their lights flashing in unison. The throng buzzed toward me and I screamed, ducking to the ground.

"Katie!" His pen swiped through the drawings in his notebook.

There was a sound like an explosion, hundreds of tiny lives shattered at once.

The firefly stars rained down around me, falling like a firework in slow motion.

The sadness was overwhelming, watching the cloud of lights drop. I reached out my palm and caught the bodies in my hand. They felt lighter than air, empty. Nothing.

I felt faint as I watched them, as their lights blinked out one after another. I didn't feel right at all.

The world spiraled and I heard Tomohiro shout. Things were moving sideways, like I was dreaming.

I was falling, the dark tree branches rising above me.

I heard the loud thump as Tomohiro caught me, as his arms hooked under my shoulders and grabbed me, lowering me softly under the huge bonsai.

"Katie," he said, but his words echoed. Above me the stars blinked in and out, floating down.

"The stars are sharp," I heard myself say. I could feel them cutting into my wrists.

Tomohiro swore and lifted the waistband of his shirt, shrugging it over his head and tucking it around me to cover my bare arms. Then he was gone, and I was left to stare upward at the raining fireflies. Above them, dark clouds rolled slowly toward Mount Fuji's shadow.

The last of the lights blinked out, and the field was dark again. I breathed in and out slowly—something was wrong with me. I brushed the grass with my fingers, trying to hold on to concrete feelings, to pull myself back from wherever I was.

"Katie," Tomohiro said, his warm hands smoothing my hair out of my face. "Are you okay?"

"I don't know. I feel weird."

He reached out for a can of milk tea and pulled the tab back with a crack. He pressed against my back as I lifted my head a little. The sweetness of the cold drink trickled down my throat.

He put the can aside and leaned over me, trying to lift me onto his lap. His stomach was warm against my cheek, his upper body lean and muscled from kendo training. The moonlight danced along the multitude of scars down his right arm. I reached up and traced along the edges of them, some smooth, others jagged.

It was when my hand pressed against his upper arm that we both saw the blood trickling down my wrist.

The shock of seeing it brought me back from everything.

"What happened?" I said, blinking. I sat up, but dizziness ripped through my head and I leaned back into the warmth of Tomohiro's skin.

"The fireflies bit you," he said. "I'm sorry, Katie. *Che,* I screw up everything."

"I'm bleeding," I said, but already Tomo was rustling in his pocket for his handkerchief. The poor cartoon elephant, who'd been drenched in the ink fireworks at Abekawa Hanabi, now sopped up my blood as Tomo gently wiped at my wrists.

"I don't get it," he said. "The bites aren't deeper than paper-cuts. They'll sting, but they shouldn't be serious. Maybe you're allergic or something."

He hesitated, his eyes wide.

"What is it?"

"Nothing," he said, wiping at my arm again.

I snatched the handkerchief from him.

"Katie," he said, trying to pull it back.

My body froze.

I was bleeding ink.

9

My heart raced. What was going on? I threw the handkerchief as far as I could. "I'm bleeding ink, Tomo. Why am I bleeding ink?" I looked at the bites on my arms, and each one had a tiny trickle of black spilling out of it.

"Katie, it's okay, don't worry. Has this ever happened before?"

"Of course not," I said, my voice wavering. Tears blurred my vision. "What's happening to me?"

"Okay," he said. "Let's just stop the bleeding first, and then we'll figure it out, okay?"

I was shaking. I'd seen ink trail down Tomo's arms, but I'd never seen him bleed ink. Why the hell would *I* bleed ink? Why now?

And I couldn't pretend anymore that I was normal. Jun's theory was right. There was ink in me.

Tomo used his shirt to mop at each of the bites, pressing until they stopped. He was quiet while he dabbed at them, gentle and careful, deep in thought. The last two bites had actual blood on them instead of ink, which was little comfort, but still.

"Looks like they stopped," he said.

"Has that ever happened to you?" I asked quietly. "Did you ever bleed ink?"

He shook his head. "Never."

"Great," I said. "Fantastic."

"I'm sorry," he said. "I've been such an asshole. Asking you to come with me while I dealt with a buildup of power. What did I think was going to happen? Stupid."

"It's too late for that kind of thinking, Tomo. And in case you didn't notice, you're not the only one with Kami abilities."

"But how could you be a Kami? I don't get it," Tomo said.

I squeezed my eyes shut, my cheeks flushing with guilt. There had to be a way to tell him what Jun had told me, without letting him know I'd gone to him for help, right?

"Niichan—Yuki's brother—he called me a manufactured Kami," I lied. Better to say Niichan than Jun.

Tomohiro's eyes widened. "A what?"

"I wasn't born Kami," I said. "Well, I was, but...by accident. My mom ingested the ink when she was pregnant, and somehow it got into my system. I asked Diane, and she confirmed it. I mean, that my mom had eaten something sketched and gotten really sick."

"Why didn't you tell me before?" he whispered. He looked ghostly pale, like the koi.

"I tried," I said. "But you were sure I wasn't a Kami."

"Yeah, but I've never heard of that before. A man-made Kami, I mean."

"It's weird," I said, "but I guess bleeding ink proves it. So what do we do now?"

"I don't know," Tomo said. "But I'll protect you. I promise. I know I keep screwing it up, but I'll figure out how to control it." He pounded the bottom of his fist into the earth. "Shit! Nothing works the way it's supposed to. I lose control when I draw, I lose control when I don't—what the hell am I supposed to do to protect you?" His eyes flickered in the moonlight. They looked dark and glossy, like he was going to start crying. He looked frantic, filled with frustration. It broke my heart.

"You will," I said, reaching my arm up to his cheek. "And I'll protect you, Tomo. Once we find a way."

He looked down at me, his eyes glimmering with the tears he held back. They were going cold again, certain. I knew that look. He was closing down, separating himself from me.

"We're dancing around in a minefield, Katie," he said. "If I care about you, how can I keep hurting you like this?"

I wondered the same thing about myself. Didn't I have the strength to stay away from him?

"We'll find another way," I said. "I don't want you to stay away."

He pressed his hand on top of mine. "I don't want to," he said. "I don't. I can't."

I wrapped my other arm around his shoulder, pulling myself up. He rested his arm on my back, lowering himself to meet me halfway. *"Yabai,"* he whispered, *We're screwed,* and then his lips were on mine, and my thoughts shattered.

He collapsed on top of me, his warm chest pressed against mine. I ran my fingers along his scars and he shuddered, making a soft noise deep in his throat. The spikes of his copper hair tickled against my jaw as he kissed my neck. His back felt like fire as my fingertips moved across it.

Any attempt at thinking straight was consumed. This was probably why Diane didn't want me in empty fields with gorgeous boys, but I didn't care. I wanted everything to spark around me, everything to glow.

Glow. There was a weird glow in the distance.

"Tomo," I said, and the tone of my voice stopped his trail of kisses. He looked up, his spiky hair prickling my neck gently as he turned to see what I saw.

The ink that had caught on the wind like glowing embers had drifted to Mount Kuno, the one at the top of the ropeway. The ink dust held in the air there like a glimmering cloud, right over Tokugawa's shrine.

Every time the dust drifted down to the visible roof of the *roumon* gateway, there was a flash like lightning.

"*Kuse,*" Tomo whispered.

"It's like a giant bug zapper," I said, watching the lightning flash.

"I don't get it," he said, running a hand through his bangs. "What's the link with Taira and Tokugawa? I have nightmares about them all the time, I couldn't enter that gateway—and now the ink is being pulled over there? What the hell does it mean?"

"Taira and Tokugawa were both Samurai Kami," I said. "That's gotta be it."

"Samurai Kami?" Tomo said, looking at me funny. "What are you talking about?"

Oops. Guilt-trip two for talking to Jun.

"Niichan said," I tried, "there are different kinds of Kami. Imperial Kami, descended from the emperor, and Samurai Kami, from the clan families. They started out from the same ancestors, but they were kind of at war with each other. Maybe you're related to Taira and Tokugawa."

Tomo looked skeptical. "I've never heard of that. And if I

was related to Tokugawa, why did the gateway take me out and the *inugami* try to leap off the wall?"

"Maybe you're descended from his enemy, then?"

"A demon, as always," he sighed.

"I didn't mean that," I said. "You could be from a different samurai family."

"If there *is* such a thing as Samurai Kami. Katie, can we tell each other everything from now on? I don't get why you wouldn't tell me all this stuff Niichan told you."

He was right, and I panicked, looking for an escape out of my nest of lies.

"You weren't exactly nice to me when I came back from Miyajima," I said, deciding to lay the guilt on thick. "Remember the love hotel and a certain plot to push me away?"

He looked like a wounded puppy, and then I felt bad for using it against him.

"Fine," he said. "But no more secrets, okay?"

"Okay," I said. We watched the dust flash against the gateway until the glow of the ink was gone. "Let's hope someone will think it was some kind of freak storm," I said. "No one's really up here but us anyway."

"Katie," Tomo said, resting his hand on top of mine on the ground, "maybe we can try it again. You know, when you're ready."

"The shrine gateway?" I said, and Tomo flushed a little pink.

"I meant the love hotel." He stared at me through his bangs, his eyes intense.

Oh. My whole face flooded with heat. "Um, uh…"

He burst out laughing. "Flustered again, Greene," he said, ruffling my hair as he stood up. "I have that effect on girls."

"Shut up," I said, throwing his shirt at his face. "And put

some clothes on. No one needs to see that." He grinned and caught the shirt, pulling it over his torso. He grabbed his notebook and shoved it into his satchel, and I reached for my bag from school. He leaned over and kissed me on the cheek as we headed toward the bus in the darkness of night.

"You know what, Katie? You're just as dangerous as me."

I wondered just how true that was.

My *keitai* went off just after I'd pulled on my fuzzy pink pj's. I'd spent too long soaking in the bath, thinking how everywhere he'd touched tingled with the memory of it. He must have been thinking the same. I grabbed the phone and pressed the green talk button.

"Got your clothes on this time?" I said.

"Uh...Katie?"

Oh god. The color drained from my face.

"Jun?"

"Sorry, I... Were you expecting another call?" I could practically hear the blushing across the phone.

"No! No." So awkward. "It's just a dumb joke. Never mind. What's up?" Wait. He hadn't seen the dust clouds on top of Nihondaira, had he? We should have been more careful with Kami and Yakuza all over the place.

"I was just calling to see how you're doing."

"I'm okay," I said. "Thanks for the other day." I sat down on the edge of my bed, flipping through the leftover homework on my comforter.

"Of course," he said. "How...how is Yuu doing?"

"Oh. Are you calling me to recruit him for your cult, Jun?"

"Itai," he said with a gentle laugh. His voice was charming on the phone. I could almost forget the cold look that some-

times glazed over his eyes. Now he sounded warm and pleasant. "That hurts. I thought we'd moved past that."

"Well, some of us have," I said. "Tomohiro is still worried about you, Jun."

"And I'm worried about him," he said. "Are things still under control? He seemed pretty...unstable that night."

"I don't know," I said. Having Jun help me with my connection to the ink was one thing, but talking to him about Tomohiro felt weird. "He's okay. He was kind of having issues because he stopped drawing, but it's taken care of now."

"So he is still drawing," Jun said quietly.

"It's fine," I said defensively. "It's under control." Except that it wasn't really.

"A talent like Yuu's? I doubt it. He was powerful enough for the Yakuza to reach out. I saw what he was capable of that night—that's why I'm so worried."

"But you said he can learn not to be dangerous, right? To control the ink?"

Jun hesitated. "Those aren't the same thing. He'll always be dangerous. Stable powers just make him more interesting to the Yakuza."

"Is that what happened to your dad? He had stable powers?"

Jun went silent for a minute. I could almost feel the chill. When he spoke again, his voice took on a dark edge. "His control of the ink was stable, yes. But it was pathetic compared to Yuu's power. He used to draw money for them, and some weapons. Mostly they had him draw drugs, because the people who took them got too messed up to complain whether my dad had screwed it up or not."

I almost didn't want to know. It seemed too dark a world to even peer over the edge at.

"Yuu can't control the ink until he accepts what he is. Then the ink will stop fighting him; if he can embrace his ability—his destiny—and not run from it, he will be dangerous, but in control."

Now I was silent. I knew Tomo would never stop fighting the destiny Jun was talking about.

"Anyway, I wanted to make sure you were okay. We talked about a lot. I was worried I freaked you out."

"You didn't," I said. "And it's true, Jun. You were right. I talked to my aunt, and there was a weird incident. My mom ate a sketched dragon fruit. She almost died."

"Hontou ka?" Jun said. "Really?"

I nodded, even though he couldn't see me, and stretched out on my bed, on top of my homework. I stared at the little bites on my arms and legs from the fireflies.

"And another thing," I said. "Jun, I got a bugbite tonight. It's dumb but...I'm kind of scared."

"Scared?" his voice jumped, louder in the receiver. I felt a little surge of warmth to know he was so worried about me.

"Where it bit me on my leg, I...I bled ink. What does it mean?"

There was silence. Had I said something wrong?

His voice was cold, determined. "What bit you?"

"A firefly," I said, my heart starting to race. Why was he acting like that? Was it something bad? Oh god...was something seriously wrong with me?

"He drew it, didn't he?" he said sharply. He took a deep breath. "The firefly. You were with him while he was drawing."

It felt invasive. Why did I have to report to him? He sounded jealous, really.

"You know what?" I said, shaking. "It's not your business. Forget I said anything."

His voice boiled over. "Do you think this is a game?"

The words startled me. "I don't have to answer to you, Jun."

"This isn't about me," he said. "Every minute you spend with Yuu, you put both of your lives in danger. You put the whole world in danger. Did you forget what I said about him being a time bomb? Why are you playing with matches, Katie?"

"You don't know that." I sat up, hugging my arm around my knees.

"I don't," he said. "But you know, don't you? He's getting worse. The fireworks at the festival, the fact that you flinched when I sketched a glass of *water*, that you're bleeding ink."

"What am I supposed to do?" I said. "Leave Japan?"

"Yuu is being taken over by his Kami side before he can control the ink. That could be fatal, to him or to you. Have there been any other signs? Blacking out, maybe? Worse nightmares? Unexplained sketches or weird anxiety?" Maybe not the last two, but everything else…

"No," I lied, shaking. "He's fine."

"Katie, if you're bleeding ink, it means the ink is trying to seep over to Yuu. He's a magnet and he's awakening every part of it in you. If he doesn't come to me for help, you'll get hurt, and the rest of Japan will follow. It's not a game. You have to stay away from him."

The tears started to blur in my eyes. A life without Tomo… I couldn't.

His voice was gentle velvet, smooth and sweet. "I know you…you have feelings for him, Katie. But if you stay with him, it will destroy you both. And I don't want that to happen."

"There's no way?" I said. I knew he was dangerous, but

I'd never thought he'd hurt me. But the kendo practice—he would've if Ishikawa hadn't been there.

"I'm sorry," Jun said. "Unless Yuu will let me help him, I don't think he will ever be…safe."

"But if…if he joins you? Then he'll be okay?" I couldn't believe I was saying this.

I could hear Jun's breathing over the phone. "I need your help to convince him. With him, Katie, the Kami could regain what's ours. Taking control would become instinctual—he'd become what he's meant to be."

He wouldn't get better, then. He'd become the monster he feared.

"But until he accepts his destiny, you'd need to stay away. He'll probably react to the distance, and that might make it worse at first, but the most dangerous thing you can do is go back to him. It's like a drug, like the ones my dad drew for the Yakuza. It will feel like taking it away from him is the most horrible thing you can do to him, but if you stay with Yuu, it will kill him. It will."

I didn't know what else to say. Tomo was a Kami. There was no way around it, no escape from the truth.

"I'm so sorry," Jun said.

"Look," I said, "I…I have homework."

"Katie—"

"Ima deru yo," I blurted out. *I'm hanging up now.*

He paused. Then quiet as a breath, he said, *"Wakatta." I get it.*

I beeped my phone off and tossed it on the floor.

The tears poured down my face, ugly sobbing tears.

I'd thought I could build a life here, with Diane and Yuki and Tomohiro.

I was wrong. I'd lost Tomohiro, just like I'd lost my mother.

The ink should have killed me when it had the chance, before I was born. What was the point of living a life of nothing but loss? How could I choose my own life when it kept stopping me in my tracks?

I cried, but there was no solution. There was no way out of it, nowhere to go.

To save him, I had to let him go.

10

"Katie-san, can I see you for a minute?"

Yuki, Tanaka and I stopped at the classroom door. Suzuki-sensei leaned against his desk, looking at me expectantly.

"Catch you in the courtyard," Yuki whispered, ducking out of the way.

Tanaka patted me on the shoulder as he followed her.

I approached Suzuki's desk slowly, ready for another part of my life to fall apart. Didn't he realize my heart was breaking? If he sent me to an international school, that would be the end of me. I would just rip in two.

"Katie, I wanted to talk to you about your latest assignment," he said, passing my math homework back to me. My paper was marked up in red. Instead of check marks, Japanese teachers made circles on the correct answers and crosses on wrong answers, like tic-tac-toe.

I stared at the sea of red loops.

"I don't understand," I said. "These are all...right."

"Yes," Suzuki smiled. "You've always been strong at math, Katie, but what I'm pleased about are these." He flipped the page to the word problems and pointed to one of my answers. "I noticed you using a lot more kanji in your responses, and I'm not the only one. Your biology and history teachers have been pleased, too. You're working hard—we can see that."

A wave of relief washed over me.

"Thank you," I said, bowing slightly.

He nodded and took the paper back, placing it on his desk. "But you're still not at the level of the other students, Katie. You still have a long way to go."

"I know."

"You're proving to me you can do it, but it's going to take time. And it's already October. The school year is over in February. If you don't want to go to an international school, I would suggest you consider retaking a year of high school."

My ears rang. He couldn't have said that, could he? "Retake?"

"I just want to make sure you're ready for exams when they come round," he said. "I've heard that Watabe and Tanaka are helping you at lunchtimes, but they have their own entrance exams to worry about. You can't let yourself be a burden to them."

"I'll work harder," I said. "I don't want to retake."

"I'm not forcing you," Suzuki sighed. "But as your home-room teacher, I'm just concerned for your well-being. If this is what you want, then you'll need to focus. No distractions. Consider cutting back on club time, friend time, relationships, and spend more time on your studying."

Great. The world was conspiring against Tomohiro and me. "I'll think about it."

Suzuki nodded. "I just want the best for you, Katie. Like I do for all my students."

"I know," I said. "Thanks."

I went into the hallway, heading toward the *genkan*. My cheeks flushed with embarrassment. Good, but not good enough. But I'd been working so hard on those kanji. The *genkan* was full of loud students, and it felt stifling and claustrophobic. I grabbed my shoes out of my cubby and burst out the front door, where Yuki and Tanaka were waiting for me.

They weren't alone.

Tomohiro grinned at me, his bangs fanned over his deep hazel eyes.

The resolve in me started to crumble. God, why did he have to look at me like that?

"Katie-chan!" Tanaka said, waving me over. Like I hadn't seen them. I couldn't see anyone *but* them.

I walked over, standing awkwardly beside Yuki.

"O," Tomohiro said, a casual Japanese hello.

"Hi," I said, my heart pounding. He frowned, looking at me carefully. He knew something was off.

"So, I was just telling the boys the news," Yuki said. "Niichan is visiting for the week."

"That's great," I said. "It must be nice having him home."

"Oh, he's not on holiday or anything," she said, waving her hands around. "He's been working at Sengen Jinja, sort of like a friendly ambassador from Itsukushima Shrine or something. They're like sister shrines."

"Where's Sengen?" I asked as Tomohiro paled. *Jinja* meant it was a shrine, which meant Shinto instead of Buddhist. Which, of course, meant *kami.*

"In Aoi Ward," she said. "It's only a few blocks west of Sunpu Park. Soooo..." She looked conspiratorially at me. "I thought we could double date over there and drop in to say hi to Niichan."

"Double date?" Was she kidding?

Tomo folded his arms and leaned against the stone wall of the courtyard. "A double date to visit your brother, Watabe?"

he said. "That's not exactly romantic." He was trying to discourage the shrine visit. What if he blacked out going through the gateway?

Yuki flushed. "Well, it's not really a double date. Tanaka and I aren't really together anyway."

Tanaka pressed his glasses up his nose, his cheeks turning pink. "It's basically a chance for Yuki to spy on you with Katie, Tomo-kun," he said. Yuki gasped and reached over to smack him in the arm.

Tomohiro grinned. "That sounds more likely, Ichirou. So let's go for coffee instead, okay?"

"I can't," Yuki said. "I have to visit my brother. My mom sent me with this." She held up a *bentou* box wrapped beautifully in a light blue *furoshiki* cloth. "Come on, it's a huge shrine. Katie's never seen it, and it's a romantic spot."

"Romantic?" I said. "A shrine?"

Yuki shrugged. "Sure. It's beautiful, right? Tokugawa built the shrine, you know. He was this super important Shizouka samurai. The torii gateway is huge and there are lots of nice gardens."

Tokugawa. Oh god. Now I saw why Tomohiro was fighting the plan to go there. Could he even pass through into the shrine?

"Guys, I have a lot of homework," I said. "And I'm sure Tomo has to study for entrance exams."

"Oh, I see what you're doing," Yuki said. "You're trying to sneak off so you can go to a love hotel, right?"

"Yuki!" I stammered. Tomohiro just grinned. He leaned forward and wrapped his arms around me, pulling me back toward him. His touch jolted through me, the closeness of him sending waves of heat and sparks through my body.

"Would you prefer we started here?" he said slyly.

Yuki and Tanaka turned beet-red.

I struggled in his grip. "You're embarrassing, you know that?"

He laughed and kept me close to him. I was pressed tightly against him, and all I could think about was last night. And Jun's warning that I had to stay away.

"Tomo-kun?" A timid, shy voice.

Shiori stood at the front gate, her stomach totally swollen and huge.

"Shiori. What are you doing here? Is everything okay?" Tomohiro said. He loosened his grip and I slipped away, but not before Shiori saw. Her cheeks flushed red and she narrowed her eyes.

Yuki noticed and flushed with protectiveness for me. She turned to Shiori. "You're not supposed to be on school grounds if it's not your school," she snapped, her hands on her hips.

"I'm sorry," Shiori said, a sweet smile on her lips. "And I'm standing by the gate, right? So it doesn't count."

"Yuu-san has a girlfriend," Yuki said. "So back off already."

The smile vanished from Shiori's lips.

"Easy, Watabe," Tomohiro said. "She knows Katie is my girlfriend."

"Then why is she here?" Yuki mumbled.

"I just need to talk to Tomo-kun," Shiori said.

Tanaka nodded at Shiori. "Do you remember me?" he asked. "I used to be in Calligraphy Club with Tomohiro in elementary school. You used to walk home with us sometimes."

Shiori looked at him, tilting her head. "Oh. Kind of."

"He told me you were like his sister," Tanaka smiled.

Shiori looked pale again. "Oh."

"Che," Tomohiro muttered, walking toward her. "What is it?"

"I just wondered, because I called last night and you were

busy." Her eyes flicked to me and narrowed. "Actually, you're always busy. I wanted to make sure you were okay."

"I'm fine," Tomohiro said. "I'm just… Things are different now." He looked at me, and my stomach flipped over. I felt so awkward, like I was a horrible person. I didn't mean to get in the way, but even now seeing them together gave me such a bad vibe. If I wasn't here, if I put distance between myself and Tomo, would they be together?

"I get it," Shiori said, looking sad.

"Hey," Tomohiro smiled. "*Genki dashite.* Cheer up." He tucked her hair behind her ear, and my insides lit on fire. "The baby will be here soon and then *you* won't have time for me."

How was I supposed to stay away from him? I couldn't even watch him with another girl.

"I'm done with school," Shiori said. "Too many comments, and it's getting too hard, so they've asked me to stay home until the baby's born. Today was my last day. I thought you might want to go for dinner so the day isn't a total loss. Maybe *shabu shabu?* My treat."

"I—can't," Tomohiro said. "We're going on a double date."

I blinked. Was he really going to put himself at risk to prove a point to Shiori? But I felt relieved. I'd been scared he'd say yes as a way out of the danger of the shrine.

"Oh," she said quietly.

"Shiori, I'm sorry," Tomohiro said. "Listen, let's go for coffee this weekend, okay?"

"Sure," she said, and she looked ready to slip away, like she was made of air, just drifting away on the breeze.

"Wait," I said. The word was out before I could stop it. Tomo was sacrificing for me…I could sacrifice for him, too. "Tomo can go."

"Katie, I'm not looking for permission," he said. "I'll go to the shrine with you."

I shook my head. "No. Go with Shiori, Tomo. It's her last day of school. Don't let her be alone in this, okay?"

Tomo looked at me, his eyes filled with conflict behind his copper bangs. *"Demo..."* he said quietly.

"Ii kara," I said. "It's fine." I trusted him, and it was the perfect excuse not to go to the shrine. Plus, looking at Shiori reminded me of the time Tomohiro had shut me out to protect me. It felt crappy. I didn't want him to shut her out. I didn't want her to feel alone in the world, even if she'd said those awful things to me on the train.

"Okay. Shiori, let's go." He didn't take his eyes off me the whole time, maybe seeing if I'd change my mind.

Shiori looked relieved. She unfolded, stopped hunching over her belly and smiled. "Let's go, Tomo-kun," she said. She wrapped her arms around his arm, hugging it tightly, and looked at me, a mean smile of satisfaction on her face. It was brief, but I saw the look she gave me. She let go and walked past the gate, disappearing behind the stone wall. She didn't like me being close to Tomohiro and had thrown this in my face like a victory. Yuki had seen it, too.

"Yuu-san," Yuki piped up, and Tomo stopped walking. "It's not yours, is it? The baby?"

My stomach lurched.

Tomohiro's voice was dark. "Watabe, I get that you want to protect Katie. But I want to protect her, too. So you can lay off."

Yuki narrowed her eyes, unfazed. "Yuu."

"It's not mine," he said. "Okay?"

Yuki nodded slowly. "But if you hurt Katie, I'll break you. Got it?"

Tomohiro grinned, shaking his head so his copper spikes

danced around his head. "Got it," he said. He slipped out of sight, and then they were gone.

"Let's get going before we lose anyone else to social drama," Tanaka said.

I grabbed Yuki's hand and squeezed it as we walked toward Sunpu Park. She squeezed it back.

There's no one in the world like your best friend.

The large red torii towered above us at the entrance to Sengen Jinja. I got why Tomo had wanted to avoid this place—you couldn't get in without going through the torii or the *roumon* gate at the other entrance. Behind it stretched a huge complex of buildings, brightly colored in reds and greens and gold. It was like Tokugawa's shrine on Mount Kuno, but larger.

Yuki and Tanaka passed through the gateway easily, chatting with each other and laughing. I stepped toward it, thinking of the ink that had bled from my firefly bites.

I wouldn't trigger it, would I? Was it possible to pass out the way Tomohiro had, to be rejected by the shrine's security system or whatever it was?

I squeezed my hands into fists and walked slowly through the gateway. The bright red beam towered above me, the paint peeling in strips, the wood underneath it gray and chipped. I waited for some sign of the ink, a tug or a whispered voice or something. But nothing happened, and then I was on the other side.

I sighed quietly, walking quickly to catch up with Yuki and Tanaka. I was still me. I was still human. Maybe there wasn't enough ink in me to trigger the alarm. Or maybe alone I just wasn't a danger.

I followed Yuki and Tanaka to a small gazebo-type building. The green-tiled roof sloped against the four red beams, painted with gold trim. Inside the gazebo stood a long basin, carved with snaking dragons on the sides. I shuddered, re-membering the coiled dragon in Toro Iseki. Along the top of the basin were rows of bamboo cups on long wooden sticks.

"The *chouzuya*," Tanaka said, lifting one of the ladles. He dipped it into the water, and Yuki put her hands out over the water. I did the same. Tanaka poured the cold water over our hands and it dripped off our fingers into the basin.

"What's the *chouzuya* for?" I asked, reaching into my book bag for my hand towel. Everyone carried them; mine was pink and blue with a big yellow star on it and some cute cartoon kids. It made me think of Tomohiro's elephant one, and I tried to shake the thought away. He was with Shiori right now. They were having dinner. *God, I'm such an idiot. Why did I tell him to go?*

"Just ritual," Yuki shrugged, drying her hands and stuffing her towel into her bag.

"It's a cleansing thing, isn't it?" Tanaka said. "Purifying for the shrine or something? I don't really know."

That was the way a lot of things in Japan were. You just did them; you didn't ask questions.

We wandered through the buildings, looking for Niichan. Straw ropes draped over the doorways and shrines, white paper thunderbolts hanging from the cords like jagged branches. Everywhere I looked was something sacred to the *kami*. No wonder Tomo hadn't wanted to come here.

I peered into the *roumon* gate to see if Niichan was by the other entrance to the shrine, but all I could see were the cars zooming down the street.

I turned back to the main grounds and gasped. A dragon of gold loomed over the gate, his horns pressed against the ceiling. Above him dark swirls of plaster trailed along the red beams. They looked...they looked like ink.

"You found the *Mizunomi-ryu*" came a familiar voice, and I jumped. I looked beside me to see a smiling face.

"Niichan!" It was Yuki's brother, the one who'd hosted us at his house on Miyajima Island at the beginning of summer. The one who'd shown me a moving painting at Itsukushima Shrine, a painting that only came alive for Kami.

"Katie," he grinned. "Nice to see you again." He wore a pair of dusty jeans and a loose white shirt with a green polo unbuttoned over top. *"Genki?"*

"I'm doing well," I said.

"This is one of the treasures of the Sengen Shrine," he said, pointing up at the golden dragon. "The Mizunomi Dragon."

"Mizunomi," I said. *"Mizu* as in 'water'?"

He nodded. "He was a dragon formed by koi," he said. "They were so determined to climb a waterfall that they didn't believe it was impossible. So they kept trying, and when one reached the top, the *kami* turned it into a dragon."

My heart nearly stopped. The koi fighting each other that Tomo had drawn—they'd been biting each other's tails and circling. If he'd left them, would they have turned into a dragon?

"Good thing this guy is here," Niichan said, his voice quiet. "When the shrine burned down, this dragon supposedly came to life and splashed water all over the fire. He saved the shrine for Tokugawa. It's not actually true, of course. Just a legend." He had a look in his eyes, and I knew this was more than a myth. There had been Kami in this place.

"It's not true," I repeated, and he nodded slowly. We understood each other.

"Niichan!" Yuki shouted, and she and Tanaka came running.

"Oh, Yuki," Niichan laughed, ruffling her hair. "Ichirou. Nice to see you again."

"You, too, Watabe-kun," Tanaka said.

"Please," Niichan laughed. "I keep telling you. Call me Sousuke."

"Here, from Mom," Yuki said, holding out the cloth-wrapped *bentou*.

He took it from her, swinging it back and forth. "Thanks. Praying for exams while you're here?"

Yuki rolled her eyes. "Please, like I need to."

"You need to," Tanaka said, and Yuki smacked him.

"Just bringing you the sandwiches, and we thought Katie might like to see the shrine."

"Anything else I should see, Niichan?" I said quietly. One look at him and I knew he'd understood what I meant.

"Yeah," he said. "I can show you a few things."

He led us into the main building, passing by full-size model horses, painted a milky brown and tethered to either side of their red stalls.

"They escaped during the fire," he said. "But came back when it was safe."

Did he mean it? Had they come alive? I thought the ink could only move drawings, but after I'd seen the *inugami* on the building growl...I didn't know anymore. Anyway, the horses were painted—was that enough?

"Niichan, what are you saying?" Yuki said, looking embarrassed.

Niichan chuckled. "Just old stories."

It was dark inside the main building, and I could barely make out the different urns and paintings plastering the edges of the room.

"Maintenance," Niichan explained. "The main hall's off-limits until they get the lights fixed."

I looked up at the lights, and I saw what he'd brought me here to see.

A dragon exactly like the one Tomohiro had drawn was painted on the ceiling.

He had been painted in coils of serpentlike scales, his eyes never leaving me as I moved around the room. Clouds of shadow swirled around him, flecks of gold glinting inside them.

"It's him," I said quietly. My body shivered like ice had trickled over me.

"Who?" Tanaka said.

Crap. Had I said it out loud?

"The dragon who saved this shrine," I said. "It wasn't the gold one at all, was it?"

Niichan laughed as he led us out of the building.

"Tokugawa's hardworking servants did that. Dragons cause trouble."

Of course, because the ink dragon wouldn't put out a fire. He was ready to eat me when Tomo had drawn him in the field. He wasn't exactly a do-gooder.

That's when I realized what Niichan was telling me.

The ink dragon had started the fire. Maybe he'd knocked over some candles, maybe he'd even breathed fire. I didn't know, but I was certain of one thing—he'd tried to kill Tokugawa, just like he'd tried to kill Tomohiro. They'd both drawn him.

I felt hopelessness then. I excused myself from the group and wandered the shrine grounds, the gravel crunching under my feet.

Generation after generation of Kami, hunted by the ink that marked them. It never stopped until it got them in the end. It would never stop until it got Tomohiro. Until it got me.

Why? It didn't make sense. I rounded a patch of trees, following the path away from the painting of the dragon. I passed a stall filled with *omamori,* protective charms from the shrine for every possible need—good grades, health, finances, love. The girl behind the table smiled at me, her bright red *hakama* skirt and white top making her look like a colorful *kendouka.*

I waved a hand at her to tell her I wasn't interested in buying the charms and kept walking, deep in thought.

I thought Amaterasu had been the protector of Japan. Why would she want to destroy it? Weren't the Kami her descendants?

The trees broadened here, and there was another building, almost forgotten. An elaborate phoenix painted in rainbow colors perched on the doorway, and the nearby trees were wrapped with thick Shinto rope hanging with white paper thunderbolts.

I sat down, leaning my back against the tree. I felt so lost. Tomohiro was cursed. The Kami hadn't found a way out in centuries. What hope did he have?

I had to stay away from him. At least that way, he'd have a long life before the ink got him.

Shit! Why did I have to think like that? Why did it have to be so difficult? Why did I have to lose everything, too?

"Katie?" Niichan's gentle voice came from the trees. I looked over and started to get to my feet, but he waved at me to stay where I was.

"Where are Yuki and Tanaka?" I asked.

"Wandering around the grounds looking for you," he said. "I told them I was going to eat my sandwich. Mind if I sit?"

"Why are you telling me these stories, Niichan? I thought you didn't want me to think about the Kami."

Niichan frowned, sitting on the ground beside me. He rested the neatly wrapped *furoshiki* on the ground and pulled at the ties until the cloth dropped to the sides around the polished black *bentou*. "The weight of it is heavy on your face, Katie. Anyway, Yuki can't keep her mouth closed, remember? She's told me you're dating a senior at your school, one who likes to sketch and gets into fights. I'm only guessing but...I think it's related."

"It's too dangerous," I said. "I know that now."

Niichan nodded, lifting the lid from the *bentou* and placing it gently on top of the cloth. "Yuki thinks the world of you. I don't want to see you get into trouble."

"I don't get it, Niichan. Why are the Kami so dangerous? Aren't they supposed to protect Japan?"

"Whoever said that?"

I stared at him, surprised. "Isn't that what Shinto is all about? People pray at the temple for protection and good fortune from the *kami,* right? Like, good grades, good health, stuff like that."

"Or do they pray to appease the *kami?* Are the *kami* giving good things or withholding the bad? Do you think the ancient beings of Japan care about our modern judgment calls of what is desirable?"

"I don't get it," I said.

"What we consider justice isn't what justice was even a hundred years ago," he said. "And the *kami* go much further back than that. It's hard to understand what they want, but they were always fighting with each other. Maybe they want to protect Japan. Maybe they want it back from us. And maybe they just had so much power in them that in human hands it's out of control."

"The last one sounds likely," I said. "It's more than he can handle." My face went pale. "I mean—"

"I already guessed," Niichan smiled, lifting one of the sandwiches from the box. "But keep the secret better from others, okay?"

I got to my feet, walking toward the shrine. The sun was starting to set, and the glow of it caught on the phoenix feathers. "So which shrine is this?" I said, touching the red support beam with my hand.

"*Otoshimioya,*" he said. "Actually, this is the shrine that has the most in common with Itsukushima where I work."

"It doesn't look as big as the ones back there."

"It's not the principle building." Niichan took a bite from the sandwich and waited until he finished chewing. "But it's for a daughter of Susanou, like in Miyajima."

"That's the *kami* of storms, right?" I said, running my hand down the beam.

He took another bite. "Yeah. Amaterasu's brother." He reached for another sandwich, his hand bumping the lid of the *bentou.* It clanked into the box and the sound startled me.

"Amaterasu," I said, staring at the phoenix. Niichan grunted agreement behind me.

"They didn't get along," he added. "Susanou controlled storms, but he was also the ruler of Yomi, the World of Darkness. Kind of like Hell, I guess."

A thought appeared in my head, slowly, the idea blurry and strange. But it sharpened as I thought about it, until I could barely contain it.

Oh my god.

What if Amaterasu wasn't the only one with descendants?

11

The world spun with the thought in my head. What if there were Kami descended from Susanou? Wouldn't they be as evil as he was? Wouldn't they be at war with Amaterasu's Kami?

"Niichan," I breathed, my throat thick and parched. He looked up from his sandwiches. "Are all the Kami descended from Amaterasu? For sure?"

"Yeah," he said. "Of course. I mean, I think so. Why?"

"What if they weren't?"

"Katie. It's time to step away from all this, okay?" Niichan wiped the back of his hand across his mouth, the sandwich crumbs tumbling onto his jeans. "Stay away from the boy at your school. It doesn't matter who he's descended from. You already know he's dangerous. Please, if not for your sake then for Yuki's. Just let it go."

I opened my mouth to answer, but Yuki and Tanaka appeared from around the trees.

"Katie," Tan-kun said, waving at me. "We've been looking everywhere. We're heading back to the station."

Yuki crouched behind her brother. "Niichan, you knew

we were looking for her. Why didn't you tell us you were over here?" She smacked the back of his head with her hand.

"I-te!" he snapped, rubbing his head. "Jeez, Yuki. I'm eating my sandwich. You want me to choke?"

I was numb, barely able to pretend everything was fine. What if Tomohiro was descended from Susanou? Maybe... maybe he really was a demon. That was why he struggled with his power, wasn't it?

"Let's go," Yuki said.

Jun had drawn a glass of water and nothing had happened. He'd drawn the snakes and they hadn't turned on him or us.

"Katie's daydreaming," Tanaka laughed, reaching for my wrist and pulling me along.

Jun wore that spiky bracelet, but I hadn't seen as many scars on his arms. Ikeda had some scars, too, but Jun...the only wounds I'd seen on him were the welts where he'd carved the kanji into his skin.

Tomohiro was something else. Jun was right. He'd always been right.

We went through the torii gate and toward the station.

"You're so quiet," Yuki said. "Everything okay?"

"It's fine," I said.

"I knew Tomo-kun should have come with us," Tanaka laughed. "She's been love-struck by your brother."

"Gross!" Yuki squealed.

Tomo. I had to call him. I had to tell him.

But I couldn't. He was with Shiori, and I was with Yuki and Tanaka. And what would I tell him? *Bad news, I've figured out you really are doomed. You're descended from the* kami *ruler of Hell.*

I tried to calm myself down. It was just a theory. I didn't have any proof, except that it all made sense.

When we reached the station, Yuki and Tanaka waved

goodbye. I waited for a minute, staring at the road home. Tomo would still be with Shiori, but I couldn't keep this to myself.

I took off running, but not toward Diane's.

It was nearly dark when I reached Katakou School. It was stupid of me to come. Jun wouldn't still be here, would he?

I stood by the gate, unwilling to step onto school property. I'd seen the way Yuki had got on Shiori's case. I know she'd been trying to protect me, but I didn't want to risk a student scolding me that way.

I peered past the gate to the bike racks for the school.

Jun's sleek black motorbike was parked beside them.

The school was still lit up for various clubs. It wasn't unusual to have activities running so late at a Japanese high school. Anyway, it was only just past dinnertime—not that late, even if the sun was setting.

I walked across the courtyard, hoping the darkening sky would hide the color of my uniform.

I passed a group of girls carrying tennis rackets and suddenly recognized one.

"Hana?"

Hana looked up, a racket in her hand and a tennis ball in the other.

"Hey, the American girl," she said. "Takahashi's friend. Sorry, I can't remember your name."

"Katie," I said. "Is Jun—is Takahashi around?" Which name did they really use, anyway?

"Yeah," she said. "Prefecture tournament is this weekend. He's drilling the younger *kendouka*."

Hana led me to the gym, but everything was silent. She opened the door and peered in. "Practice is over, I guess."

So I'd missed him. "But his motorbike's out front."

She shrugged. "Maybe he's getting changed. You could wait for him if you want."

"Thanks," I said. We walked back to the courtyard, and Hana waved as she left with her Tennis Club friends. I sat on a bench beside the bike racks, watching his motorbike and waiting. I looked like some stupid girl with a crush, I knew that. I bet that's what Hana thought, especially after I'd called him Jun, but she hadn't said anything about it. Maybe she liked that I used his first name, the way I used hers, reminding her of her time in California. Or maybe she was just being polite.

Susanou. Why hadn't I thought of it before? Tomo wasn't like the other Kami. He couldn't hide his power the way they could. He was falling apart in front of me. The huge vacant eyes, the *shinai* he was willing to strike me with…it was Susanou. It had to be.

I heard footsteps and the school door slamming closed. Jun. His earring glinted in the dusk light, his blond highlights almost glowing against the darkness of the rest of him. He'd changed out of his school uniform into a pair of dark jeans and a T-shirt, a fur-lined vest overtop. The fur was a bit much, but I guess I really didn't understand Japanese fashion. It looked kind of cool, or extravagant or something, like he was a J-Pop idol.

He approached his motorbike, throwing his book bag over the handle. That's when he noticed me on the bench, as he hunched over his bike.

"*Bikkurishita,*" he breathed. I'd startled him.

"Jun," I said. The name was strange as I said it. *It's our secret.* But calling him Takahashi would sound weirder and get me another lecture. "Sorry, it's me."

"Is everything okay?" he said. "Yuu—is he—"

"He's okay," I said. "But I needed to talk to you."

"Of course." He sat down beside me on the bench, a little too close, and it was like the heat of him turned my face red. I wanted to move away, but it would come across as rude. And it wasn't like I was uncomfortable—I just felt guilty. Here I was running to Jun yet again behind Tomo's back.

But Tomo was the reason I was here.

It was all I could do to stop my voice from wavering. "I was at Sengen Jinja today, the one near Sunpu Park. And there was this shrine for this *kami* Ohisa-somebody. I can't remember." He listened to me in silence, his eyes staring into mine. I wished he wouldn't look at me like that. I turned to look at his motorbike. *Phew.* That was safer. "She was the daughter of Susanou. And I started to wonder if...if maybe..."

"You're shaking," Jun said, his voice gentle.

I ignored him. "So remember we talked about Imperial Kami and Samurai Kami? What if that's not the main difference? What if not all Kami are descended from Amaterasu?"

At first his face was stone, his eyes cold and dark as he thought.

"Amaterasu is the only one the imperial family ever claimed lineage from," he said at last.

"Yeah, but who would want to admit to being descended from Susanou? I mean, no one is going to make that announcement. And there's no royal family without scandal, right?"

"*Che,*" he swore, the way Tomohiro often did. The thought made me feel guilty. "So you think maybe Yuu is descended from Susanou?"

"Well, I mean, I'm not saying he's evil," I said. I felt sick to my stomach to hear Jun say it. I hoped I hadn't given him some kind of ammo. "But maybe that's why the ink won't be controlled. I mean, when you drew that glass of water, noth-

ing happened. Can I ask you something? Your arm. Do you…
do you have scars like Tomo does?"

Jun shifted on the bench so he faced me. Our legs were almost touching, and I could feel the warmth of him next to
the cool breeze of night. He lifted his right arm slowly, twisting it so I could see the underneath of his wrist. It was hard
to see in the darkness if the skin looked normal. "Here," he
said, taking my hand. His touch sent a jolt through me. He
placed my fingers near his elbow and gently traced them down
to his wrist. His skin was warm, his arm strong like Tomo's
from all the kendo training. My fingers ran over the rough
edges of the scars.

So he did have them.

"Most Kami have at least a few," he said. But there were
lots of them that bumped under my fingertips. Jun had had
his share of accidents. "It's been a while," he said. "They're
not fresh the way they are for Yuu."

"Oh," I said. I pulled my hand out from under his grip. I
was glad it was dark. I hoped he couldn't see the deep pink in
my cheeks. My heart sounded like it was going to beat right
out of my chest.

"But the lack of control Yuu has, the explosive power…
you could be onto something. I'd never thought of it before.
Susanou…" He lifted his left arm to brush away the bangs
that trailed over one eye, the spikes on his black bracelet
gleaming in the starlight. "The *kami* of storms, earthquakes
and Yomi, right?"

I nodded. "The World of Darkness. My friend's brother
said it translated to 'Hell.'"

"Has Yuu ever called up any of those?"

I thought for a minute. The storm surrounding the dragon

he'd drawn. The earthquakes I'd felt when I first moved to Japan. And…Hell?

"Wait," I said. My pulse leaped and I felt sick to my stomach. "When the Yakuza tried to take Tomohiro away, the ink made this…this giant demon-face thing. It was really freaky. I didn't see it clearly but…it scared the hell out of Ishikawa."

"There's your answer," Jun said. "My god. He's not a normal Kami."

My heart ached. He really was the demon he'd feared. It was all worse than he even realized. I felt tears blur in the corners of my eyes. "What can we do?"

"There's got to be a way to stabilize his power. In the meantime, the best we have is for you to stay away from him. Don't do anything to provoke the ink."

I nodded. He'd started drawing again, so that would help. I'd find ways to be busy, so that he wouldn't react too strongly to me pulling away. It was horrible, but it had to happen.

"Katie," Jun said, resting a hand on my shoulder. "You're not alone in this, okay? We're going to help him."

"I know," I said. "Thank you."

Jun nodded. "I'll find out what I can, okay?"

"Okay."

"Katie, you look terrified. Let me take you home and you can get some rest."

"It's just…it's a lot to take in," I said. I could barely hold back the tears. I blinked, and one streamed down my cheek.

It was like being told to stay away from your own soul. How could I?

"Hey," Jun said. His fingers brushed my cheek as he wiped the tear away. "We'll figure this out, okay?"

I nodded, hoping I could hold the tears back until later.

He took my fingers gently and pulled me from the bench.

He rested my hand on the motorbike with his own fingers on top, lingering just a moment too long before he went back to the *genkan* to get his extra helmet.

I felt so alone as I waited in the dark. Couldn't he just hurry up so I could go home and cry my eyes out?

When he came back, he strapped the helmet on me and I straddled the bike behind him. We sped toward Shizuoka Station together and then past. I shouted my address at him and he drove me all the way home. I held on to him the whole time, like he could help me make sense of things. The wind whipped my tears away, numbing the pain.

On the steps of the mansion, I turned back to him. "Thanks," I said, my voice like a ghost.

"I'm here for you, okay?" he said. *"Tomodachi kara."*
Because we're friends.

"Yeah," I said. *"Tomodachi kara."*

He grinned, and then he zoomed down the street, and there was nothing left around me but darkness.

"Katie, is that you?" Diane yelled from the living room. I pulled the door closed behind me and kicked off my school shoes. She appeared in the hallway, her face crumpling with concern. "Have you been crying? Your eyes are puffy."

"I'm okay."

"It's that Yoshida boy, isn't it?"

"Yuu, Diane, not Yoshida. And no."

Diane smiled. "You're an awful liar, Katie. Listen, I've had my share of boy trouble. I know."

The tears spilled over; I couldn't stop them.

"Oh, hon," she said and pulled me into a tight hug. She smelled of strong perfume, but I didn't even care. I held on to her, too. "What's he done? I'll snap him in two."

I pulled back and shook my head. "It's not his fault," I said. "It's just not going to work."

Diane sighed and nodded. She kept her arm tightly around me and led me to the living room. We sat down on the edge of the ugly purple couch, but that just made me think about how Tomo and I had held on to each other that night after the Yakuza, how we'd fallen asleep on the tiny couch clutching each other. I cried harder.

"It'll get easier," Diane said, patting my back. "These cultural differences...they're not as big as they seem."

She didn't know. How could she?

"I'll make you some tea. Would you like that?"

"Yeah," I sniffed.

"And I think we had some matcha cookies left. Just a minute." Diane disappeared into the kitchen. Fixing things with food, like always. But nothing sounded better than a hot glass of tea.

From the hallway, my *keitai* went off.

I ignored it.

It buzzed again.

I dragged myself to my feet, walking toward the bag and pulling the *keitai* out.

Texts from Tomo, of course. The words were blurry through my tears.

How was Sengen? Thought about you the whole time. Tomo

My hands shook as I held the phone. God, he was so perfect. Why did he have to be a Kami? Why did it have to be like this?

I turned the *keitai* off and slid it back into my bag.

"I'm sorry," I whispered.

★ ★ ★

I avoided him at school the next two days, taking on extra cleaning duties and getting Yuki to cover for me when he showed up at our classroom. "She already left," she'd told him, when I was actually cleaning sinks in the bathroom. She said he'd swiped his bangs out of his eyes a little too hard and then left without a word. "He looked totally confused," she'd said. "So why are we avoiding him?"

"I just need some space," I'd said, which she'd translated as me being annoyed that he'd gone for dinner with Shiori. I'd reminded her it was my idea, but what else did she have to hold on to? She had no clue about the real reason.

Friday night, I received another text from him.

Did something happen? You okay?

I didn't know what to say. I didn't want to push him away. It seemed easier to just say nothing.

I hope you can still make it to the tournament tomorrow. Or you owe me shabu shabu and a night of wild passion. You hear me? Tomo

"You jerk," I said aloud. It stung avoiding him like this.

Fine, I typed back. I'll come to the tournament. Jeez, keep your pants on, Romeo.

A moment passed, and then my phone buzzed.

I'm not making any promises.

How the hell was I going to stay away? He was so lame it was cute.

12

The next morning I got ready early, putting on my new pink blouse and lacy beige skirt with my soft pink ballet flats. It wasn't so much that I was dressing up for him. I was trying to blend in more with the other girls, and here, supercute and girlie fashion was the way to go.

Okay, so it's not like I didn't hope he noticed how adorable the combo was.

Wow, Katie. What happened to staying away?

Great. So my resolve was going to last all of five seconds?

I headed toward Katakou School, where the prefecture tournament would be held. The stands were already thick with crowds when I arrived, and I searched for the best possible place I could sit to watch the matches.

I stepped down to the next aisle and just about tripped over a girl's purse.

"I'm so sorry!" I blurted out and the girl looked up at me. She wore a bright red dress with a lacy sweater. The skirt of her dress ruffled out like a ballet tutu but was way too short, so she'd paired it with leggings and a pair of cute sandals.

"Shiori?" I said, her presence throwing me off. "You came to watch kendo?" She seemed too…delicate for it somehow.

"Not kendo," she smiled. "I came to support Tomo-kun." Of course. I hoped she wouldn't ask me to sit with her. It seemed so awkward.

Instead, she said, "I wish you could sit with me, but there's just no room here. Maybe somewhere in the back?" She said it pleasantly, like we both didn't notice the slight it was.

I noticed. And it was almost worse than having her ask me to sit.

"No problem," I said. "Um, I'll just…"

"Greene!" I looked down the row and saw Ishikawa, his bright white hair sticking out in the crowd like a kendo flag.

"Excuse me," I said, a little smug. It felt good to be invited, even if it was by Ishikawa. I sidestepped down the row and collapsed into the seat beside him. "Hey," I said. "You were allowed to leave the house for this?"

"No, but since when has that ever stopped me?" He wore a white dress shirt with a red tie and khaki pants. The shirt was so thin I could see the bandage patched over his shoulder and the colorful outlines of the tattoo on his arm. "I'm doing better, but I couldn't miss this."

"Everything…okay?" I said. "You know, with the—"

"The police?" he said. He waved a hand in front of him and I looked. Four cops stood on the sides of the gym, dressed in black with official white bands encircling their arms just above the elbow. "Nah. They keep questioning me, but I'm not going to talk."

"What are they doing here?" I panicked. They weren't going to arrest Tomo, were they?

"Relax," Ishikawa said. "After today, their whole conspiracy theory will be blown to smithereens. Anyway, if Takahashi and I are here cheering for Yuuto, it won't look suspicious for him, right? No malice, no motive."

"Those are big words for a rice ball," I said, flicking him in the shoulder.

"I'm not a rice ball, Greene. Do you know the meaning of the *myoji* for 'Satoshi'? *Wisdom.* It's *wisdom,* jackass."

"Uh-huh," I said. "Do you know what irony is? Because your mom did."

He laughed. "You're as bad as Yuuto."

"So Ju—Takahashi is here, too?"

"Over there." He pointed a few rows down, where Jun sat with a group of kids. They laughed and joked as they waited for the first match to start. Some of them were dressed in school uniforms, holding banners in blue and green.

I looked past them nervously to the police. One of them, a woman constable, was talking to the referee. I hoped Ishikawa was right. I was tired of worrying about what they might find out.

The *kendouka* entered the gym in a line and the crowd rose to their feet, cheering. The competitors wore full *bogu,* but I noticed Tomohiro right away. The way he walked, with confidence and grace. The way he held his *shinai* with just the right amount of tension. He looked beyond the league of any of the others. He looked like an ancient samurai.

"Yuuto!" Ishikawa screamed, waving his arms in wild circles. *"Ganbare!"*

Tomohiro looked up and saw both of us. I couldn't see his expression through the *men,* but he saw us, together, cheering for him. Maybe that was enough.

I took a deep breath. *"Ganbare!"* But the crowd had quieted down, and my voice rang out in the silence. Trust me to embarrass myself.

"Aaaand now the whole gym knows you're in love with him," Ishikawa said. "You have quite the pair of lungs. Impressive."

"What about you?" I smirked. "You were as loud as me." I'd just meant it as a gibe, but I realized what I'd said the minute the words were out.

"Yeah, well," Ishikawa said, his eyes soft as he stared straight ahead at the *kendouka*. "It's you he heard."

My heart hurt a little, but I wasn't sure why. I wanted to ask if he was okay. "Ishikawa, are you—"

"His best friend," Ishikawa said. "So shut up."

"*Kendouka,* in position!" the referee called.

Tomohiro was up first, against a junior from Katakou. I could hear Jun's voice as he called out, cheering for the boy I didn't know. Tomohiro advanced as he shrieked a *kiai*. He galloped across the floor toward him and smacked the *shinai* toward the *kote*.

"Point!" yelled the main referee as the three of them lifted their red flags.

"Already?" I said.

Ishikawa laughed. "Yuuto's gonna mop the floor with that kid."

He wasn't kidding. It was an easy match for Tomo. The *shinai* clacked together as the two circled in the arena. Tomohiro lunged, and the boy barely blocked it. But he stepped too far into the move, and Tomohiro snuck his *shinai* underneath for a hit to the *dou*.

Next up were two girls from a school we didn't know. And then a boy from Suntaba against a girl from Katakou. The matches went on and on, but every time Tomohiro went up, the competition had no chance. He was in perfect form, focused and quick, his attacks precise and calculated.

I wasn't the only one who noticed. The police muttered to each other below us.

But they couldn't suspect him just because he was winning, could they? That wasn't fair. He hadn't done anything. I mean, on purpose. We *had* been responsible for Jun's fracture, but not to put him out of the tournament.

Match after match, Tomohiro got faster, sharper, more vicious. I shook when he screamed his *kiai*—had he always sounded so frightening? A whistle blew as his *shinai* accidentally lunged toward an opponent's leg. When had he ever got a penalty warning like that before?

The match ended, and the crowd clapped wildly. He was heaving each breath in now, exhausted. He lifted the *men* from his shoulders to cool off.

That's when I saw his deep black eyes, the pupils large and empty.

"Oh shit," I said.

"Greene," Ishikawa said, clasping my shoulder. "Such language."

"Look, moron," I said quietly. "His eyes."

Ishikawa breathed out. "Oh shit."

"Like I said. What are we going to do?"

"That's why he's getting so aggressive. It's like when he attacked you in practice."

Tomohiro was on his last match of the tournament now, lunging again and again. His elegant form and careful thinking were gone. He attacked viciously, without thought. It was like he wasn't even the same person.

"Yuuto!" Ishikawa yelled out, but it didn't faze him. He nudged me in the arm. "Snap him out of it, Greene."

"Tomo-kun!" I yelled. I could feel Shiori's eyes on me as I yelled. And then Jun turned around, startled by the sound of my voice. "Tomo-kun, stay calm. *Faito!*" But it was like he couldn't hear me.

He raced toward his opponent, turning his back to us. And then I saw that the *tenugui* headband wrapped around his copper hair was dripping with black ink, trailing in raindrop lines down his back.

Jun noticed, too. He rose to his feet, looking at me frantically.

We couldn't reach him. He was going to lose control right here. Some scary ink thing would explode around him and the police would arrest him, maybe worse. He was a demon, Susanou's descendant. He was capable of anything.

"Tomo!" I shrieked, my whole body shaking. I felt so helpless.

Jun curled his hands into fists and turned to face the tournament. Tomohiro's opponent was running scared now, dodging every deadly attack. The referees looked antsy, ready to call Tomo on any violation they could.

"Yuu-san, *faito!*" Jun chanted, and the sound of it startled me. He said it over and over in a steady rhythm. "Yuu-san, *faito!*" He curled his fingers into fists, shaking them up and down in time with the chant.

Beside me, Ishikawa joined in. Then Shiori.

And then the whole crowd added their voices.

Jun was trying to reach him. He was trying to break him out of it. The crowd chanted as one loud voice.

"Yuu-san, *faito!* Yuu-san, *faito!*"

The boy stumbled and fell backward in the arena. Tomohiro lifted his *shinai* into the air, the way he had with me in practice. I watched, unable to move. My heart beat in my ears, and my pulse raced.

And then the ground started to shake, just a little. I looked at Ishikawa, alarmed.

"Just a tremor," he said. "Keep chanting!"

But it wasn't just a tremor. It was moving in time with my pulse.

Tomohiro screamed out, his *shinai* throttling downward. The boy winced as it approached. The referee's whistle started to blare in his mouth.

"Tomo!" I shrieked.

Tomohiro stumbled, almost falling on the boy. The whistle died off, cut short. The earthquake stopped rumbling.

The boy quickly lifted his *shinai* up and struck Tomo's *dou.*

"Point!" yelled the referee, the white flags rising.

The *shinai* dropped from Tomo's hand, landing in a splatter of black ink. I gasped, but no one else seemed to see it. Tomo had lost, and the boy had won. That's all anyone focused on.

Tomo fell to his knees, the *shinai* gently rolling back and forth on the gym floor. He reached his hand out to the boy and said something we couldn't hear. The boy took his hand and Tomo pulled him up. They put their arms around each other's backs and raised their free hands to the crowd in triumph.

Everyone cheered loudly.

"Nice move, Yuuto," Ishikawa said quietly, and he was right. Tomo had won the crowd over; they'd forgotten what he'd almost done. He was the gracious loser now. He was the good sport.

I looked where the patch of ink had bled around his *shinai,* but it was gone, as if I'd imagined it. But sometimes the others didn't see the ink the way I did; Ishikawa hadn't said anything. But Jun turned to look at me, his lips pursed in a tight line. He'd seen it, too. Maybe only those with ink inside saw it.

Only Kami. And artificial inductees.

I wasn't sure which was worse—belonging, or not.

"Come on, Greene," Ishikawa said, rising to his feet.

"Where are you going?"

"Are you stupid? Tomo needs us right now. The match is over—let's go." He grabbed my hand and pulled me along the row. Shiori and her bright red ballerina outfit were long gone. We twisted toward the door and down the stairs to the gym floor.

I hesitated, unsure if we should be down here. Wasn't this kind of an official area? But Ishikawa slammed his palms against the gym doors and walked in, determined, his eyes lit as if they were on fire.

The gym lights shone brightly into my eyes. All the *kendouka* were milling around, gathering their supplies, going over their point totals with the coaches. In the corner I saw Watanabe-sensei with the young *kendouka* from our school. Tomo was sitting on a bench beside his navy-and-white sports bag as he chugged down a bottle of water. His headband was draped across the wooden seat beside him, and his copper spikes pressed against his head, slick with sweat.

"Tomo," I said, stumbling toward him. I sat beside him on the bench, resting my hand on his back as he twisted the cap back onto the water bottle. Ishikawa dragged a chair toward us and straddled it backward, resting his hands on the back of the chair and his chin on the back of his hands.

"Yuuto, you okay?" His eyes gleamed, and I had to look away.

"Fine," Tomohiro said. "But I had to throw the match."

Ishikawa nodded. "You had no choice. You couldn't exactly win every time. That's a little suspicious."

"It was the ink, wasn't it?" I said. Why were they pretending it hadn't happened? "You lost control."

Tomo stared at the police, who were pretending not to watch him as they circled the gym. His voice was just above a whisper. "Could we talk about it later?"

But I couldn't let it go. "That boy," I said. "You almost put him in the hospital."

Ishikawa snorted, thumbing toward himself. "Wouldn't be the first time he put a boy in the hospital."

"Shut up, Ishikawa." I rested a hand on Tomo's. "What happened?"

"I don't know, okay?"

"Did you stop drawing again?"

"Katie," Tomohiro snapped, and I didn't like the way he said my name. "I can't talk right now."

Why? I wondered. The police wouldn't know what we were talking about. But I was mistaken. Shiori appeared suddenly, dressed in her deep red and tulle. She'd even painted her nails a glittery red to match. She held a white towel in her hands, and she looked past me like I didn't exist. This was why we couldn't talk now, not the police.

"Here, Tomo," she said. "Your towel."

"Thanks," he said, grabbing it from her and wiping at his face.

Ishikawa looked as pissed as I felt. "Shiori, could you give him some space?"

"It's fine," Tomo said, and I felt my cheeks burn. It wasn't fine. I didn't like her being here. I didn't like her calling him Tomo.

"I think maybe it's you two who need to give him space," said Shiori. Her voice was like stone; I'd never heard her sound like that before. "What do you expect to do for him, Satoshi? You want to get Tomo-kun mixed up in the same trouble you're in?" Ishikawa opened his mouth but said noth-

ing; his eyes burned. He lowered them to the gym floor, and
the disappointment stung. Why didn't he talk back? Tomo
didn't say anything, either. He sat there panting, the towel
wrapped around his neck, his fingers twisting and untwist-
ing the water-bottle cap.

So I spoke. "That's hardly fair, Shiori. You don't know
what happened."

She looked at me with hard eyes, and for the first time, I
truly saw the revulsion there. "All I know is things changed
when you got here. Tomo was fine until then."

Everything froze. A million replies screamed in my head
but I couldn't get them out of my mouth.

"Shiori," Tomo said.

"It's true," she snapped. "You used to be happy, Tomo! You
used to joke around all the time when we were together. Now
you look like you haven't slept in weeks." I thought about
how happy they'd looked at the festival, Shiori's pet goldfish
swimming endless circles in that plastic bag. Nowhere to go,
just around and around. *We can't be together. We can't be apart.*

"He's going through a lot right now, okay?" I said, rising
to my feet. "You wouldn't understand." Shiori was shorter
than me, but she stared me down anyway, her hands resting
on either side of her pregnant stomach.

"You're the one who doesn't understand. You're a *gaijin,*
Katie, a foreigner. You don't belong here." I felt like I'd been
slapped. Her voice trembled, rising louder and louder. "You're
making his life miserable, don't you see that?"

"Shiori!" Tomohiro shouted, and even the police on the
other side of the gym looked at the sound of it. Shiori's cheeks
flooded with a red that matched her dress. Her eyes blurred
with tears.

"You know what, forget it," she said, her voice wavering, and she turned to leave the gym.

I don't know why I followed her. I was pissed off, humiliated, but there was something about her pain that was so familiar. Being alone, being rejected—I couldn't let her go. I was the reason Tomohiro had stopped answering her calls. I was the reason he'd pulled away.

"Shiori, wait," I said, meeting her at the doors to the gym. The tears ran down her cheeks now, her mascara started to blur in the corners under her eyes. "I'm sorry, okay? Look, we're all worried about Tomohiro. He needs all of us right now."

She blinked, reaching into her purse for her hand towel to dab at her eyes.

"You don't get it, do you?" she said. "We've known each other since we were born. Our moms were best friends. How long have you known him? And you know what's best for him and I don't? You're in the way, Katie, not me."

She didn't even know the half of it, how I was causing these violent outbursts of ink.

"Shiori, listen—"

Her voice wavered. "I'm sick of listening. I'm sick of waiting by the phone while he's out with you. Do you know what I've been through for keeping this baby?" Her voice took on an edge to it, sharp and wavering, as she spoke just below Tomo's hearing. "Do you know what it's like to enter your homeroom and your desk is missing? To have your textbooks burned in the chemistry room when you're eating lunch? To have *slut* and *whore* and *ugly bitch* written on your locker in permanent ink?"

My body tingled with numbness. I didn't know what to say.

Shiori grit her teeth, her eyes flashing. "My phone goes off all night with messages to kill myself. Do you have any idea how hard it is to carry on like that?"

"I'm so sorry," I said. "Shiori, I'm sorry." I'd had no idea it was that bad. It made me sick to my stomach.

Tears had welled up in her eyes, but she clenched her fists at her sides.

"All I had left was Tomo…and you've taken him from me. Leave us alone, Katie. You've done nothing but screw up our lives. I'll take him back." She narrowed her eyes. "I'll make you know what it feels like."

She turned and pushed through the doors, and I stood there, my body feeling like it would burst in every direction at once. I was horrified, and I was stunned. I shook as I tried to keep it together.

The doors opened again, startling me. It was Jun, his silver earring sparkling in the bright gym lights. His blond highlight clung to his cheek, and his cold eyes gleamed from under the sway of his jagged bangs.

"You okay?" he said.

I nodded, although I was far from fine.

Behind me, I heard Tomohiro's voice, dark and unfriendly. "Takahashi." I turned and saw him approaching with Ishikawa. "Get away from Katie."

Of course; he didn't know why I looked so upset. He probably thought Jun was threatening me or something.

Jun held up his hands and smiled. "I'm just here to see how you are, Yuu," he said. "That was a tough last match—you okay?"

"I'll be better when you leave," Tomo countered, and Ishikawa grinned, hunching his shoulders as he put his hands in his pockets. I shuddered. He wouldn't bring his knife to the match, would he? No one was that stupid.

"Easy," Jun said, nudging his head slightly in the direction of the police. They were watching, two of them muttering to each other. I could imagine what they were saying now. The victims and the suspect, all together, and Tomo threatening Jun once again. "We want to look friendly, right?" Jun was right. We didn't want them zeroing in on him.

Ishikawa folded his arms and tilted his head back. "Then you better be going."

"I just wanted to see if you were okay," Jun said. "I saw your little blackout."

Tomohiro smirked. "None of your business."

"When it involves Katie, it's my business."

Tomo's eyes lit with fire at the bait. "Stay away from her."

Jun's eyes were cold, unforgiving. "What if she doesn't want me to stay away?"

"You're dreaming, jackass." Tomo narrowed his eyes as he breathed deeply, his body shaking with the effort to restrain himself.

Jun smirked. "Oh really? Ask her. She deserves better than a spoiled demon brat who can't control his power."

"Fuck you, *bakayaro!*" Tomo lunged forward and pushed Jun's chest hard with the palms of his hands. I gasped as Jun stumbled backward, his bangs loosening from behind his ears and fanning across his face. He tilted his chin down, glaring at Tomo as he clenched his fists at the side. Tomo moved toward him again.

"*Ochitsuite,*" Ishikawa warned, grabbing Tomohiro's arm. "Calm down." Tomo yanked his arm out of his friend's grip and stepped toward Jun.

The police had noticed. Two of them were walking over from the far end of the gym.

I grabbed Tomohiro's other arm, squeezing myself in front

of Jun to put distance between them. "Tomo, take it easy, okay? Did you even notice who started the chanting that broke through to you? Jun saved you out there!"

Tomo's face twisted like he'd been punched. Then it hit me. *Oh god.* I'd said *Jun* instead of *Takahashi.* Taking Jun's side while calling him that would be totally humiliating. My body coursed with mortified embarrassment.

"I mean, Takahashi helped you." I tried to fix it, but it was too late. I couldn't take it back. It was more than a hit to Tomo's pride. It meant Jun and I were on friendly terms. He could see that.

Tomo stared at Jun and shifted his weight back and forth, snorting out deep breaths as he restrained himself from fighting.

"Yuuto, the police," Ishikawa warned quietly.

Tomo stood rigid for a moment, then narrowed his eyes at Jun. He spat, "You're not worth it." His shoulder butted against Jun's as he stormed toward the doors. Ishikawa stared with his still-burning eyes at Jun, but Jun's were like ice. I couldn't tell how he was feeling.

"Next time I'll pound your face in," Ishikawa told him, and then he was gone, calling out to Tomohiro as he trailed him out of the gym.

The police had reached us. "Everything okay here?"

"Fine," Jun said, putting on a fake smile. "Just a disagreement."

"Pretty loud disagreement. Was he threatening you?"

Jun shrugged. "Kendo matches take a lot out of you. Yuu-san is just exhausted, I know that."

"Takahashi Jun, the kendo champ, right?" the policeman asked. When Jun nodded, he continued, "How's that wrist healed up?"

I tensed. Jun could destroy Tomo now.

"Fine," Jun said. "Can't believe I was so clumsy to fall down the stairs."

The policeman frowned. "Hmm. Well, hope to see you compete again soon."

"Of course," he answered. The police retreated, and then Jun and I were alone.

Jun tucked his highlights behind his ears and then tried to transition the movement into a subtle hand on my shoulder. I didn't mind, though—I was too shaken up. "Are you okay?"

Everything was a mess. Maybe Shiori was right—every time I tried, I just screwed up everything.

"I don't know." I felt like screaming and crying at the same time. That couldn't be too healthy. "Why did you say that, Jun?"

His shoulder slipped from my hand and he tugged nervously at his earring. "I'm sorry. I shouldn't have said it like that. It came out wrong."

I sighed, rubbing my temples.

"Let me make it up to you," Jun said. "We could go for coffee?"

I don't know if he meant it in a friendly way or something more, but I snapped. It was too much.

"Look, can you just give me some space?" I couldn't stop myself. "Tomo's my boyfriend, Jun, okay? We're together. I can't go for coffee with you."

I'd overdone it.

"Okay," Jun said, his voice quiet. "I get it."

"I need some air," I said, pushing through the gym doors. What I needed was to find Tomohiro and apologize. What a stupid thing to be sorry for—calling another boy by the wrong name, when I wasn't even used to such a cultural rule—but I couldn't leave this mess the way it was.

I twisted through the hallways of Katakou School, feeling guilty I knew the layout so well. I headed into the courtyard, where the crowds were milling in and out from the tournament.

It was easy to spot Tomohiro and Ishikawa in the crowd thanks to their dyed hair. They were outside the gate of the school, turning north toward Ishikawa's house. I hadn't missed them, then; I had time to make it right.

"Tomo!" I shouted, but he couldn't hear me over the crowd. As I pushed my way through, I saw two guys approach them on the street. They didn't look like kendo spectators. They wore T-shirts and ripped jeans, and one had a gold chain around his neck. The other had a sprawling tattoo on his shoulder, like the one on Ishikawa's arm.

Oh crap. Yakuza? Here? My mind raced. But they looked too young to be Yakuza, no older than Ishikawa. Maybe they were Yakuza-in-training like him. Whatever they were, their eyes were hard as stone and their fists huge. This couldn't be good. I inched closer to the gate, scared for them to see me, fighting the urge to run the other way.

The tattooed guy folded his arms across his broad chest. "Well, well," he said. "The squealer and the freak."

"He's not a freak," Ishikawa said. "And I didn't squeal."

"That so?" said Gold Chain. "Why did the police visit you in the hospital, huh? You think we didn't notice?"

"Hanchi says you haven't answered the guys' calls," added Tattoo. "Sounds like someone's loyalty's wavering."

"I'm still on bed rest, man," Ishikawa said.

"Looks like it," said Tattoo.

"Look, let's just go, Sato, okay?" Tomohiro said. The two

of them stepped forward to leave. Gold Chain shoved Ishikawa back roughly, and Tomo tensed.

"What's the rush?" Gold Chain grinned. "We're not done talking here, Freak." He stepped closer to Ishikawa, so that he was just about breathing into his face. "What'd you tell the police, huh, Satoshi? You tell them we shot you? You tell them what you've been up to?"

"I told them nothing," Ishikawa said. "You guys can trust me. You know that."

Tattoo let out a cold laugh. "We don't know nothing. We know you ran out on us after that stupid snake trick your Kami friend pulled."

"He didn't run out," Tomo said. "He was shot. He had to go to the hospital."

"Shut it, Freak," Gold Chain said, and shoved Tomo roughly. Tomo stumbled backward, his bangs falling into his eyes as he stared at the ground. I wasn't sure if I should get closer. My body tingled remembering the fear of being trapped in the back of a Yakuza truck. I didn't want to draw their attention, not again. I stood frozen. The rest of the crowd scattered down the other side of the street, pretending they hadn't seen what was happening. I guess they thought it was a gang brawl. They didn't want to get involved, and I was just like them.

"Stop it," Ishikawa said. "Look, as soon as my shoulder's better I'll call in, okay? Cut me a break, will you?"

"He won't call in," Tomo snapped, stepping toward Tattoo. He stood close, their angry faces almost touching, his breath making the boy's hair stir. "He's done. Find another pawn."

"Restrain your boyfriend, would you, Satoshi?" Tattoo said. "He doesn't seem to realize who he's talking to."

"Oh, I know," said Tomo. "I'm talking to garbage."

"Least we're not freaks," said Gold Chain.

Tomo laughed, and the sound of it chilled me. I didn't like this side of him, the side that relished the darkness of the ink. Descended from Susanou, king of Hell. I shuddered.

"There are advantages to being a demon," Tomo breathed, his eyes gleaming with dark delight. "I can draw nightmares you can't even fathom. And I'm not like the Kami you've employed before. I'm dangerous, unstable. You saw that, right? So you know I could make your life hell if you don't walk away. Now."

They stood, breathing, silent. I clung to the school gate, watching.

"I got it," Gold Chain said, unfolding his arms and stepping back. Tomo had done it. He'd scared him. He'd scared me, too, hearing him talk like that. Jun was right. He really was a weapon. He could be.

Tomo nodded to Ishikawa, and the two walked past the Yakuza.

That's when they jumped him.

13

Gold Chain went for Tomo, and Tattoo leaped at Ishikawa. Their arms swung as they tangled on the street amid the gasps of onlookers. I could hear the pounding of fists against Ishikawa's stomach, while Tomo dodged a blow to the face and returned a punch to the nose. It was a flurry of limbs and sounds, all awful. The metallic smell of blood filled the air as Gold Chain's nose splattered red onto the concrete. Tattoo punched Ishikawa hard in the shoulder and his white shirt swelled with dark red, the gunshot wound reopened. I had to call someone, but it involved Yakuza and Kami, and the police would mean more trouble for us. I couldn't. I stood there, unsure what to do next. I couldn't get involved—I had to stay away.

No. I didn't come back to Japan to stay away. It wasn't so I could watch Yakuza beat up Tomo while I stood there helpless.

I wasn't helpless. I was a Kami, too. I could do something.

I stepped forward and then hesitated.

Ishikawa was on his knees, hunched over as Tattoo punched him in the head. His fingers reached into his pocket.

No, Ishikawa. Don't.

He pulled out the knife, thrusting it at Tattoo who backed off.

"Oh, you're dead," Tattoo snarled, pulling a knife of his own.

Tomohiro pushed Gold Chain away, reaching a hand out to his friend. "Sato!" he cried out, and suddenly ink dripped down Tomo's neck, pooling on the back of his shirt.

"Tomo!" I shouted.

A pair of strong hands pulled me back.

"*Da-me,*" she hissed. "Stay out of it."

"Ikeda?" I looked at her.

"The crowd," she said, her fingers pressing deep into my shoulders. "You'll only make it worse if you get involved. Yuu will lose control of himself."

I watched as the ink curled around Tomo's back, feathering out into the start of raven-colored wings. She was right—it had to stop, but I couldn't be the one. If I was in danger, something awful would happen here, in front of the crowd. The ink still looked like blood, but any second now, it was going to look like something unexplainable.

"We have to do something," I whispered.

"I know," she said, "but we can't. Just wait."

Then I heard the voice of the woman constable as the police from the kendo match dashed past us. "*Yamenasai!* Stop right now!"

In a blur of limbs, the police tackled the four of them, dragging them away from each other as they flailed. Ishikawa's knife clattered to the ground and he cried out as the policeman yanked his arm backward, his gun wound bleeding down the front of his shirt.

"Katie," said a warm voice, and then Jun was beside us. "Ikeda. Thank you."

"Of course," Ikeda said. "I wouldn't want things to get

worse for all of us. It's bad enough with the attention Yuu Tomohiro is drawing to us."

I glared at her, and Jun did the same. "Too much," he said coldly.

She grimaced, releasing my shoulder and stepping away.

I watched in horror as the police subdued the brawl. It was one thing to see them slam Gold Chain and Tattoo up against the wall, but Tomo and Ishikawa...they weren't criminals. They didn't deserve this.

"That idiot," Ikeda said. "He should never have pulled that knife."

She was right.

One of the policemen grabbed Tomo and shoved him hard against the wall of Katakou School. His bruised cheek scraped against the cement as the cop pressed Tomo's face into it, looking to see if he had any weapons on him.

Tomohiro squirmed under the hold, his back slick with ink. His left eye was pressed against the wall and forced closed, but the other was open, and he saw me in the crowd.

Tomo. I looked back helplessly. Everything was unraveling.

A police car pulled up and they pushed the two Yakuza into it, slamming the door on them while the woman constable talked into her radio. A second car approached, and they opened the back door of it.

"No," I breathed.

Tomo watched me as long as he could—as they hauled him away from the cement, as they led him to the car. He stumbled over the curb, but wouldn't take his eyes off me.

"Tomo!" I cried out.

"Shh!" Ikeda jabbed me in the arm. "Don't get involved in it now, Katie."

"Ikeda's right," Jun said. "I know it's hard, but she's right."

I fell to my knees as the police slammed the car door and got in the front. This couldn't be happening. It couldn't. Would they charge him? Would they connect Ishikawa's and Jun's injuries? And worst of all, would Tomo keep the ink under control?

The crowd muttered around me, watching the drama unfold. Behind me, I felt Jun's hands rest on my shoulders, hesitantly at first, only awkward ghosts of fingertips. But then he curled them around my shoulders and sighed, his breath warm against the back of my neck.

Tears blurred in my eyes as the cars sped away. I didn't know what to do. There was nothing I could do. Maybe if I hadn't humiliated Tomo inside, maybe he wouldn't have left, and then…

I squeezed my eyes shut. "It's all my fault."

"It's not," Jun said. "The Yakuza were waiting for him. I told you—they never leave you alone."

"Is this what they did to your dad? Waited for him?" The tears spilled over, leaving cold trails on my cheeks. I felt Jun's hands tense. The smell of the falling maple leaves on the *momiji* trees swirled on the breeze. "I'm sorry. I didn't mean to be nosy."

"It's okay," he said. "That's not what happened."

I stood shakily and stepped onto the road. "Where are they taking him?" I didn't even know where to look.

"Local police box," Ikeda said. "Which for our area is probably the station by Sunpu Castle."

I had to go. Maybe it was stupid, but I couldn't just stand here gawking like the rest of the crowd. I had to do something.

I started running.

"Katie!" Jun shouted, and I stopped, looking over my shoulder. The wind was colder outside than I'd expected; I wasn't dressed for it with my bare legs and short sleeves. "At least let me drive you."

I nodded and we raced toward the bike racks and his waiting motorcycle.

The street whirred below us as Jun drove to the police station. I clung to him, the feel of his hips familiar now after all the rides. The wind held such a bite, and I wondered when exactly the summer had faded away, when the fall chill had taken over. Maybe just today, when I wasn't paying attention.

The horizontal traffic light changed to yellow, and Jun sped up. He darted through traffic carelessly, and if it wasn't him, I would've been worried. But I'd seen the way he moved in his kendo matches. It might look careless, but each move was carefully articulated. I bet his driving was the same—designed to intimidate, but he was always in control.

He parked in front of the police station and I tugged my helmet off, hanging it over the handlebars of the motorbike before Jun even cut the engine. He followed behind me, up the stairs of the dark glass police station.

I hesitated at the front doors.

"You going to march right in?" Jun chuckled.

"It's not funny." My throat felt dry from the cold wind that had battered against us on the drive over.

"Come on," he said, and he leaned his whole body against the door. It reminded me of the way they'd pushed Tomohiro against the wall—his face squished, his bangs covering one eye. Jun's blond highlight looked black against the shadow of the door. For once, his eyes didn't look so cold.

"Thanks," I said and followed him inside.

It was a blur of activity and artificial lights inside. Someone behind the desk wrote important-looking notes, and police milled about looking busy. But I saw Tomo and Ishikawa right away, the two of them sitting with Gold Chain on benches near the desk. Tattoo was missing—interrogated first, maybe, or whatever it was police did.

I opened my mouth to call out for Tomohiro, but Jun grabbed my shoulder, shaking his head no. His earring glinted in the fluorescent lights as his head shook back and forth.

"Stay calm," he said, "so the ink stays calm."

I nodded. "Tomo," I said, my voice wavering. He looked up, his eyes wide and surprised. Ishikawa looked up, too, his shirt a stained mess. There was blood trickling from the corner of Tomo's mouth, and I wanted to wipe it away. He was looking at Jun now, and then me, but he didn't speak.

"Sumimasen," shouted a policeman, and I jumped back, startled and grateful for Jun's reassuring grip. "Can I help you?"

"He's my brother," Jun said smoothly as he pointed at Tomo, and I blinked, my eyes huge. He was lying to the police. Oh god. We were in so much trouble. "I wanted to make sure he was okay."

The policeman smirked. "You think I don't know you, Takahashi? I watch kendo. I saw you in the nationals last year." He lowered his voice. "And I'm surprised you didn't recognize me. I've been to your house twice to interrogate you."

My heart stopped. We were going to get arrested for lying to the police. *Shit!* How did I get into this mess?

But Jun just laughed. "I was only having fun, *keiji-san*," he said. "But really, he's our friend. The other guys jumped him, you know."

"Listen, you know I don't trust a word you say," the detective said. "Not back then, not now." Back then? What did he mean? At the hospital? But it seemed more serious than that.

"You're lucky I don't haul you into that room and ask you some questions. About your wrist, for one."

"I fell down the stairs," Jun grinned, his eyes gleaming. Good grief. He enjoyed skirting danger as much as Tomo did.

"Not with that fracture you didn't," the detective grumbled. "And I bet I know who to blame for it, too." He motioned at Ishikawa, Tomo and Gold Chain on the bench, and my heart flopped over. "I couldn't lay anything on you then, and I can't now. But don't think I'm not watching. Now get the hell out of my station."

"What are you going to do with them?" I asked timidly. He stared at me, anxious. He didn't think I spoke much Japanese. I could see that. A *gaijin* watching police protocol was making him nervous.

"If you mean the two with anime hair, they'll be fine," he said. "We've called their parents to pick them up when we're done getting the information we need. The others have a… complicated record. And the rest isn't your business. Now out."

"Thanks, *keiji-san,*" Jun said. He slid his fingers down my arm to grab my wrist; the motion of his warm fingertips made me shiver. "Come on," he said gently and walked through the doors of the station. Tomo watched us go, his eyes on Jun's grip on me. The doors shut behind us and Jun collapsed on the first step. I sat beside him and let my eyes glaze over. None of this felt real.

"What the hell were you thinking, lying to the police?"

Jun laughed. *"Sumanakatta,"* he apologized. "I don't think much more of the police than I do of the Yakuza. They both let me down back then. Those detectives and I go way back."

"He said that, too. What did he mean he couldn't lay anything on you then? When we… When your wrist broke?"

"I'm slippery like a koi," Jun laughed, looking across the

street to the murky moat of Sunpu Park. "'Back then' meaning when my dad died. They tried to say I was involved with
the Yakuza, too. Bunch of bullshit, of course. I'd never join
those bastards."

So that's why they'd had such strong suspicions that Jun's
and Ishikawa's incidents were related—they could both be
traced to the Yakuza. And now thanks to this fight, so could
Tomo. Jun's voice turned so cold when he talked about the
gang that it was almost frightening. It made me think of the
way he'd asked Tomo to draw Hanchi dead.

"You didn't…you didn't kill any Yakuza, did you?"

"What?" His eyes were pools of cool black ice. "Of course
not."

"It's just that you asked Tomo to…to kill Hanchi."

"Ah." Jun leaned back on the step, his palms pressed against
the concrete. "Well, I would like him dead, yes. He was the
one who employed my dad before everything went to hell."

"Why—" I couldn't believe I was asking this. "Why didn't
you just do it yourself?"

"Katie," Jun said, his voice velvet. "Is that what you think
of me? I thought if Hanchi would leave me alone, I'd leave
him alone. But when he went after Yuu, I realized something.
He's never going to change. He'll keep exploiting Kami any
chance he gets."

I stretched my legs out, rolling my heels from one side of
the concrete to the other until my toes tapped against it, like
mini windshield wipers.

"You want to stay, don't you?" Jun said after a minute.
"Until Yuu can leave."

"Yeah," I said. "You don't have to, though."

"I'll stay."

"It could be a long wait."

"I know."

I looked out over Sunpu Park. The leaves had turned golden and crimson, ready to be lifted off the branches by the swirling autumn wind.

"Did you tell him yet?" Jun asked.

"Tell him?"

"That you're a Kami."

He said it so matter-of-factly, like it wasn't complicated. "I'm not a Kami, Jun."

"You know what I mean."

"Yeah, I told him."

"And about Susanou?"

Susanou. Wouldn't it be dangerous to tell him that? "I didn't think he was ready to hear it." Jun nodded. "Anyway, I don't know for sure. It's just a theory."

"It makes so much sense, though," Jun said. "I don't know why I'd never thought of it before."

I wrapped my arms around myself. "Does that mean your Kami cult doesn't want him anymore?"

Jun's eyes flashed with hurt. "Hey," he said. "That's not fair. We're not a cult. I didn't ask to be born into this heritage, but I'm a Kami...it's my fate." He drew his knees up to his chest and rested his chin on them. "We've inherited great power, and we can't ignore it. I'm glad this is who I am."

"It's hard to know what to use that power for, though."

Jun shook his head. "The world is corrupt. Look at those thugs who attacked Yuu just now. You saw the ink running down his back—it was crying out for justice."

"We have a system for that," I said. "You're not supposed to take it into your own hands."

"The system is broken, Katie. Not just criminals, but the way we treat each other. By now you must have seen the bullying in the schools." I'd seen a bit, not so different from the bullying I'd seen back in New York. But Shiori...she was suffering, I knew. "Everything is rotting. We need the old system—justice by the hands of the ruling *kami*."

"Do you know the *kami* stories?" I'd done enough internet searches to recognize the similarities with other types of myths. "They're not exactly model rulers. They're always throwing dead horses at each other and stuff."

"That was Susanou—once," Jun laughed. "And besides, Susanou isn't always the bad guy he's cracked up to be."

I blinked. I hadn't heard that before. So Tomo wasn't...evil? "What do you mean?"

"Think way back," Jun said. "Mongol invasion, a long time ago. They took China—*kyu!* They took over Korea—*zashu!* And they're on boats, coming for Japan."

I rolled my eyes. "Are the sound effects necessary?"

"And then what happens? *Bashan!*" More of Jun's effects, but the sound of this one startled me. He waved a huge arc with his hand. "Huge wave and a giant storm. The rain falls in sheets, and the thunder booms from the sky. The boats crash into the shores, the Mongols drown. *Kamikaze,* it was called. The divine wind. A *kaze* sent by *kami*."

"*Kamikaze* means something different now," I said, which sounded stupid the minute I said it, but too late.

"It still has the same idea, though," Jun said. "Saving others through your own sacrifice. Susanou saved Japan that day, if you want to think about it that way. Samurai were on the shores waiting to fight the Mongols. There would've been hundreds of Susanou's descendants among them."

"There's no way to know for sure," I said, but I still sighed in relief. Susanou might be evil, but he still wanted to protect Japan. So maybe Tomo's nightmares were worse, but he had the same goals as descendants of Amaterasu. Which meant there was hope at the end of that storm.

"*Maa, ne,*" Jun mused. "I guess not."

The only part we didn't talk about was how many lives Susanou had taken to keep Japan safe. How many men drowned in the rains that day? Is that what Tomohiro would do someday? Could he really kill people with his abilities?

And is that what Jun thought? Make them pay, no matter who got hurt in the process?

"Yuu and I would make good princes," Jun said after a minute. "And you would rule with us, Katie."

I stared at him—was he for real? His lip curled up into a smile, and I couldn't tell if he was serious or not.

"Are you joking?"

His eyes gleamed. "Maybe. I guess I have to make it through entrance exams first, huh?"

I couldn't get a straight answer out of him. How much did the thoughts consume him—justice, corruption, revenge? Is that what he thought about as he lay awake at night?

We sat in silence for a bit, sprawled out on the police-station steps. The sun dipped low in the sky and the world turned golden, then shadowy. I wrapped my arms around myself and pulled my legs close.

"*Sa-me zo,*" Jun said, the tough-guy way of saying *It's cold.*

"*Un,*" I mumbled, a casual Japanese yes. Sometimes it felt easier to fit in than others. But thinking of myself as a Kami… as one of them…I couldn't picture it.

"I'd give you my jacket, but I'm not wearing one," he grinned. "Wait there." He ran around the side of the building, where I could hear the faint hum of a vending machine. When he came back, he placed a hot can of café au lait in my hands. I breathed in the sweet steam, burning my tongue with the first sip. The heat raced all the way down my throat, warming me from the inside.

"Thanks," I said. "You know, you really don't have to stay."

"I know," he smiled. "But I want to be here with you, even if it's because you're waiting for him." He motioned at the doorway with his coffee.

"Jun," I said.

"I know. I'm pathetic."

"Not at all. I—"

A car pulled into the parking lot and startled both of us into silence. A man opened the passenger's side and got out, and at first I wondered who must be driving. A flash from my old life, before I remembered that the right was the driver's side in Japan. Life in reverse, nothing the way I thought it would be.

It was Tomo's father, looking like a somber version of his son. He wore a tight-fitting suit with a dark tie, his black hair slicked down neatly and his face hiding any trace of emotion. He walked up the steps with grace and pride, like he was going to some really important meeting, not at all like he was going to pick up his son from the police station. I almost felt sorry for him, except I knew none of it had been Tomo's fault. His dad must have known that, too. He knew what kind of person Tomo was.

He walked straight past us, not recognizing me in the dark, and through the glass doors. I rose to my feet, hurrying toward the closing door. It was made of glass and we could see through it easily.

His dad stopped at the desk and spoke to the person taking the important-looking notes. Then he waited. They must be getting Tomohiro. Relief pulsed through me. He could go home.

Tomo appeared from the side, escorted in handcuffs by

the woman constable I'd seen earlier. *Handcuffs*—my heart raced at the sight of it. She undid the cuffs and he swung his arms forward, rubbing his wrists with his fingers. The back of his shirt was stained with dried ink in the shape of sprouting wings. I hoped to god it had stopped there. It could just look like blood, right? From here the tiny wings looked kind of like handprints. Maybe.

Tomohiro's dad stepped forward toward his son. At first I thought he was going to hug him, but I was wrong. He swung his hand back and slapped Tomohiro so hard across the face that I heard the sound of it from outside the glass door. Tomo's face twisted from the blow, his head falling limp as he stared at the tiled floor. I gasped a breath of cold air; the café au lait burned at my fingertips.

"Who the *hell* do you think you are?" shouted his dad. "Humiliating me like this! Causing trouble for others. What the *hell* is wrong with you, Hiro?"

I thought the police would stop him or something. You couldn't just slap your own child in a police station, could you? But they weren't doing anything. Tomo's dad bent over in a deep bow, his face as red as if he'd been the one slapped. *"Moushi wake gozaimasen,"* he shouted, which I knew was a super-formal apology. After a moment he yanked Tomohiro's arm and pulled him into an awkward bow. Tomo didn't say anything at first, so his dad smacked him across the back of his head.

I winced at the impact, and Tomo raised his hand instinctively to rub the spot, but he didn't say a word, not even that it hurt.

"Apologize properly!" his dad shouted, and Tomo bent over, his face a map of black and blue from the fight, a new pink bruise forming on his cheek and a lump on his head. I saw his lips move, but I couldn't hear him from out here. He was apologizing, though. I knew.

"It's late," one of the police said. "Get him home and get some rest."

His dad bowed his head sharply and then turned toward the door. Jun and I backed up as he came through, his face flushed pink.

Tomohiro followed. I could smell the sweat and dried blood, the stale air from the police station. I knew his skin would be warm from being indoors, and I longed to reach out and touch the bruises on his face. I wanted to run my fingers over them, to wish them away. Tomohiro looked at me for a moment, and then his eyes flicked away, down to the ground.

"Tomo," I said, but he walked right past Jun and me, following his dad down the steps. He got in the driver's side—no, the passenger's side here—and the car rumbled to life, its headlights as bright as the ghost-white koi Tomo had drawn.

Jun curled his fingers around my elbows, but I was glad, because I felt like I was going to collapse.

I felt like I'd lost something, like everything had come undone.

Across from us in Sunpu Park, a maple leaf broke from the tree and drifted into the murky, cold moat, spinning lightly as it swirled on the surface.

14

I called Tomo when I got home, but his *keitai* was off. I phoned his home number once but hung up when I got scared his dad would answer.

I couldn't get the image out of my mind, the way his dad had slapped him—the sound of it, the veins protruding in his dad's neck as he screamed at him.

And the way Tomo didn't fight back at all. The way he just stared at the floor, like nothing mattered anymore. Like he was as lost as I felt.

When had it all started to fall apart like this? I thought I'd come back to fix things, but I felt like it was all turning to sand in my hands, slipping through my fingers.

I slumped down at my desk and pulled out my notebook for kanji practice. I might be falling apart, but I couldn't afford to let my studying drop. There was no way I was going to an international school, and there was no way I was leaving Japan. I copied the kanji until my wrist ached.

Then I found myself doodling names, checking characters in my dictionary when I got stuck.

渡部雪。Watabe Yuki. 田中一郎。Tanaka Ichirou.

石川智。Ishikawa Satoshi. I smirked. The kanji for his first name really was "wisdom."

勇智宏。Yuu Tomohiro.

I stared at that one for a while. I wrote it a few more times.

Then I wrote my name beside it. ケイティグリーン。Katie Greene—unlike the others, written only in phonetic kana. No elegant kanji. No deeper meaning to the characters.

I dropped my pencil and flopped onto my bed, staring at the ceiling.

What had the police asked Tomo? He'd looked so defeated. Were things okay? Had they asked about the ink on his back or more about that night with the Yakuza?

I clicked my light off and lay in the darkness. The weather had turned too cold to turn on my air conditioner, and the room felt unsettling in its silence. I drifted in and out of sleep, imagining all kinds of nightmares that might materialize before me.

None of them did. Weird dreams, sure, things that didn't make sense. Sparring in a kendo match with Yuki and baking a strawberry shortcake with Tanaka. I jolted awake, and I swore I could still smell the berries, feel them crushed against my fingertips in bright red stains. I fell back to sleep and dreamed of Ishikawa at Tokugawa's shrine on top of Mount Kuno, the painted *inugami* snarling as Ishikawa poured water from a bamboo ladle over his bleached hair. He flung a ladle of water at me and I leaped out of the way as it splashed against the stone beneath us. I woke when my body slammed against the tatami on my floor.

Grumbling, I pulled myself back into bed. I hadn't slept this badly since Mom died. Was Tomo okay? I almost called him right then and there, at four in the morning. But I was awake enough to know it was a bad idea, and I tossed my phone back onto my mini study table, falling back to sleep.

I dreamed of Jun, leaning against the tree at Nihondaira, lazy fireflies flitting through the sky. These ones didn't bite; they just hummed in the air like live sparks from a fire, deep red and orange in color. Jun wrapped his arms around me tightly and I leaned against him, smelling the sweetness of cherry blossoms, the sharp pine of the rosin on his cello bow, the fresh lemon of his oiled *shinai* blade.

I jolted awake, and for a moment I couldn't move, paralyzed by the guilt at such a thought.

"They're just stupid dreams," I whispered into the darkness, but it wouldn't take away the pink from my cheeks. It wouldn't slow the heartbeat I could hear in my ears.

I checked the clock—five-thirty.

Was Tomo awake? Was he lost in the nightmares of the Kami? He couldn't possibly be sleeping worse than I was.

Well, maybe. At least I wasn't getting chased by *inugami* in my dreams.

I tossed and turned until the sun rose. I heard the roar of the shower as Diane got ready for the day, but I didn't budge. Life seemed better today if I didn't get up.

After a while she knocked on my door and slid it open. My room was the traditional room of the apartment, which meant a sliding door and tatami floors. I even had a little alcove with a fake plant and a scroll in it.

"Katie?" she smiled. "Sleeping in?"

"A rare occasion here," I mumbled. We usually had to go to school on Saturdays, too, for club activities.

"I'm going out with some teacher friends. I promised we'd meet up today—do you need anything before I head out? Breakfast or anything?"

"I'm fine," I said, rubbing at my eyes.

"Did you sleep okay?"

"Not so much." No point in denying it—I probably looked like crap.

"Listen, why don't you call up Yuki or something? Get your mind off this boy."

Yeah, right. My problems were way past mere boy troubles.

"Sure," I said. "That's a good idea."

She smiled. "Positive you don't need anything?"

"I'll be fine. Have fun."

Diane nodded and slid my door shut. I listen to the clunk of her shoes, the door clicking shut, the keys jingling in the lock.

I rolled around in self-pity for another couple minutes and then stumbled out of my room, searching the kitchen for food. I put a slice of thick toast in the toaster oven, watching the machine brighten with white-hot light as it seared the bread. When it dinged, I burned my fingers sliding the toast onto a plate and drowned the white crust in glistening honey. I gulped it down with a cold glass of black-bean tea.

Then I heard a thump against the front door. It wasn't so much a knock as the sound of a body colliding with the wooden frame.

I froze, every part of me tingling with adrenaline. After a minute I tiptoed to the door, peering through the peephole. I could see Tomo's copper spikes—matted and unbrushed—scrunched against the door, the rest of his body folded under him.

"Tomo," I gasped, pulling the door inward. He slumped onto the *genkan* floor in a mound, breathing heavily. I knelt beside him, resting my arms on his shoulders. He lifted his head like it weighed a hundred pounds.

"Hey," he panted.

"'Hey'?" I repeated. "You collapse at my door and you say 'hey'?"

His face was a map of bruises from the fight with the Yakuza, his nose a little puffy around the edges, his cheek swollen. I could finally do what I'd wanted at the police station. I traced my fingers along the bruises, but he winced.

Then I saw the cuts on his arms. Little jagged lines formed a star near his elbow and dried ink crusted around them like blood. It looked like a...a dog bite.

"What the hell happened to you?"

"Close the door first," he said, pointing at our pale green entryway. His jeans and sneakers stretched into the hallway where he'd collapsed. I hooked my arms under his and heaved. He pushed against the floor and I pulled him backward. By the time I made it to the raised floor, I was wheezing and sweaty.

"Okay, explain," I said, clicking shut the front door. "This isn't just from the Yakuza fight. I'm pretty sure they didn't bite you."

He pressed his elbows against the floor, rocking himself sideways until his upper body was upright. "I'll be fine. I just need a minute."

"Tomo," I said, running my fingers over the bite marks. "What happened?"

"I couldn't sleep last night," he said. "Every time I drifted off, the nightmares shocked me awake. I dreamed of them again, Katie. The *inugami*. They were coming for me. I raced along the shore of Suruga Bay, by the strawberry farms. Up the thousand steps to Mount Kuno."

We'd taken the ropeway to Kunozan Toshogu Shrine, but there was another way up, by climbing the steps up the steep mountainside by the water.

Tomo inched away and rested his back against the raised

floor of the hallway. He lifted his palms, twisting them back and forth as he remembered. "There was blood on my hands," he said. "I think I'd..."

I was glad he didn't finish the thought. I didn't want to know. "Real or dream?"

"I don't know. Dream, I think. There's nothing on them now. I've had sick nightmares before, Katie, and they've always been horrible but...this one was so vivid. I reached the *roumon* gate, the one that knocked me out last time. But this time it crumbled around me. I broke it."

"You were stronger than the security system," I said, and he nodded. He ran a hand through his copper hair, and the golden dust of ink sprinkled onto the floor.

"And then the *inugami,* the one you saw growling. It was alive, Katie. It came at me with a mouthful of teeth." He raised the bite marks toward me.

The chill raced through me, everything feeling like pinpricks.

I whispered, "It was a dream, right?"

His voice was quiet, gentle. "Then how the hell did it bite me, Katie?"

My voice shook. "I don't know."

He curled his legs slowly under himself, resting his bitten arm against the edge of the raised floor. I reached out to support him, walking him down the hallway toward my room. The couch was too small and he looked like a mess. He needed to lie down.

I slid my door open, wishing I'd tidied things up a bit. I nearly tripped over my phone on the tatami. I helped him onto my pink comforter and he grunted as he swung his legs over.

"Just a minute," I said and raced into our shower room, grabbing a fresh washcloth and wringing it out in the sink. I sat down beside him in my pajamas, dabbing the crusted ink away from the bite marks. The wounds were pink, and he winced as I mopped at them.

"*Domo,*" Tomohiro said through gritted teeth.

"You're welcome," I said. "You look like an ink painting yourself, Tomo. You're bruised black-and-blue, and you're so pale." I felt stupid after I'd said it.

"*Oi,*" he said, but his voice was faint. He was only giving me the reaction I wanted.

"Sorry," I said. I wiped up the last of the ink on his arm and lowered it back down.

He reached for my hand, curling his fingers around mine. "I haven't told you everything."

My mind buzzed with possibility. My skin felt cold as ice where his fingers touched mine.

He looked at me carefully, his bangs spread across the tips of his eyelashes. "When I woke up...Katie, I woke up at Kunozan."

"What?"

"I was there. The gate wasn't damaged, but I was on the other side of it, just inside the trees at the back of the shrine."

My throat was dry. I wanted to go into the kitchen and get my black-bean tea, to pretend none of this had happened. "You were sleepwalking?"

He sounded frustrated. "I don't know." Had he blacked out and gone the whole way to Nihondaira? Maybe it had felt like a dream because he wasn't in control—maybe the Kami side of him had taken over again.

His fingers pulled away from mine and ran through his bangs, pushing them back to his ears as he lay back. "How much was a dream?" His voice got louder, agitated. "I don't even fucking know what's real anymore, Katie. What the hell is happening to me?"

"Hey," I said, my voice shaking. "It's okay. Just lie down for a bit. We'll figure it out."

He grabbed at me, his arms wrapping around and pulling me close. He smelled of warm spice mixed with the sourness of dried ink. My head pressed against his heart, listening to it beat in my ear as his breath tickled against my forehead.

"I'm scared," he whispered, and he was so vulnerable in that moment that he was almost someone else, that I almost couldn't recognize him.

He clung to me until he fell asleep, his chest rising and falling slowly on my soft pink comforter.

It was an hour before he woke up, his eyes opening first and looking around, trying to figure out where he was.

I sat up from the *zabuton* cushion where I'd been hunched over my laptop, searching the internet for any help I could find. Sleepwalking, *inugami,* Susanou, Yomi—none of them had yielded any help. Apparently no one had ever been bitten by a dream before, or whatever it was that had happened.

"Tomo?" I said quietly, lifting my laptop to my table and snicking its lid shut.

"Katie," he said. "How long was I asleep?"

"Not that long." I lifted myself onto the comforter beside him. "Are you feeling better?"

"Yeah," he said. "A lot."

"Good." I'd been worried that being near him would make his nightmares worse.

He scrambled upright, leaning his back against the wall. "Did I…? I collapsed in your *genkan,* didn't I? Oh god. I'm such an idiot."

I scrunched up my face in confusion. "Yeah," I said, "how dare you fall over bleeding in my doorway? What are you talking about?"

"Scaring you. I didn't mean to scare you."

"I'm not scared," I lied. "I'm used to this by now."

"That's not a *good* thing, you know."

"I'm fine with it."

Tomohiro lifted his hand and traced his fingertips down my cheek. I leaned in and pressed my lips again his. The world was sweetness; why did everything feel right when we were like this?

He pulled back just a little, his words floating across my lips. "So this is your room, huh? Where's the giant poster of me?"

"I'm getting it laminated."

He grinned and laced his fingers through my hair, the feel of it sending buzzing happy pinpricks shooting through me.

I stared at the trail of scars up his arm.

"What happened with the police?" I said quietly.

He sighed, shaking out his bangs and leaning back against my wall. "That feels like years ago. Tousan was so pissed."

"I gathered that," I said. I couldn't get the image of him slapping Tomohiro out of my mind. It was so horrible, so cold. What bothered me most was the truth it revealed—Tomo's dad was more worried about his pride than his son.

"You saw," he said, his voice hollow, his eyes tired and red.

I shook my head. "I just saw the way he stormed to his car." At least I could save him some embarrassment. "I called you last night, but you didn't pick up."

"He took my *keitai*. Scared I was going to call my goons and come up with more evil plots." He laughed, but the sound was hollow and filled with scorn.

"How much trouble are you in, Tomo?"

"I have bigger problems than the police," he said, lifting his arm to inspect the dog bite by his elbow. "Sato was in way more trouble than me. They said I was a first-time offender and I didn't use a weapon. Plus when they found out who my dad was, they figured I'd just made a bad choice of friends. They wanted to know why Takahashi was hanging around the police station waiting for me, whether we're both involved in gangs. But at least they figure there's no deeper meaning to my injuries, like gambling on the tournament, so for the moment the pressure's off."

I bit my lip, feeling awkward. "I told him to leave."

"It's not my business."

The guilt pulsed through me and I felt like I would be sick. Somehow him not caring was worse than him getting upset. "Tomo, there's nothing more to it."

"You've become close, though."

"*Chigau,*" I said, shaking my head firmly.

He snorted, trailing his finger down my cheek and onto my lips. "*Usotsuki,*" he accused me, and he was right. I was a liar.

"I wanted to find out more," I blurted. Maybe now was the right time to tell him everything. He was falling apart anyway. Maybe we needed some new info to get the ink in check. "He told me I might be an artificial Kami, that my mom might have ingested the ink. He was right, Tomo."

"What else did he tell you?"

"About the Samurai and Imperial Kami."

Tomo smirked. "He'd like that kind of hierarchy. I suppose he's an Imperial type. An emperor or a prince or some shit."

Wow. He'd hit it on the head. But I didn't like the snarky way he'd said it.

"Actually, he thought you were both Imperial Kami." Why was I defending him? "But I have my own theory."

"Which is?" He tilted his head to one side and his bangs slanted across the tip of his ear. I reached out and tucked them behind it, unable to stop myself.

This was the moment. And it was hard.

"I've been thinking that maybe not all Kami are descended from Amaterasu."

Silence. He didn't understand yet what I was saying.

"There are other *kami,* right? Why should Amaterasu be the only one with children?"

"Of course the others had children," Tomo said. "But not human children. Hell, not even all of Amaterasu's Kami manifest the ink. Why look to other ancestors?" But he sounded uncertain. I could see him processing the idea as he spoke.

"Okay, but she's the *kami* of the sun, right? And your drawings have nothing to do with sunshine, Tomo. Storms, yes. Rain, yes. Earthquakes. Lightning. Dragons and demons."

He laughed once, like he couldn't believe me. "Because that's what I *draw,* Katie! You want me to doodle a sun with a pair of sunglasses on? What about the wagtails and the butterflies? The horse? What about the koi?"

I took a deep breath. "Koi can turn into dragons, too. And one time Amaterasu's brother threw a dead horse at her to frighten her."

His eyes went dark then, not alien and vacant like when the ink took over, but like they'd been extinguished. He was staring at me, but I felt like he couldn't really see me. They were cold, like Jun's.

"Her brother," he said, his voice flat. "You think I'm descended from Susanou. The gatekeeper of Yomi."

"I don't know." I reached my arms out wide as I shrugged. "It would make a lot of sense, wouldn't it? Why the ink is so destructive to you, why everything that happens to us relates back to things associated with Susanou."

"Not everything relates back."

"And the shrines you keep dreaming about. Itsukushima Shrine, the one Taira rebuilt—it's dedicated to daughters of Susanou. And Kunozan, where the *inugami* attacked you. It was built by Tokugawa, right? And Tokugawa restored the Sengen Shrine for another of Susanou's daughters."

Tomohiro sighed loudly, burying his head in his hands. "That's messed up," he said, his voice muffled through his fingers. "So I really am a demon, is that what you're saying?"

"I'm not," I said. "I—I just—"

He looked up slowly, his eyes cold and angry.

"You're telling me I'm the heir to the ruler of Yomi, Katie. The World of Darkness. Hell. What does that make me?"

My body buzzed with the adrenaline of telling him the truth, the horror of it. I wanted to be sick. I wanted to run and never come back.

"I didn't say that," I said.

"You're scared of me," he said. "Look at you."

"I'm not." My voice practically squeaked like a mouse.

"Then that's it," he said. "If you're right about this, I'm beyond redemption."

"Look, I'm sorry. I'm not trying to be horrible. I know it's coming out that way. I just want to figure this out so I can help."

"I'm not saying it doesn't make sense," Tomo said. He lay back and rested his arms on the back of his head, his elbows jutting out to either side of my pillow. "But it means we're right back where we started."

I lay down beside him, and he draped an arm over me

without speaking. He didn't hate me, then. "Back where we started. Meaning…?"

He looked at me, and his eyes were deep and beautiful. I wanted to kiss his eyelids, to turn my back on this nightmare and lie beside him forever.

"Meaning," he said, "that you need to run like hell from me."

The tears brimmed in my eyes as I nestled into his warmth. Our legs and stomachs were little explosions of heat where we touched. The spikes of his hair tickled the tip of my ear.

"I don't want to," I whispered.

He kissed the top of my head.

"You have to, and you can't look back."

"I'm sorry." I hadn't meant to break us. I thought there would be hope in figuring it out. But Tomo was right. How could there be hope or exile from what he was? He was falling apart before our eyes.

"*Gomen,*" he said into my hair. "I'm so sorry. I should never have dragged you into this. God, I was so selfish."

"No," I said. "I wanted this. I still want this."

"*Gomen,*" he said again.

And then it was over.

15

I could barely drag myself up for school the next day. How could I face math and biology and chemistry when my world was crumbling? I considered being sick for the day, telling Diane I had a fever and staying under the covers and pretending the world had stopped spinning. But I couldn't hide from this forever. If I stayed home, it would look bad to Suzuki-sensei, and it would be yet another red circle on my list of reasons to go to an international school. I couldn't lose the rest of my life, and so I pulled out my school uniform and tied my red handkerchief around my neck, desperate to hang on to the fragments I had left.

Besides, at least I could see Tomo at school.

Running the other way was not going to be easy.

I walked to school slowly, my blazer buttoned against the fall chill and my kneesocks pulled as high as I could stretch them.

I thought maybe Tomo would have early-morning kendo practice for the seniors, but of course he had the day off, since the prefecture tournament was finished. So when I walked past the Suntaba School Gate, he was there at the bike racks, leaning against the wall and talking to Ishikawa. Their bruised faces matched like a sad pair of twins. Tomo had his blazer completely buttoned, too, and his sleeve cuffs turned down. He'd have to with all those bruises and bite marks.

I watched the two of them together for a minute. A girl stopped to talk to them, her black hair curling around her shoulders. It was like an electric shock pulsed through my whole body. She moved on with a friendly wave, the talk completely innocent.

Oh god. What would it be like when Tomo got a new girlfriend? My heart twisted and felt like it dropped into my stomach.

But he wouldn't, I told myself. It was too risky, so I didn't have to imagine it. He'd be alone…but that was a horrible thought, too.

His eyes caught mine across the courtyard and I felt frozen, thinking of the first time I saw him at the gate that day, the way he'd slouched like he was doing now. He stepped toward me like he had that time. He shoes made the same *click-click-click* on the courtyard concrete. The breeze picked up the scent of his vanilla hair gel and the miso still on his lips from breakfast.

I wanted to kiss it off, but instead I stood and tried to breathe. I watched the *momiji* leaves swirl lazily from their branches and down to the roof over the hundreds of bikes parked in the racks.

"*Ohayo,*" Tomo said, his voice velvet and honey and *mirin* syrupy sweet. I couldn't stand it. I wanted to collapse into his arms.

Instead, I breathed in. And then I breathed out. And my

heart beat in my ears and clawed at my sides like a caged dragon.

"Morning," I said. It felt like a flock of wagtails pecking at my arms and legs.

"Doing okay?"

"Yeah." The sour sound of *furin* chiming in my head.

"I brought you something." He reached into his blazer pocket and pulled his hand out in a fist so I couldn't see what he was holding.

"A breakup present?" I didn't mean to say it out loud, but it was hard enough talking to him right now. Why was he giving me a gift? I thought he'd wanted me to run the other way.

He shook his head, not meeting my eyes. *"Oi,"* he said. "It's not like that. We don't have a choice." He moved his hand toward me and waited, so I held out my palm. He opened his hand, his fingers brushing against mine.

It was like living in one of the Basho haikus we'd learned in Japanese class. The beauty of the dying flower.

On dead branches
Crows remain perched
At autumn's end.

The gift fell from his opened hand into my palm. It was a tiny pouch made of pale yellow fabric, with pink cherry blossoms weaving through the cloth. At the top of the pouch hung a little golden bell and then a braided pink-and-yellow strap for attaching it to a bag or phone. Pink kanji were embroidered on the front, reading from top to bottom.

厄除守

"It's an *omamori*," Tomo said. "A charm from Sengen Jinja. I picked it up this morning."

"You made it through the gate?" I said, but he shook his head.

"I went around." He winked, like it was funny.

It wasn't.

"It reminded me of the *yukata* you wore to Abekawa Hanabi. That moment when I knew we didn't have to say goodbye."

My throat was dry, my voice cracked. "We are saying goodbye, Tomo."

"I know," he said. "But I didn't know that then. I just knew we had possibility. The possibility to choose."

It seemed so long ago. I remembered the stall with the *furin* chimes. *The sound of possibility,* the vendor had said. The chance to choose how your life would go.

"Give me your *keitai.*"

I reached into my book bag and handed it over. He looped the charm strap through the top of my phone, the little bell jingling like a lost cat.

"What does it say?" I said, looking at the kanji.

Tomo's lips were dry. He looked like he hadn't slept all night.

"*Yaku-yoke mamoru,*" he said. "'Protection from Evil.'"

The chill of it broke my heart. "You're not evil."

"I am," he said. "I am."

I didn't know what to say. I wanted to break into a million pieces. He put the phone back in my hand. The little bell jingled.

"May I walk you to class, Katie?" My name melted like sugar on his tongue.

"Okay," I whispered.

We walked stiffly beside each other into the *genkan.* We changed our shoes in silence, on opposite sides of the room assigned to our school years. We joined up in front of the door to the school. He slid it open, and I stepped forward to walk through.

His fingers slid around my wrist and tugged me back gently.

I looked at him, the touch of his warm skin shocking me out of my defenses. I couldn't handle this. We needed to just rip the bandage off, didn't we? This was torture.

We were standing where I'd seen him for the first time, on the stairs where Myu had slapped him, where his drawings had rained down around me.

"*Suki*," he whispered, his eyes gleaming. *I love you*.

"*Suki*," I said.

And then his fingers slipped away from my wrist, like sand in the empty top of an hourglass. Our time was up.

"Sayonara," he said. No one ever said that kind of goodbye except when things were final, when they were over.

"No," I said in English. I refused to say it. I wouldn't. I stepped up onto the school floor and turned toward my room. He followed me like a ghost. •

I walked slowly, not wanting to reach the room. Then it would be over.

It was already over.

Everyone stared at us as we passed. I guess we both looked like a wreck. But they were staring way too intently—how would they know we broke up? I touched my hand to my face. Was something up?

Tomo noticed, too, and glanced at me with a confused look.

Maybe they'd heard about the kendo tournament? But no one was congratulating him on his incredible matches or perfect form. No one was saying anything loud enough that I could hear.

They were whispering.

"Something's wrong," I said, and we peeked in the next classroom.

A group of second years stood staring at the front of their

homeroom, hands dropped to their sides or covering their mouths. None of them paid attention to us arriving.

I stepped into the room.

Giant kanji made of thick ink dripped on the front wall of the class, spanning the chalkboards from floor to ceiling. The ink oozed slowly down the characters like blood and pooled on the floor with an oily sheen.

Demon Son, it read. *You cannot hide.*

"Oh my god," I whispered, my eyes wide. I'd never seen anything like this before.

Behind me I heard a crash, and I turned. Tomo was shaking, his book bag on the floor with its contents spilling out. His eyes were huge and horrified.

"Katie," Tanaka sang from the hallway, walking over to us. "Tomo-kun." He grinned. "Wrong classroom, dorks."

"What the hell is this?" I said, pointing at the ominous kanji.

"Some kind of stupid prank," Tanaka said. "It's in all the classrooms."

Tomo's words wavered, his voice barely audible. "All of them?"

"Yeah."

Tomohiro bolted across the hallway, and I followed. He raced in the doorway, where another group of students stood gawking at their ink-coated chalkboard.

There is no escape from betrayal. You will kill.

I lifted my hand to my mouth as I started to retch. This couldn't be happening.

Tomo burst from the room and raced down the hall; I chased after him. He sped toward my classroom, 1-D. He slid the door open so hard it slammed into the wall.

I entered the room behind him.

There is only death. She must die.

It couldn't mean me, could it? It couldn't.

My legs collapsed under me.

Someone caught me as I went down. All I could think was how different his arms were from Tomohiro's.

"Katie!" Tanaka said. "You okay?" Tomo couldn't take his eyes off the board.

I steadied myself against Tanaka. He was strong for someone so lean and willowy. He helped me stand as Yuki twisted between the rows of desks to reach us. "I know," Tanaka said. "It's bad. But don't get too upset, okay? It's just a stupid prank."

I wish.

Yuki rested her hand on my shoulder. "Who would do something like this?"

Suzuki-sensei entered our classroom, stopping abruptly as he stared at the giant kanji.

There was silence for a moment while he was as stunned as the rest of us.

Tomohiro looked deathly pale. I could see his hands shaking from here.

Suzuki's face turned bright red. "Who is responsible?" he said, his voice boiling over like a rice cooker.

No one answered. I chanced another look at Tomohiro. He needed to get out of here before people noticed him. He didn't belong in our classroom; what if they accused him of writing the kanji? Tanaka had told me before that Tomo's calligraphy style was really easy to pick out. Was this it? And was this his fault? Like the fireworks, this was ink that had spun out of control. It had to be him—it couldn't be anyone else.

"Who is responsible?" shrieked Suzuki, and the sound jolted the class to movement.

"We don't know, sir," Tanaka said. "It's in every classroom."

"Tanaka, get the headmaster."

Tanaka nodded, then looked at me with concern. "Will you be okay?"

Yuki reached for my arm. "I'll help her," she said. "Go." I looked at her gratefully. I probably wouldn't collapse again, but I was glad to have her beside me.

"Yuu Tomohiro," barked Suzuki. "Get to your own classroom. Now."

Tomo didn't move. He stared at the board, transfixed.

"Who did this?" Tomo said, his voice wavering.

I stared at him. What did he mean? He knew it was the ink, didn't he?

His voice shook with anger. "Who the *hell* thought this was funny?" He looked around the room, his eyes narrowed and fiery. My stomach flipped with fear. *Don't lose control,* I pleaded in my head. *You'll only make it worse.*

"Yuu," Suzuki snapped. "Out."

"Maybe you did it," said a voice at the back of the classroom. Everything turned to ice as I stared at the student who'd spoken up. "We heard what happened at the prefecture tournament," he said. "The ink that splattered on the ground when you knocked that boy over. You could write kanji like these. Didn't you used to be in Calligraphy Club with Ichirou?"

So someone else had seen it, and now everything was unraveling.

Another student chimed in, "I saw the police take you away after. I heard you bashed in Takahashi's hand so you'd win."

"That's a lie," I said before I could stop myself.

"I heard he had to transfer schools because he almost killed a kid," said another classmate.

"Enough," ordered Suzuki. "Yuu, to your classroom. The rest of you, keep it to yourselves until the headmaster gets here."

We don't know who's responsible, and pointing the finger at each other won't help."

Tomohiro shook, heaving in deep breaths. He stared at the last boy who'd spoken. "You don't know anything," he said. "I didn't do any of this. I would never hurt anyone." His eyes flashed to me. "Never."

"You did," the boy said. "You almost killed him."

"It wasn't me!" Tomo shouted. "*This* isn't me!" He stormed to the front of the classroom, knocking over the desks in his way. They crashed to the ground on their sides. I cringed against Yuki at the sound of it.

"Yuu-san," Yuki called out, but he didn't listen.

He reached for the huge kanji that said 死, "death." He pressed his palms against the chalkboard and smeared the ink around, blurring the strokes of the kanji together until it said nothing at all.

"*Yamenasai!*" ordered Suzuki, but Tomo didn't stop. He moved on to the next, his hands stained black as he crossed out the kanji. It splattered around like a modern-art project, dripping down his arms onto his white school shirt and the cuffs of his blazer, dripping onto his bare skin where the top buttons had been left unbuttoned.

"Yuu, *yamenasai!*"

The tears blurred in my eyes as I watched him. He stalked out of the room and to the class across the hall, swiping his hands through the ink on their wall, the blackness of it dripping in his hair and onto his gold buttons.

"*Chigau!*" he yelled. *It's different,* it meant. *It's not true. It's not who I am.* Every meaning of defiance held in that single word. "*Chigau! Chigau!*"

"Tomo," I cried, staggering across the hallway. "Stop."

He looked at me, and the pain in his eyes hurt so much that I felt it. I could feel the pain in my heart, as if it were my own.

His body heaved with his breath, and then he took off running down the hallway. I followed; I couldn't lose him, not now.

"Tomo!" I shouted, but he didn't slow down. I could hear his cries of anguish as he raced through the hall, leaving a trail of ink behind him.

He entered the boys' change room by the gym, where he always prepared for Kendo Club. I pushed the door in behind him. I thought for a minute and locked the door behind me. If he was going to be taken over by the ink, then I needed to salvage what was left of his secret.

Along the white tiled wall ran a row of faucets, all sharing the same deep troughlike sink. Tomo fumbled with the tap, his slippery ink-covered hands shaking too much to turn it on. The tears streaked down his face, carving lines through the splatters on his face, trailing along the edges of the bruises.

The tap finally turned, and he reached his hands under the flow to wash the ink away.

But there was no water.

Ink poured from the faucet, spraying against the bottom of the trough and coating Tomohiro's hands black.

He wailed and turned on the next faucet, and more ink poured out.

"Tomo," I said, reaching for the faucet near me. We turned them all, and the ink flowed in. I twisted the handles shut but they kept pouring, the trough filling up with blackness, ink spilling over the sides and dripping onto the floor.

Tomo let out a scream and hit the side of the trough with his palms. He turned and slammed a bathroom stall door as hard as he could. It swung inward and crashed against the wall, the sound echoing around the change room. Tomo dropped down by the trough, his feet flat and his arms wrapped around his knees. He let out a strangled sob. "I'm not evil. I'm not."

I bent down beside him and wrapped my arms around him, the ink warm and slippery against my blazer sleeves.

"I know," I said. "I know." But I didn't know. I wasn't sure. The more I saw, the more I thought it might be true after all, as horrible as it was to admit.

"I didn't choose this," he said, his voice frantic. "I never chose this. Why am I being punished when I didn't have a choice?"

Someone pushed against the locked change-room door, and we looked up, eyes wide.

"Yuu-san!" Headmaster Yoshinoma banged against the door, his voice gruff and serious. "Open this door."

"I can't let them see me like this," he whispered, his inky fingers linking with mine. "What am I going to do?"

I looked at the door on the other wall of the change room that led to the tennis courts. "Run," I said. "Go somewhere safe."

"Where do I have that's safe?"

More banging on the door. "Yuu!"

"Go," I whispered harshly. "Home."

"I can't. My dad's home until lunch and he'll kill me if I show up during school hours. And I can't go to Toro Iseki."

"Nihondaira, then."

"How the hell am I going to get so far?"

"It's quiet up there, isn't it? It's safe."

He nodded.

"Go ahead, and I'll meet you there later."

His eyes widened. "You can't. What if it gets worse? You have to stay away, Katie. Promise you'll stay away."

"You know I can't do that."

"Please." He was using puppy-dog eyes. It wasn't fair. "You can't follow. I'll text you, okay?"

"Yuu, if you don't let us in right now—"

"Run," he said. "Get out of here so you don't get in trouble."

"Too late for that," I said. "They saw me chase after you. I'll stay here and smooth it over. Just go!"

"I'm sorry." His fingers squeezed mine, the ink warm as it squelched between us. Like we were in kindergarten playing in the mud, about to get in trouble for wrecking our uniforms. I wished that was all it was.

"Go!" I hissed. The headmaster pushed against the door, and then Tomo was gone, out to the tennis courts and around the side of the school. He'd make for the bike racks, and then? Wouldn't everyone notice him stained with ink? I hoped it would dry, lift off him like sparks or golden fireflies the way it sometimes did.

"Yuu Tomohiro!" barked Suzuki-sensei's voice from the other side of the door. I went along the row of taps, twisting them off as I approached the door. It was easy now that Tomohiro had left. The last two ran clear trails of water through the ink as I turned them off. I pulled the dead bolt back on the door and swung it open. Headmaster Yoshinoma was there with Suzuki-sensei beside him, followed by Watanabe and Nakamura. They all peered at me, awaiting an explanation.

"He's not well," I said. It's the first thing I could think of. "He left. He feels sick."

"I bet he does," Suzuki-sensei said, "pulling something like this."

"*Chigaimasu,*" I said, using the polite form of the word

238 • AMANDA SUN

Tomo had shouted over and over. *It's not true. It's different.*
"It's not what you think. This is a prank, but he didn't do it."

"Then why did he run?"

The headmaster peered past me into the change room, his
eyes bulging. "And what happened in here?"

I looked carefully at the teachers. I needed a good explanation.

"He was washing the ink off, but they ran it through the
pipes somehow," I said. "Look, there *was* an incident in elementary school, but it wasn't Tomo—Yuu's fault. A dog
attacked his friend, but he always blamed himself. This is
bullying, Headmaster. It's a bullying prank. Yuu wouldn't do
something like this."

I paused, hoping they'd believe me.

"Katie, back to class," Suzuki-sensei said at last. "This doesn't
concern you."

Like hell it didn't.

"Suspend him, I think, and possible expulsion," muttered one
of the teachers, and another nodded in agreement.

"But—"

"Back to class *now*," Suzuki-sensei said, and I knew I had lost.
I nodded, walking toward my classroom.

But as soon as I was around the corner, I dashed for the
genkan. I pulled my shoes on quickly, waiting to be discovered, but with the chaos no one seemed to notice. I snuck a
peek at Tomo's cubby—empty, his notebook and shoes gone,
his slippers scattered on the floor by a trail of black ink. They
must have fallen out in the hurry. I shoved my uniform loafers on and raced into the courtyard, tucking my hair over my
shoulder to try to conceal it.

Sneaking out of school sucked when you were the only
blonde girl.

The ink trail stopped at the gate of the school. I thought about hiding in Sunpu Park until Tomo was ready for me to join him in Nihondaira. He would text me eventually to meet up, wouldn't he? Was it really too dangerous to be near Tomo? No—it scared me more to think that he was up there on the mountain alone. What if he fell apart? What if he lost himself?

But it was more than I understood, more than I could handle. I needed help. Whether Tomo liked it or not, we couldn't do this alone.

I turned sharply down the street and ran toward Katakou School.

16

I raced through the courtyard, the crowds sparse with all the students in class. I could phone Jun's *keitai,* but that would get him in serious trouble with his teacher—if he even heard it ring.

I stopped at the entrance to their *genkan.* How would I find Jun? I didn't even know his classroom.

I could hear voices from the side of the school, girls chatting and laughing. I walked around the side of the school to look—maybe they could help me. I started preparing myself for the mortifying questions I'd ask. What if I got in a lot of trouble for being on school grounds during classes?

But this was big. I thought of Tomo cycling toward Nihondaira—panicked, not sure what was real, what was a dream. Not sure what was going to happen to him, or to me.

I reached the school tennis court. Girls in white shirts and green shorts, the school PE uniform, bounced tennis balls on their rackets, up and down, never going anywhere, always the same, hoping they wouldn't drop them.

Please don't let my world drop.

And then I recognized one of them, the girl I'd met a few times in the courtyard of the school. She caught sight of me, too, as I shyly pulled away from the side of the building.

"Hana," I said, but my voice was too quiet for her to hear me. She made some excuse to her friend and jogged over, her hair pulled back by a white terry-cloth headband that was too tight for her head.

"Katie," she said in English. "Everything okay?"

"Not really. Do you know what class Jun is in? I need to talk to him."

She looked over her shoulder at the group of girls, who were pretending to play tennis while eavesdropping and whispering about me. "You could get in a lot of trouble for being here during class hours."

"Believe me, I wouldn't be here if it weren't important."

She hesitated a minute. "I think he's in Hasegawa's class," she said, "but I'm not sure. But you're in luck—we've been given a free period this morning to work on our demos for the upcoming school festival."

Right—the music he'd been practicing with Ikeda. It was hard to imagine he had a normal school life. It was hard to remember any of us having a normal life.

"You remember the music room?" she said, and I nodded. "Go one door farther, and you'll find the auditorium. I bet they're practicing in there."

"Thank you," I said.

"Just try not to let anyone see you and your friend, okay? And don't tell them I helped you."

What friend, I wondered? She must mean Jun. "No problem," I said and she smiled, raising her racket behind her head, her other hand gripped around the tennis ball.

"You could be really good for him, you know?" she said.

"He just hasn't been the same since his dad— Anyway. See you later."

"Oh, we're not—" I said, but she'd already turned back to her tennis practice. I turned and sidled along the building, trying to look as inconspicuous as a blonde *gaijin* in a different school uniform *can* look sneaking around a wall. How long ago had Jun's dad died? Did everyone know what had happened except me? I thought about what Jun had said at the police station, how he was recognized wherever he went. Had journalists like my mom dug at his life story and published in the newspapers? I wished I'd thought to search him on the internet the way I'd searched Tomo. I wondered what I'd find.

I eased through the *genkan* and down the maze of hallways toward the music room. Whenever I came to a classroom, I ducked under the row of windows and crawled. I felt like a moron, but a stupid thrill ran through me anyway. I felt like I belonged in one of those police dramas Jun liked as my elbows skimmed the cold vinyl floors of the school.

I thought of Tomo in the wide-open space of Nihondaira, the sky above him. It had looked dark on the way over from Suntaba, like it was going to rain. Was he sitting beneath the giant bonsai tree waiting for me? I crawled faster.

I reached the last classroom and hurried down the hallway to the music room. I went one past to the auditorium, which had multiple doors for entering. I approached the closest and pulled the cold metal handle.

The door opened to darkness and warm, musty air. It smelled stale and slightly metallic, like gum and spit, like old sweat on fabric and carpets that needed replacing. I walked soundlessly between the rows of seats. The floor sloped down to the stage in front of me, where three soft spotlights lit up the stage just past a glow. My eyes adjusted, and then I saw him.

Jun sat in a black chair in the middle of the glowing lights. He wore his white dress shirt and navy pants, his blazer crumpled over the side of the stage with his book bag leaning against it. There was a strip of black against his wrist where he wore the studded bracelet that covered some of his Kami scars. As he moved under the spotlights, the spikes around his wrist and the earring in his ear glinted like some sort of broken Morse code I didn't understand.

He held his cello upright and the bow spanned the instrument, poised the way he held his *shinai* before a match started. I looked for Ikeda and a black piano to materialize in the shadows of the stage, but she wasn't there. Jun and I were alone in the darkness, in the thick air heavy with silence.

He drew the bow across the cello.

The richness of the wood vibrated through the air, the sound so deep I could feel it in my heart. The panic I'd arrived in retreated to the back of my mind for a moment. His life was so composed and peaceful next to the one I was living. Jun was a calm lake; Tomo was a waterfall. And I was the water, swept every which way, unable to shape myself into what I wanted.

The tone of the cello lifted through the auditorium. The notes were quick, always returning to a deep constant sound in between the higher melody. The tone was mournful and joyful at the same time, bittersweet doom with a note of hope in it. Beethoven, maybe? No...I knew this piece. Mom had listened to it before when she was writing a piece on a local cello player who'd joined the New York Philharmonic.

Bach. That was it. One of his cello suites. The deeper notes resonated in my rib cage. It was beautiful, but sad. It sounded like everything could just fall apart.

I walked toward the stage, and then a glint of gold in the balcony caught my eye. I looked up, and my eyes widened.

Ribbons of ink danced in the air, fluttering like slow-motion streamers on castle turrets. They shimmered with a rainbow sheen of oil, rippling with each note Jun sounded from the cello. They draped around the room like scarves, twirling and wafting on the air. When they touched each other, little puffs of gold dust sparkled down like dull stars.

I'd never seen the ink do something like this. And Jun wasn't even drawing. It was like when Tomo had said the ink was using him as its canvas. Jun was the canvas now, and the ink was painting beauty around him.

The Bach suite came to an end, and Jun started into the next one, his eyes closed. But he blinked them open as his fingers trailed up the strings, and then he saw me there, watching him.

The notes of the cello stopped. The silence closed in around me.

"Katie," he said, and the ribbons melted into the air, nothing left but a golden dust falling from the sky like smoke from a firework.

"Jun," I said, feeling exposed all of a sudden. The ink on the chalkboards came back to me, Tomo's awful cries of anguish as the taps poured ink into the trough.

Jun frowned, seeing the look on my face. *"Doushita?"* he said, angling the cello away from his body. He lay the instrument down beside his chair. "What's wrong?"

"It's Tomohiro," I said, and the oddness of using his full name wasn't lost on my ears. Just like I'd tried to appease Tomo by calling Jun by his last name, now I was trying to smooth things over with Jun by distancing myself from Tomo. Just to be polite, of course. That was all there was to it.

"Did something happen to him?" he asked. He moved from

his chair toward me and then sat on the stage, his legs dangling over the side and his fingers curled around the edge. If he reached out his foot he could easily tap it against my elbow.

"At school," I said. "When we got to class, there were ink messages written on all the chalkboards. Huge kanji, from the floor to the ceiling. It was awful. They all said things about death and betrayal, that there was no escape."

"Che," Jun swore, reaching to rub his earring between his fingers. "Everyone saw it?"

"They think it's a prank."

"Where is he now?"

"Nihondaira. I thought he'd be safe there."

Jun nodded as he watched me. "Would you like me to drive you there?"

"Oh." I hadn't even thought he'd offer. *Yes.* "I can't yet. I promised him I'd stay away until he texted me it was safe. What if I make it worse?"

Jun was silent, which didn't surprise me. He'd been saying that since the beginning, that I would make Tomo lose control until he wasn't himself anymore. Until the Kami desires took over.

Oh god. It was happening, wasn't it? This was the moment he'd warned me about. My pulse raced in my ears. Tomo was being taken over by the ink. Would he look at me and see nothing, no recognition of who I was? Would he…would he hurt me?

The tears flooded my eyes before I could stop them. It wasn't the kind of cry I wanted to have in front of anyone, let alone Jun. It was a cry that was ugly and strangled. I couldn't stop myself as the sob racked my body. I tried to hold the next one in, but that only made it bubble out in an awkward sound.

"Katie," Jun said, and he pushed himself off the stage with

his palms. He rushed toward me, his footsteps soft against the plush carpet. His arms wrapped around me and the warmth of him enveloped me.

The sob choked in my throat from the surprise of it. It felt strange; his body curved differently against me than Tomo's did, just enough for me to think, *This isn't Tomo. It's someone else.* A dumb thought, maybe, but it's what my brain mustered in the moment.

Jun's arms draped across my back, his chin curved around my neck. He spoke quietly, his mouth right beside my ear.

"All these tears," he said. "All these tears Yuu has caused you." His arms were strong but gentle, the lick of blond at his ear distracting and too bright as it pressed against my cheek.

His low voice was warm against my skin. "I wouldn't make you cry, Katie."

He moved his head back, his melted eyes looking into mine. I could barely see him, the tears lingering in my eyes as I looked on in stunned silence.

Then he pressed his soft lips against mine.

Warmth and guilt collided in a jolt that sent me reeling. My heart pounded in my chest. A tear that had rolled down my cheek pressed against his cheek from the closeness of us. He smelled like lemons and *yuzu* fruit, like ink and rosin. The combination made me feel just a little ill, but even worse—I kind of liked it.

I had to stop the kiss. Even if Tomo and I had broken up, which I wasn't completely sure was the case, I knew this was wrong. Feeling this way was wrong. But as I stepped back, Jun stepped forward, and our lips stayed touching. His arms moved from my back until they were draped lazily over my shoulders, his hands clasped behind me. I tried to muster the strength to pull away from him again.

It was wrong to be tempted by something like this. Tomo needed me. Even if we couldn't be together, even if he'd told me to run the other way... I mean, Jun was a Kami, right? He'd only cause me the same trouble.

Damn it, why haven't I pulled away yet? It was like we were both lost, like we couldn't remember what was real. Some kind of strange dream.

I tried to step back again and my *keitai* fell from my pocket. The little bell on the charm Tomo had given me jingled as it hit the floor.

Jun pulled away from me at the sound, resting his forehead against mine.

"I'm sorry," he whispered. "I shouldn't have done that."

"It's okay," I said and then realized that was a stupid thing to say.

Standing here near the spotlights blotted the rest of the auditorium into darkness. Jun had messed up my hair when he'd hugged me. He smoothed it out and tucked it behind my ear, the cool tips of his spiked bracelet grazing against the skin.

"It's not," he said. "I'm not the kind of guy who goes after someone's girlfriend. Please don't think that. God, I'm sorry. I just— *Suki da kara.*" *It's because I like you,* he said, the guilt heavy in his words.

He didn't say anything for a moment, and then I realized he'd confessed his feelings. What was I supposed to do?

Refuse him politely. "I'm sor—"

"It's okay," he said, his hands dropping to his sides. "I just... It kills me to see you hurt like this, Katie. I want to be the one that protects you. Not him." He ran a hand through his hair as he sighed.

I bent down and picked up my phone. The little bell on

the charm tinkled as I shoved it back into my pocket. *Oh god, Tomo. I'm sorry. I'm so sorry.*

"I have to go."

"Of course," Jun said. "Let me drive you to Nihondaira."

"I don't know if that's a good idea."

"I've ruined everything, haven't I?"

"It's not that. I just—"

My phone started to buzz just as Ikeda burst in the auditorium door.

"Jun," she said, racing down the sloped aisle toward us. "What the hell's going on?"

"Ikeda," Jun said, his nose scrunching up as he said it.

I opened my *keitai,* wondering if it was the text from Tomo I was waiting for. I felt like crap. Kissing another guy while he was having a meltdown alone. I was the scum of the earth.

"You guys weren't alone," Ikeda said.

Jun tilted his head. "What are you talking about?"

My eyes went huge as I saw the text.

A photo of Jun and I kissing. It couldn't be.

"Some pregnant girl from the girls' school north of Suntaba," Ikeda panted. "I recognized her uniform in the hallway. When I asked what she was doing in the auditorium, she ran."

"Oh my god," I said. "It was Shiori." That's what Hana had meant when she said *you and your friend.* Shiori had followed me here.

I turned my phone to show Jun the picture and the text that went with.

Tomo deserves better. Break up with him or he'll be the next to see this photo.

Ikeda saw the photo and looked at the floor, her face flushing with color.

"Shiori's actually blackmailing me," I said in disbelief. Was she that desperate?

"Where did she go?" Jun asked Ikeda, but she shook her head.

"I lost her," she said. "I wanted to make sure you were okay, so I didn't follow her."

I raced my fingers over the buttons, trying to think what to say.

Tomo and I broke up. Don't send the photo.

It was true, sort of. I needed to talk to him first. If he saw this photo in the state he was in now...

"I have to get to Nihondaira," I said. "Now."

Jun nodded. "Let me drive you. Bike's out front."

"I'll come, too," Ikeda said, but Jun shook his head.

"We're fine," Jun said. "Stay here in case Hasegawa-sensei comes looking for me. Say I had to get new strings for the cello. Anything."

"Sensei's not going to come looking for you," Ikeda said, reaching for Jun's arm. "What are you talking about?"

Jun flinched away from her touch; he meant it to be subtle, but I saw it. I saw the way Ikeda's face fell.

"Just stay here," Jun said. "Katie, let's go." His fingers wrapped around my wrist and tugged me forward. I looked back as he pulled me toward the auditorium doors. I saw the hurt on Ikeda's face. I saw her hands curl into fists as she looked down at the carpet.

Jun and I hurried toward his motorbike, while my phone buzzed with another text.

Liar. You're still with Takahashi. You took Tomo from me. Now I'll take him from you.

"Shit," I said, straddling the bike as Jun passed me a helmet. "She's going to send Tomo the photo."

"He could lose his mind to the ink if she drops that on him now," Jun said. "Hurry."

I nodded, tugging the helmet strap too tight. It pinched my skin as Jun revved the bike to life.

I should never have listened to Tomo and stayed away. I should have been with him in Nihondaira from the beginning.

I had to make things right now.

I hoped I wasn't too late.

17

I clung to Jun's waist as we sped up Nihondaira Mountain. It felt strange and awkward to hold him after what had happened, but I tried to ignore it. I had to reach Tomo before it was too late. I'd made a mess of things.

The sky melted into grays and shadows as we ascended the mountain.

"What's up with the sky?" I shouted into the wind. It had been sunny this morning—why the sudden gathering of clouds?

"It's Yuu," Jun said. "Remember the storm he pulled up with the dragon? He's causing some kind of weird weather up here."

What was he drawing? What was the ink drawing on him?

Jun pulled into the deserted parking lot by the ropeway to Kunozan. It was empty up here, cold and silent.

I got off the bike and yanked the helmet off my head, placing it in Jun's waiting hands. "I'll take it from here."

"You're joking, right?" He pulled off his helmet and his black-and-blond hair flopped out to the sides. "What if he got the picture text? He's already in bad shape from what you told me. If he's going to destroy himself, there's no way I'm going to stand by and let him take you with him."

I hesitated. That's what he'd almost done, wasn't it? With the *shinai* in kendo practice and the words on the chalkboard. *She must die.* Did it really mean me? Could the ink really kill someone?

"Jun," I said quietly. "Remember when you asked Tomo to kill Hanchi? On paper?"

He stared at me, his eyes cold and his head tilted in confusion, like he couldn't believe I was talking about this.

My throat felt too dry. "Can he really do it? Can a Kami really kill someone like that?"

"They can," Jun said calmly, and my heart dropped to my stomach. "Most Kami can't. But some…yes."

"How do you know?" I said. "Did the Yakuza ask your dad to…to kill someone?"

Jun looked annoyed, his face flushed. "It doesn't matter how I know. It matters that the Yakuza don't ever get their hands on someone like Oyaji again."

The term he used for his dad…it was tough and a little unkind. He should've said *otousan* or *chichi*. It was subtle and probably nothing, but it made me feel weird.

"Jun, what did they make your dad do? I have to know what a Kami is capable of."

He shook his head. "You don't understand. My dad screwed around with the Yakuza and got burned. I won't let Yuu hurt you, okay? That's all you need to know. Go help him before he self-destructs."

He was right. I couldn't waste more time on this.

"Okay," I said and took off down the curved road toward the clearing and the giant bonsai tree.

The clouds were so thick they blotted out all sunlight. It was like a solar eclipse up here, and I stumbled over my feet in the dark as I ran. Thunder rumbled in the distance.

I reached the clearing, but it was pitch-dark. Only the ghostly glow of Mount Fuji's snowcap in the distance gleamed with light.

"Tomo?" I called, my voice wavering. I swallowed and tried again. "Tomo?" He didn't answer. I walked toward the tree to see if he was sitting there.

He wasn't, but his black notebook lay among the roots. Its covers bulged with a stack of torn pages inside. The cold autumn wind twisted my hair in front of my face and I tucked it behind my ears. The jagged edges of pages poked out at odd angles. He'd done a whole collection of drawings—why tear the pages and then stuff them back into the notebook?

Come to think of it, he'd made excuses about these torn sketches before. He hadn't shown them to me. He'd been irritated when I asked to see them and shoved them deep into his bag while he changed the subject.

Jun had listed the signs of losing control to me on the phone. Blacking out, worse nightmares, over-the-top anxiety—unexplained sketches.

I pinched the edge of the cover with my fingers and pulled it open to the loose pages.

I gasped.

It was me. He'd sketched me.

Some were on notebook paper, tiny sketch pads or napkins, one on *genkoyoushi* grid paper. Not always the same pose, but all had the same terrifying look that filled me with dread. He'd drawn me in a long kimono with phoenixes and hundreds of flowers sketched onto the fabric. In some of the drawings I was holding a giant shield or something with weird designs, like a gold disc that reached from the ground to my waist. My hands rested on the top of it, the long kimono sleeves draped over it almost touching the ground.

Each of the drawings was unfinished, a final line missing that joined my ear to my chin or the waist of the kimono to the ground.

The cold wind gusted again, and the kimono in the drawing spread to either side, billowing like a cloak around the sketch of me. The wind scattered the stack of drawings and they tumbled through the field in every direction.

"Shit!" I yelled, racing after them. I caught a few, but they swirled every way; I couldn't catch them all. One lodged in the branches of the tree high above.

"Katie?" Tomo said, and then I saw him at the edge of the clearing. He held one of the escaped drawings and he stared at me in surprise. Trails of ink had dried on his arms, but his face and hands were washed clean, probably from the nearby pool.

"Tomo, the drawings!" I said. The wind slowed and the papers floated down to the soft grasses. Their corners tugged in the breeze.

"You opened my sketchbook?"

Shiori's threat was momentarily gone as I stared at the drawings I'd managed to catch. At least Tomo was talking coherently. Maybe he hadn't seen the picture of Jun and me yet. And this was a much more serious problem. I didn't know why, but every nerve in my body pulsed. *Run,* they said. *Run like hell.*

"What are these?" I managed, the drawings crinkling as my hands shook.

He didn't answer me.

"Tell me! What the hell are these?"

"Amaterasu," he said.

"BS," I said. "These are drawings of me."

He said softly, "I know."

Me as Amaterasu. My blood turned to ice. Thunder rumbled in the distance.

Tomo walked toward me, stooping as he went to pick up the scattered drawings. "For a month I've been waking up with a pen in my hand and a new sketch in front of me. The nightmares that went with them were horrible. I've never drawn things like that in my sleep before. I've had ink splattered on the walls or dripping on the floor, but never a finished drawing."

"They're not finished," I said. "One line's missing in each of them."

"I know, and thank god."

"Why didn't you tell me?" I shouted.

"I didn't want to freak you out, okay?" he snapped back.

"Well I'm freaked out!"

"That makes two of us."

"What do they mean?"

"I don't know," Tomo said.

"They're creeping me out."

He ran a hand through his hair. "I was scared to destroy them. In case…something happened to you. So I collected them and tried to keep them safe."

Why would he draw me as Amaterasu?

The idea jolted through me like electricity.

"Tomo," I said. "I'm a manufactured Kami."

"I still don't like that term."

"Fine, but who are most Kami descended from? Amaterasu, right?"

He blinked, and then he got it, too.

"You're descended from Amaterasu," he said.

"The ink in me makes you stronger because it's more power

to add to yours," I said. He was standing so close now that I could feel the warmth of his body as it protected me from the cold wind around us. "But you're descended from Susanou."

"Which means we're enemies," Tomo said. "And that's why the ink's attacking you."

"And why we can't be together," I said. "Oh my god, Tomo."

"It can't be," he whispered. He dropped the stack of drawings and they took to the wind again, scattering across the field. He fell to his knees, his hands pressed against the cool grass.

I fell to my knees, too, placing the drawings I'd collected in the notebook and closing the cover. I couldn't believe it—after all this, after everything we'd vowed to change. We couldn't take our lives into our own hands. We'd never had a chance to be together.

The silence of the clearing suddenly filled with the revving of a motorbike. It got louder as it approached, and then the headlight beamed against us, blindingly bright. Tomo looked up, surprised.

What the hell was Jun doing? He'd promised to stay away.

But there were two people on the bike, and the bike wasn't Jun's. It was black with a blue stripe along the side, not quite as sleek in its build.

A second bike, Jun's, throttled around the curve of the road.

"Katie!" he called out, but I could barely hear him over the rumbling of the idling motors. Both bikes shut off, and the driver and passenger of the first one got to their feet, lifting the helmets from their heads. The passenger rested a hand on her swollen, pregnant belly.

Shiori and…and Ikeda.

"Shiori?" Tomo said, staring at them. "What the hell is going on? Did they hurt you?"

Of course. He'd think Jun and Ikeda had brought her as some kind of bargaining tool for him to join the Kami.

But I knew better. I knew why she was here.

Jun slammed his helmet against the ground as he stormed forward. "Ikeda, what's going on?"

"Katie's been keeping something from you, Tomo-kun," Shiori said.

"Stop it!" I shouted. She had no idea what she was doing, the damage she could cause.

Jun grabbed Ikeda's arm and swung her around to face him. "What are you doing?" he hissed.

"I went looking and found her in Sunpu Park," Ikeda said. "She was having a crisis of ethics, you could say. I thought it would be better to bring her face-to-face with Yuu, to make sure she wouldn't chicken out."

"What the hell is wrong with you?" Jun snapped.

"She's not the only one suffering," Ikeda said quietly, looking at me. "Go on, Shiori. Set this straight. We haven't done anything wrong. We don't have anything to hide."

Shiori pulled out her phone, her buttons beeping as she sorted through her files. So she hadn't texted him after all.

"What's going on?" Tomo asked me, rising to his feet.

"Tomo, it's not what you think." My pulse drummed in my ears.

Shiori threw her phone in the air, and it came down like a shining, falling star. Tomo caught it, turning it to face him.

"There," Shiori said, her voice quivering as she held back the tears. "This is what you gave up everything for, Tomo-kun."

I watched the pain carve its way onto his face as he stared at the photo of me kissing Jun. I wanted to look away. He crouched down slowly, pressing his knees into the grass. The

LCD screen cast an eerie light on his face, bathing him in light and shadows as his eyes filled with angst.

"Yuu, it's not Katie's fault," Jun said. "You pushed her away. You made her cry."

I felt ill. Jun was *not* helping.

The look on his face broke my heart in two. I wanted to take him in my arms, but I was scared he'd push me away. "Tomo, I swear, it's not what it looks like."

"Don't try to talk your way out of it," Shiori smirked. "I didn't send him the photo." She paused, stepping closer to Tomohiro. "I sent the video."

Oh god. "You took a video? What kind of twisted person are you?"

"You're one to talk, aren't you, Katie?" she said. "You kissed for eleven seconds, if you look at the video clock. It's not exactly like you tried to stop it." Shiori leaned over Tomohiro, resting a hand on his shoulder. He didn't shrug it off, but sat there looking numb. She reached out to press the play button on the screen, to put Tomo through all of it again. She tilted her head to the side. "From the looks of it, you were quite enjoying yourself."

"You don't know anything!" I screamed. I stepped forward, too scared to reach out for him. "Tomo, let me explain. Please. Look at me." But he wouldn't look up. He tilted his face forward and his copper bangs fanned over his eyes, hiding them from me.

He flipped the phone shut, pressing it into Shiori's hands. A flash of lightning lit up the sky, and a distant thunder rumbled.

"*Betsu ni,*" he said, looking disinterested. "No big deal."

I froze, my pulse in my ears. Shiori looked stunned.

"What?" she breathed.

"I said it doesn't matter," Tomohiro said.

"But, Tomo-kun. Katie cheated on you with your kendo rival. You're telling me it doesn't matter?"

"*Sou,*" he said. He raised himself to one knee and then stood, towering over her. "It doesn't."

I glanced at Jun, who looked as puzzled as I was. Ikeda sat down sideways on her bike, her fingers tapping on the handlebars.

"Katie doesn't belong to me, Shiori," Tomo said quietly. "She's free to choose her own life and who she wants to be with. If Takahashi makes her happy…then I'm happy."

"Oh, what a load of crap," I said. The adrenaline coursing through my body made me feel woozy. "Like you'd be happy if I was with Takahashi. And you know I'm not with him. Why are you spouting this kind of philosophical garbage?"

Shiori took a step toward Tomo, taking his hand with hers. "Tomo-kun, come back with me. I would never put you through any of this." She looked down at her stomach, the bulge of it. "We can be happy."

"I don't want to be happy, Shiori," Tomo said. He pulled his hand from hers, his eyes burning into me. "I love Katie. And if that means I have to suffer to keep her safe, then that's what I'll do. If it means I have to stand aside so someone else can take care of her because I can't…I will stand aside. That's what love is."

"Tomo," I whispered. I felt fluttery and barely there, a mixture of guilt and shame and bliss.

His voice turned dark and mean. "I'm not interested in someone who would blackmail and betray her way into a relationship. That's ugly, Shiori."

The tears brimmed in her eyes.

"Tomo-kun, I just—"

"Don't call me that," he said. "Yuu will do."

The tears spilled over and she ran from the clearing, tipping from side to side with her heavy belly as she went.

"Hidoi," Jun said, turning his head to watch Shiori go. I agreed—that was cold of Tomo to do. But I couldn't blame him. The pain on his face was horrible, but I was scared to reach out to him. What if he refused?

"Get out of here, Takahashi," Tomo warned. "I don't have anything to say to you."

"I came to make sure you're okay," Jun said. "Katie told me about the ink on the chalkboards this morning. Anything you want to tell me?"

"Like?"

"Blackouts? Weird drawings you can't explain? Nightmares getting worse?"

Tomo's voice was like stone. "No." He was lying, but I didn't blame him. After seeing Jun and me kiss, he hated him even more.

"Denial won't help, Yuu."

"I'm not going to join you, so fuck off."

Jun shifted his weight as he looked at me, his eyes cold and gleaming. "Right now my concern is Katie. You're putting her in danger."

Tomo narrowed his eyes. "I never asked her to come here." The words stung, even though I knew he meant it as a way to protect me. I wanted to be here with him. I should've come by myself right away. "You might not be past using her to get to me, but I would never hurt her, so you can piss off."

"Using her!" Jun laughed. "Is that what you think? No, Yuu, you wouldn't knowingly hurt her. But you can't ignore the warnings written on the chalkboards. What if you kill her?"

"They're just threats!" Tomo shouted, rising to his feet. He curled his hands into fists at his sides. "Just nightmares."

Jun's voice thundered, "They're not. We both know that. You're a weapon, Tomo. You were created for a single purpose. Judgment. Retribution. That is all."

Tomo shook his head. "I won't accept your lies." He uncurled his hands and looked up, his eyes lit with flame. "I. Won't. Kill."

Ikeda spoke up. "That's what Jun said, too."

I whirled around to face her, and so did Jun.

Ikeda looked down at the ground, her eyes soft. "He knows, don't you, Jun? Why don't you tell Katie how you know so much about what Kami can do?"

"Ikeda," Jun said. "Not now."

"No," Ikeda said, balling her hands into fists. "I think Katie should know what happened, don't you?"

The blood in my ears hummed. What the hell was going on here? More secrets?

"Why don't you ask him, Katie? What happened to his dad? Then we'll see where your loyalties lie."

"That doesn't matter right now!" barked Takahashi.

"They need to know," Ikeda shouted. "I have stood by you through everything, Jun. I can't stand by anymore and watch everything fall apart. Yuu needs to know what the ink can do to those you love."

"What happened, Jun?" I said. Tomo flinched beside me, but said nothing.

Jun stood, heaving deep breaths into his lungs. His blond highlights almost glowed in the darkened clearing. His eyes were cold and distant. He was remembering something awful. I almost didn't want to know.

"My dad was bringing in a lot of money from his Yakuza

work," Jun said, his voice soft, younger somehow. "Until the accident. One of the guys they sold guns to didn't like the merchandise, so he came to get his money back. There was a struggle...my dad was shot." He ran a hand through his hair and leaned against his motorbike. "They didn't want to send him to a hospital because the police would get involved...so they assigned him private care from within the Yakuza chapter. A nurse. She took care of him, came into our house while Mom was at work and I was at school." His hand balled into a fist and his eyes flashed with...sadness? Anger? I backed up a step. I didn't like where this was going.

He stood up and walked past Tomo and me, standing at the edge of the little bridge over the two pools of water. Mount Fuji gleamed in the distance.

"She fell for him," Jun said at last. "And that bastard snuck around with her for months before we found out. I came home from school early one day...I'd found out that I'd passed my entrance exams for junior high." He lowered his head and then crouched down in the grasses beside the water. He shook his head, as if trying to get rid of the memory.

"Shortly after, his father ran off with her," Ikeda said.

Jun grabbed a stone from the side of the pool, flipping it over and over between his fingers. "Mom cried for months. We didn't have enough money because he spent it all on that bitch while we scrounged for bills. Do you know what it's like to try to study for exams while your mom is sobbing in the next room? Do you know what it's like to consider working for the Yakuza just to pay for your school fees?" He whipped the stone at the water and it splashed loudly. The water sprayed around him, beads of it catching in his bangs. He stood, turning to face us.

This was the worst part. I knew it.

"What did you do?" I whispered.

Jun's shoulders hunched over as he stared at the water. "It was an accident."

"Thought you didn't have accidents," Tomo said. "So I'm not the only unstable Kami after all."

Ikeda sat on the edge of her bike. "He was doing his homework. His mom was wailing in her bedroom. And everything boiled over. I've seen the notebook, Katie. It's still in his room. Pages and pages of scribbled kanji in every direction. Scrawls and torn paper. Everything underlined, smudges in dark black ink and pencil."

Jun's voice shook. "I couldn't take it anymore. What he'd put Mom and me through."

My throat was dry. I didn't like this story. I didn't like it at all. "What did he write, Ikeda?"

"'Bastard. I hate you. I want you to die. DIE. DIE. DIE.'"

"And he died," I whispered.

Jun was silent, so Ikeda spoke up. "He collapsed while shopping in Ginza in Tokyo. When the police came they recognized the nurse and arrested her for past Yakuza crimes."

"It was the Yakuza who did it," Jun growled. "If he hadn't got involved with them, he'd still be alive."

"Oh god, Jun," I said, shaking. "You…you killed your own father."

He looked at me, his eyes cold and his fists at his sides.

"*They* did," he said. "I wasn't responsible. How would I know writing a word in my own notebook would kill him? He drove me to that point!"

I raised my hand to my mouth.

"You need to know," Ikeda said, "what Kami are capable of. Go back to America, Katie. There are dark places here where you don't belong."

"You're wrong." I shook my head. "I belong here. I'm part Kami. This is my world, too."

"No, she's right," Tomo said, and I glared at him. "My drawings could kill you. Even my words."

"Did you forget Ikeda is on their side?" I said. "Of course she's going to say that. This whole story is to drive me away from you." *No,* I realized as I said it. Her story was to keep me away from Jun. It was her own form of manipulation, just like Shiori had done with Tomo. Ikeda wanted Jun to herself; that was all. She wanted to scare me off him.

It was working.

"Katie," Jun said, turning to face me. His eyes were warm, his hand outstretched. I could barely look at him; I was terrified. He'd killed someone. He'd killed his own dad. "Please don't be afraid of me," he said. "I would never hurt you. I'm not the same as I was then. I've learned to control the ink better."

He took a step toward me, and my stomach twisted. "Stay back."

The warmth in his eyes blinked out. He stood for a moment, saying nothing. Then he threw out an accusatory hand at Tomohiro.

"This is your fault," Jun snarled. The wind gusted around us, his blond-and-black hair tangling around him.

"It's always someone's fault but yours, isn't it, Takahashi?" Tomo said.

Jun's face darkened. "You know nothing. Don't you dare bring judgment on me. You killed your mother, too."

Tomo look like he'd been slapped, his eyes filling with pain.

Jun laughed. "Oh, yes, you think I didn't look up your history, Yuu? You blame yourself, don't you? She was bringing you your lunch. If you hadn't forgotten it, she wouldn't have crossed when the truck pulled out. You're just as guilty. And you nearly murdered your friend Koji by summoning *inugami*. And now your next victim." He raised his hand to me, and I shivered. "She chooses a demon over me. A dirty bastard child of Susanou's."

Tomo shook with every breath; he was pain, he was fury. "You're crazy," he whispered.

"Everything in my life has always been taken from me," Jun said. "I won't let you take Katie, too."

"She's not a thing to be taken," Tomo said. "She makes her own choices."

"You can't deny your attraction to her," Jun said. "I felt it, too. The ink flowing in her veins."

I pressed my lips together, narrowing my eyes.

"That's why you pursued her, isn't it?" Jun continued.

Conflicted expressions flashed on Tomo's face. I knew that had been a part of it, at first. The Kami blood calling out to itself. But we were more than that now. Trying to turn us against each other wouldn't work.

"She's an amplifier to the power," Jun said. "Don't tell me you didn't feel it."

My heart nearly stopped. The cold way he talked about me, like I was just an object. It started to make horrible sense— he barely even knew me. Why would he ask me out for coffee over and over? What made him so interested in me when he had someone like Ikeda who worshipped the ground he walked on?

My lips trembled as I spoke. "You didn't care about me at all, did you? You only cared about the ink in me."

"You can't be blind to the power you radiate," Jun said.

Nerves fluttered and clawed at my sides. "You used me."

Jun shook his head. "Every prince is adorned with a crown jewel. We need each other."

"I don't need you," I spat.

Jun smiled darkly. "You're wrong. You'll see when Yuu finally submits to his true lineage. It's time to face your destiny."

Tomo's voice was as dark as night. "I will never submit."

"Then I'll force you," Jun muttered, and there was a rush of ink. I could hear it, could smell its sour metallic scent. I felt like the ink inside of me lit on fire. Blackness spread across Jun's back, dripping down to the grass as it twisted and shaped into feathery raven-colored wings. The wings flapped back and forth, spraying his arms with inkblots that trickled down to his palms. They pooled in his hand and poured into the shape of a black kendo *shinai,* which he held out toward Tomo.

"You're falling apart at the seams," Jun said. "You're going lose your mind to the Kami side of you, and there'll be nothing left to do but break you."

"You can't stop me," Tomo said, his voice growing deeper, louder. "I have the power of Yomi at my fingertips. You think you can stand against me?"

I caught a whisper on the wind, like a crowd of voices speaking at the same time. It had been a long time since I'd heard it last. It gathered, louder and louder. A flash of lightning lit the clearing, and the thunder rumbled closer than before. The rain started to leak from the gray layer of clouds.

"You can't stop me," Tomo said again, and his voice had changed. His eyes were flooding with blackness like pools of ink. I was losing him.

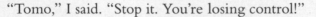

18

"Tomo," I said. "Stop it. You're losing control!"

"I'm sorry, Katie," his strange voice said, his eyes on Jun as he started to circle him. His voice echoed as if many others were saying the same words, their timing just a bit off. The ink dripped into his hand until he held a *shinai*, too. It dripped, drop by drop, into wings on his back as black as night. "This is what I am. This is what I will always be."

"Please," I pleaded.

"I will rule this world," Jun said, and his voice, too, was darker, larger. My breath caught in my throat. I'd never seen Jun lose control before, never heard him sound like that. I flashed a look at Ikeda, her face crumpled with worry, but she made no move to stop them.

Jun's voice echoed with a tone that wasn't his, the discord of the hundred voices whispering in my ears. "This is your last chance to earn my allegiance, Yuu Tomohiro. If you don't yield, I will take you down."

A sinister smile curved on Tomo's lips. "Try it."

Jun leaped at him, swinging the dripping *shinai*. Tomo's *shinai* cracked against it, and the ink splattered around them.

I backed away until the sharp bark of the tree pressed against my back.

"Jun," Ikeda finally called out. "Leave it." He didn't answer her. "Your wrist!"

Tomo heard her and struck at his weak wrist, but Jun pulled his arm back before he could hit it. He swung at Tomo and the *shinai* smacked him in the back, knocking him forward onto his knees. Ink feathers tumbled from his back and caught on the wind, lifting up into the clearing.

Jun swung his *shinai* to hit him again, but Tomo rolled out of the way and kicked at Jun, knocking him backward.

"Guys, cut it out!" I said. "This isn't going to solve anything."

"They won't listen," Ikeda said. "You said Yuu is descended from Susanou, right? And Jun from Amaterasu. That means the *kami* haven't stopped fighting for thousands of years. The warriors change, but the fight doesn't."

The *shinai* cracked together and lightning forked through the sky, followed by a loud crash of thunder. The rain started to pour from the dark clouds, smearing the ink in trails down their faces.

Jun smashed his *shinai* into Tomo's leg and he collapsed into the mud. I gasped, running forward to help him.

"Stay back!" Tomo shouted, lifting his arm up to me. Jun's *shinai* slammed into his back and he fell forward into the mud, his arm still outstretched.

"Stop it!" I shouted at Jun and pulled at his shoulder.

The moment my fingers touched his shoulder, a shock went through me like I'd touched an electric fence. Every nerve in my body alerted, like I was seeing things more clearly, more sharply than before. The rain sounded louder. The echoing voices thundered in my head. The touch jolted Jun back, too.

The ink in me was awakening. I could feel it, like noticing someone who'd been sitting quietly in the corner, watching. Waiting.

Tomo was on his feet and he dropped his *shinai,* shoving Jun back with both hands. Jun was still stunned from the shock between us and he fell easily, thumping hard against the ground.

Tomo fell on top of him and punched him in the jaw.

Jun cried out, and the falling rain turned to ink. Lightning struck the top of Mount Kuno beside us, where Tokugawa's shrine stood. Tomo looked up at the inky rain, and Jun took the chance to shove him off and get to his feet. He stretched out his empty hand, and the ink collected in it like a pool of dark water. It stretched out until he held two *shinai,* one in each hand.

"Is that it?" Jun taunted, his body hunched as he heaved in breath after breath. "I was expecting better from the Demon Son."

"I'm not finished yet," Tomo said, the ink stretching into a second *shinai* in his left hand. "You're still breathing."

"Sorry to disappoint," Jun said. And then he flapped his inky wings and lifted into the sky.

Tomo bent his knees and yelled out the loudest *kiai* I'd ever heard. He pushed off the ground and they were both in the air suddenly, *shinai* cracking against each other like some kind of synchronized movie fight.

I knew there was a style of kendo that involved a *shinai* in each hand, but I didn't know either of them knew how to do it. And maybe they didn't. Maybe they were going on pure instinct. Each crack of the swords against each other caused a flash of blue lightning and a rumble of thunder. The rain drenched the clearing, leaving puddles of ink everywhere.

"They're going to kill each other!" cried Ikeda through the bursting rain. Would they go that far?

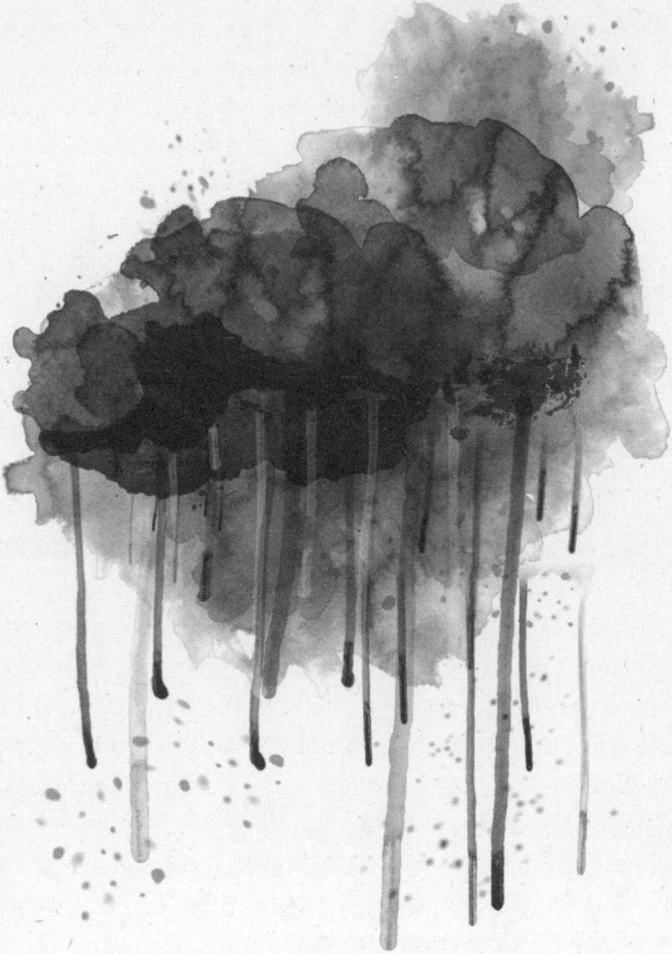

Jun would. He had.

Oh god. We had to stop them.

Tomo's copper hair was slicked to the sides of his head, the ink running through in streaks of black. The feathers on their backs melted and reshaped under the relentless pelting of the rain. Jun shrieked at Tomo, and Tomo yelled back, and they crashed into each other again, their wings beating hard against the sky. The grasses below me bowed over from the storm.

Susanou was the *kami* of storms. The harder they fought, the worse the storm would get, and I didn't know how to stop it. The clearing was flooding, and with this much ink around, what if Tomo lost his mind? I had to stop Susanou's blood from awakening in Tomo.

Ikeda was right. Susanou and Amaterasu would never stop fighting. I couldn't stand against Susanou alone. I needed an ally.

Tomo's drawings lay scattered and torn in the mud, blotted badly by the rainfall of ink. I grabbed the nearest one, but it was too smudged to be of any use. I reached for Tomo's notebook and opened the cover. All the drawings inside flailed in the storm and ripped at the pages, trying desperately to get out. The crossed-out koi were biting each other's tails in a chain, trying to form themselves into a long, sleek dragon. The horse we'd ridden in Toro Iseki was bolting and rearing, whinnying in terror. The wagtail beat his wings so hard that he flipped the pages of the notebook back to the beginning. I saw his sharp talons pressing through the layers of paper as I forced my way through the pages.

I grabbed one of the Amaterasu drawings and slammed the notebook shut. I reached for the pen hooked over the cover page.

Nervously, I traced the final line from my ear to my chin to make the drawing complete.

Nothing happened. As usual, my Kami power was too weak to do anything but send Tomo's and Jun's powers spiraling out of control. Just like I couldn't destroy the dragon Tomo had drawn, I couldn't complete his drawings either.

Jun slammed Tomo in the sky and he fell with a crash into the pool. Water sloshed up in a fury of white foam and murky ink. I crumpled the drawing in my hand and raced over. I reached the edge of the water just as Tomo came up sputtering for air, his wings melted and drowned. The pond was only chest deep, but Tomo slipped and stumbled in the pool, his energy gone. His eyes had returned to normal; the human part of him was in control.

Jun hovered above like a dark angel, watching, a black *shinai* in each hand.

I helped Tomo out of the water and onto the shore, where he collapsed.

"He's strong," he panted.

"You're stronger," I said. "You just need stay in control."

"Get away from him, Katie!" Jun yelled from above. "He'll only bring more sadness and destruction."

"Urusai!" I shouted at him. "Enough, Jun!"

He shook his head slowly. "I should've finished this the last time," he said in the voice of many, holding his two *shinai* out at angles away from his body. "He's an abomination. There were never meant to be Kami like him. He's unnatural."

Unnatural. He didn't fit in, like me. Neither of us belonged. But that meant we could carve out a space where we belonged. I didn't believe he was dangerous. I knew there was more there. Potential lay before us. Possibility and choice.

I grabbed Tomo's right arm and wrapped his fingers in a fist around the pen. I placed the paper underneath, just as Jun pulled back the *shinai,* ready to descend on Tomo.

Jun flapped his wings once, backing up higher into the air for the assault.

Holding Tomo's arm, I drew a shaky line connecting the sketch's ear to her chin.

The lightning and thunder pulsed at the same moment. It boomed in my ears so loudly I screamed.

Jun plummeted from the sky and into the second pool of water, sending angry caps of foam spitting onto the grassy edges.

The rain slowed, and it took a moment for the blinding bright light to fade. Ikeda raced to the pool where Jun had fallen, reaching into the dark waters and pulling him out.

The ground started shaking violently, the sound of it like thunder.

"Earthquake," Tomo said. "Come on!" We limped away from the giant tree in case it decided to heave itself over. Everything shook and I lost my footing, stumbling into the mud.

The earthquake stopped as Jun leaned forward on the edge of the pool. He coughed the water out of his lungs. His wings had dissolved in the water like Tomo's, his eyes clear as he regained control.

Tomo helped me upright and then stared back at Jun. At the edge of the water, the black ink that had seeped from Jun's back twisted upward, wriggling as it formed the body of a snake.

"Oh my god," Tomo said suddenly. "I'm not the descendant of Susanou."

"What?"

He slowly raised his pointed finger toward Jun. "He is."

19

"Lies," Jun barked, but Tomo shook his head and pointed toward the snake. Jun looked back, his eyes wide.

"Susanou's messengers," Tomo said. "It makes so much sense. You're the one who's dangerous, Takahashi."

"Impossible," Jun said. He splashed his hand through the ink, grabbing where the snake's neck would be. He throttled the column of black until it splashed back into the water. "I have control over my powers. You don't."

Tomo shook his head. "I don't think you do. I saw your eyes, heard your voice. You're as unstable as me. You've trained a bit.... So what? You still have the nightmares. You still black out, don't you? You've killed, Takahashi. You've gone to darker places than I have."

"I was younger then," Jun snapped. "You had your share of accidents, too."

"The earthquake," Tomo said, "and the fireworks that rained down. Even this ink rain—they didn't happen until you were here."

"So what?" Jun said. The water curved around his cheeks and dripped down his chin. "You and your dragon caused that storm in Toro Iseki. And Katie said she's felt tremors before, just her."

"It's not about starting storms or tremors," Tomo said. "You called up those snakes, like the ones Susanou fought in the myths. You want to take over Japan like he did. You're the one who takes lineage from him, not me."

Ikeda wrapped an arm around Jun but he shrugged it off, stumbling to his feet. "You don't have any proof."

"Neither do you," Tomo said.

"My control is my proof," Jun said, stretching his palms out to his sides. "My power is my proof. I'm an imperial descendant of Amaterasu. I will be a king, Yuu. And you are heir to nothing but the darkness and filth of Yomi." He spat as he spoke, and I saw the distaste in his eyes, not for Yuu, but the lack of lineage. The shallow desire for a princely line.

"You're wrong," said a voice like mine, but I hadn't said anything. It had come from the edge of the forest, where the slope cut away near the ropeway to Kunozan. I turned to look.

She was gleaming in the darkness like a papery ghost. The edges of her face and hair were Tomo's jagged pen lines, the hair left white and colorless where mine was blond. It was drawn up in a tight bun with curls that draped over the top of her head. A hairpiece of white cherry blossoms dangled down in plastic chains in front of her forehead, like the hair ornament I'd worn to Abekawa Hanabi. Her eyes were doe-like and gentle, but she held her head with confidence and poise, which made her innocent nature look like an act. She had that air to her like someone who knew way more than she let on.

She wore an old-fashioned kimono, not at all the kind worn to summer festivals. It looked more like the ones from *seijin-shiki,* the ceremony when you become an adult and don those elegant *furisode* kimonos with the superlong sleeves that reach to the ground. And believe me, those were some elaborate outfits. Flowers of every size and shape had been sketched into her kimono, all colorless and empty. The color of the kimono shaded from white to gray to black on the hem and sleeves. Large phoenixes and chrysanthemums tumbled across the skirt of the fabric, and a thick gray obi was tied stiffly around her waist.

The paper version of me, the drawing Tomo had made.

She was beautiful, more beautiful than I was, and elegant. I blushed as I realized she was how Tomohiro saw me, how he had sketched me. But was that true? He'd sketched in his sleep. I hoped I looked like that in his subconscious, full of strength and sure of myself.

"Katie?" Tomo said with caution, looking at the paper girl.

She stared at him with her large eyes, her pupils pools of black ink.

"Yes," she said. "And no."

"Masaka," Tomo whispered, and he stepped back. "The drawing…you're from my dream."

"It was the only way to reach you," she said. "It was the only way to push you toward your destiny."

Jun's voice rang out from beside the pools. "You *drew* Katie?" he shouted. "Are you an idiot? Don't you know that could hurt her?"

I felt nauseous as I looked at her. Tomo's drawings often gave me motion sickness, but not like this. I took in deep breaths of the cold air, trying to steady myself against the tree trunk.

"He didn't have a choice," said the paper girl. "I forced his hand while he slept."

"Why?" Tomo said. The ink dripped through his copper hair and down his face like black tears.

"Because you are at war," she said. "You don't know who you are."

"He's the heir of Yomi," Jun said. "Susanou's descendant."

The paper Katie looked at Jun, her eyes shining like black stones. "No. You are."

Jun laughed darkly and stumbled forward, Ikeda holding him upright. "Of course you'd say that. You're from Yuu's subconscious."

"Nevertheless," she said, "there is no escape for you." There was a beam of bright white light, and I had to shield my eyes. When the light faded, she held the giant shield from the drawing. She twisted it, with effort, the whole shield groaning as it turned in the muddy grass. It wasn't a shield at all. It was a mirror, a huge mirror lit by the same papery-white glow as the rest of the girl.

I was filled with a horrible sense of dread. I didn't want to be here. I didn't want to see this.

"Don't fear the mirror," the paper Katie said to me. "Your ink is weak, and not yours, but it *is* from Amaterasu."

But Jun was transfixed. He limped forward, stumbling. He must have hurt his leg when he hit the water. He gently pushed Ikeda away, leaving her behind as he dragged himself toward the mirror.

I could see him reflected in it as he approached. He looked the same, but his clothes in the mirror had changed. He wore a dark *montsuki,* a men's kimono, the jacket long and black and flared over the white-and-gray-striped *hakama* skirt. A white knot was tied just above the *hakama* and trailed up in two white cords that vanished under the coat.

I waited, half expecting the image to grow horns or growl at him or something, but it didn't. Nothing happened, as far as I could see.

But Jun saw something else. He gasped and fell to his knees.

"What is it?" I said. "What happened?"

The paper girl looked at me and blinked her eyes, the sound of it like crinkling paper. "He sees himself," she said. "He's always known the truth. He just refused to face it."

"No," Jun whispered, looking at his hands. His voice rose as he spoke, each word wavering. "It can't be. It's not true! They did this to me. They took Oyaji from me!"

"And Tomo?" I said. I couldn't wait any longer. "He's not descended from Susanou?"

The paper girl shook her head. "Yet there is only death for him, because of his struggle."

"Struggle?"

"Tomohiro is from two Kami lines," the paper girl said. "His father was descended from Amaterasu. His mother is the heir of Tsukiyomi."

Tomo's face turned pale.

"Tsukiyomi?" I said. "Who the hell is that?"

Ikeda spoke up. "One of the three," she said. "The three principle *kami*. Tsukiyomi was the *kami* of the moon, Amaterasu's lover. She betrayed him."

There were *three?* Oh god. I'd seriously messed up.

Tomo looked down, his eyes wide. "Tousan is a Kami?"

"One that never awoke," the paper girl said. "But the ink manifested in you, and now you war with yourself."

Amaterasu from his father. Tsukiyomi from his mother. A war within his own blood.

"Then he has a choice," I said, my heart leaping in my chest. "He can choose his fate." He could choose to align himself with Amaterasu. We could be together after all.

"There is no escape," the paper Katie said.

"There is only death," Tomo repeated, as if he'd heard her say it thousands of times. He probably had, in his nightmares.

I frowned. "I don't understand."

"There's no good or bad *kami,* Katie," Ikeda said. "The ink destroys. That's all."

"No," I said. "I don't believe it. I know Tomo. He has a choice. He makes that choice every day. Descent from Susanou or Tsukiyomi or Amaterasu doesn't matter. It's all the same."

"He can't win against *two kami,* Katie," Ikeda shouted, and then I saw the tears blurring in her eyes. "We can't even win against one!"

Jun shouted suddenly, lost in his own battle. Ink swirled around him in ribbons, not gentle like the ones that lifted as he played cello, but violent like snakes, whipping at him as he tried to push them away. *"Uso,"* he spat. "Not after everything I've been through."

"Jun," I said, tears blurring in my eyes. I hated seeing everyone I cared about in so much pain. Jun, who had always been composed and calm—to see him writhing on the ground was too much.

"I can't be the bad guy," he said, his voice hoarse, his eyes filled with tears. "I can't. I don't want to be. Everything... everything is slipping from me. I've lost everything. You've taken it from me, Yuu."

He rose to his feet, new wings spreading out in tendrils of ink on his back.

"You don't know *anything* about me!" Jun shouted, pointing at Tomo. "Anything!" He flapped his wings and tumbled toward a drawing of the paper Katie, clutching it to his chest.

"Takahashi, stop!" Tomo cried out.

With a loud, horrible sound, Jun ripped the page in two.

I screamed as a fire seared through me, as if my body had sliced in two. I dropped to the ground writhing, the world spinning around me. The ghostly glow of the paper Katie dimmed out, and all I could see was blackness. I was losing myself, the way I had when the fireflies attacked me.

"Katie!" Jun shouted as Tomohiro dashed to my side. His warm arms wrapped around me and pulled me from the ground, pressing my head to his chest. Tomo's eyes were on fire as he stared at Jun. "What the *hell* did you do?"

"No." Jun shook his head violently, his eyes wide. "It was only supposed to destroy Amaterasu."

"Katie," Tomo said, and I struggled to hold on to his voice.

Every breath was ice in my lungs, my skin like frost, but my blood was on fire, like molten lava channeling through Antarctica. I could feel it coursing through my veins. I could almost hear it. It stung, like flame spreading through me, leaving every piece of me scorched.

"It hurts," I tried to say, but it came out as a mangled scream.

"What do I do?" shouted Tomo. "Takahashi, what do I do?"

Jun hesitated, his eyes wild, his hands outstretched like he was going to wrench me from Tomo's arms. Maybe he was.

"Takahashi!" Tomo shrieked.

Jun spoke, his voice broken. "Don't let her lose control. She's linked to Amaterasu and so she felt her pain. The ink in Katie is fighting back to keep her alive. It's trying to take over, like it did in you."

"Stay with me, Katie," Tomo whispered as he hunched

over me. I wanted to reach up and sweep his bangs out of his eyes so I could see them better, but my hand wouldn't listen to me. It felt like being in someone else's body and not knowing how to work the controls.

He pressed his lips against mine, but the jolt of it made the fire spark. I jerked away from him, my body arching from the pain.

The movement made my *keitai* fall onto the grass. The little bell on the charm jingled as it hit.

Protection from evil.

How could you protect yourself when the evil was inside? Is this what it felt like to be a Kami?

Katie.

It was Mom's voice, and the sound of it stunned me.

You're not giving up, are you?

It was a memory, sitting at the kitchen table with her after a failed ballet audition. Nothing big—just a part in the class recital at the end of the year. But god I'd wanted it.

You can do this, Katie. Size it up. Move on.

"I can't," I said. "I can't."

But hearing Mom's voice reminded me who I was. The ink in me wasn't everything. It had tried to take my life from me before, when I wasn't even born. And I'd won. I'd won without even knowing. I was stronger; I could beat this.

The fire dulled, and I heaved in a breath of the cold air.

Tomo's chin rested on my forehead, bringing me back to Nihondaira, to my life.

I stared up at the gray clouds that circled the sky. Golden dust glimmered in the cracks between them, shimmering like tiny lightning strikes.

"Katie," Tomo said.

I looked at the relief on his face. Jun hung back, watching with a pained expression.

"Tadaima," I said to Tomo. *I'm back.*

Tomo laughed once and choked it back. *"Okaeri."* *Welcome back.*

"Katie," Jun said. "I didn't...I didn't mean to..."

Tomo glared at him. "Fuck off, Takahashi." He reached for the ink-stained blazer by his notebook and stuffed it gently under my head as a pillow. Then he rose up slowly, walking toward Jun. "Get out of here. It's over."

"It's not over," Jun said, his eyes cold. They looked darker than before. "Or did you miss what your sketch said? We've been enemies since the dawn of time. We must put an end to what our ancestors started."

"Jun, no," Ikeda said.

"Are you a moron?" Tomo said. "I have the ink of two *kami* in my veins, Jun. If I lose control, everyone will get hurt."

Jun stared back, his expression cold. "Which is why I have to deal with you now. I was right, Yuu. The world isn't safe with you in it."

"Jun," I said. I pressed my hands into the soft grass, pulling myself up until I was sitting. "Stop it, okay? Let's end this."

"My thoughts exactly," he said, shoving Tomo backward. Tomo growled in his throat, shoving Jun back.

Jun laughed. "I'm the bad guy, huh? Then I will make you suffer. I wanted to be a king, but if you want a tyrant, so be it. I don't care if you have the ink and blood of two *kami,* Yuu. I'm stronger than you'll ever be."

The ground began to shake. I steadied myself and rose to my feet, pressing my fingers into the bark of the tree for support. Ikeda gasped, and I tried to see what had startled her.

She was looking across Suruga Bay, past the water and the tiny boats, across to Mount Fuji with its snowcapped peak.

I watched with horror as a thick stream of ink gushed through the clean snow on the summit, staining it black. From this distance the torrent looked so small, but I couldn't even imagine how much ink was pouring down the mountain.

A matching streak poured down the left side of Fuji like a tear, carving a jagged path of darkness.

Did Jun have that much power?

His eyes gleamed. "I will make the world cry."

He lunged at Tomo, knocking him over. Sparks of gold and blue crackled around them as they fought. Jun reached his hand into the air and the ink formed into a *shinai,* which he brought cracking down on Tomohiro's arm. It jabbed into the wound from the *inugami* bite and Tomo cried out, his face crumpled in pain. He managed to kick Jun off and rise to his feet. He ran as the wings spread on his back, flapping before they were even strong enough to lift him. He started to rise but Jun grabbed him by the waist, driving him hard into the ground.

It will never stop, I thought. Jun and Tomo. Susanou and Tsu-kiyomi, the *kami* I didn't know anything about. And Amaterasu, the ink that swirled in my veins, too.

Wait. Maybe I wasn't powerless. The ink might not be my birthright, but it had been on fire a moment ago. Maybe I could use it.

I flipped open Tomo's sketchbook, but the pen was lost somewhere in the dark field. I scanned the grass, but I couldn't see anything.

The rain poured down.

The rain.

I cupped my palms together and caught the ink as it fell.

Beside me, Jun and Tomo tore into each other, blood and ink flowing, Ikeda shouting for them to stop. Tomo's eyes had gone large and vacant, and he fought with all the strength he had.

Ikeda stood near me, watching them fight with horror.

"Ikeda!" I shouted. "You're a Kami, right? Can't you do something?"

She crouched beside me. "I'm not that strong. I usually can't get things off the page."

"You have to try," I said. "I'm not strong, either, but maybe together we can stop this."

She nodded. "What do you want me to do?"

I wasn't sure. What was their weakness? Did they have one?

Susanou, *kami* of storms, and Yomi, the World of Darkness. Tsukiyomi, *kami* of the moon.

"Amaterasu," I said. "The *kami* of the sun. The shadows and clouds are making their powers stronger. Can we get rid of them?"

"I'll try," Ikeda said. She dipped a finger into the ink I cupped with my hands, and turned the page in Tomo's notebook.

日。

"That's it?" I shouted. "'Sun?'" Nothing happened.

"I told you," Ikeda said. "I'm not very strong."

"Because there's already sun," I said. "It's just hidden behind the clouds."

She cupped her hands and I poured the ink rain into them, wiping my stained hands on the grass. I dunked my finger in the ink and ran it across the page.

Please, I thought.

天照大神

Thank god I'd practiced my kanji. Thank god I knew what to write.

Amaterasu. The word glowed with a faint golden dust, then turned black again. That was it. That was the extent of my power.

Ikeda dropped the cupped ink with a splash and reached in front of me. With her stained hands, she traced the kanji I'd written, making them darker and bolder.

The word rippled, then gleamed with golden sparks. It flickered with light, the way the fireflies had.

It grew brighter and brighter, and Ikeda backed away, shielding her eyes. All around us the field glowed with crisp white light, the trees turning black and gray, like we were in a moving ink painting.

There was the loud sound of thunder crashing, and Tomohiro and Jun plummeted from the sky, hitting the ground hard. Both of them lay still, unconscious. The bright light faded, until the clearing was normal again, the colors vibrant after so much darkness. The clouds were gone, except a small patch that had floated toward Kunozan, where they zapped into nothingness with a flash of blue light.

"Jun," Ikeda cried out and raced to his side. I stared from Jun to Tomohiro. How peaceful they both looked with their eyes closed. Like they were sleeping.

Oh god.

"Tomo," I said, running to his side.

I smoothed the copper bangs out of his eyes and wiped the ink and blood from his face with the backs of my hands.

Jun moved first, groaning as he turned his head.

"Jun," Ikeda said.

"Naoki," he said, and Ikeda flushed. I wondered if it was the

first time he'd called her by her name. "Katie. Is she okay?"
He called out for me. "Katie?"

Ikeda's face fell. But I was too busy to worry about either
of them.

"Tomo," I said, but he didn't move. I put my fingers against
his lips, and his warm breath spread over them. He was alive,
then. But was he himself or still controlled by his Kami side?

He blinked his eyes open slowly, and my body pulsed with
relief to see the soft hazel of them. He was in control.

"Katie?" Tomo said quietly. He looked at me, broken and
bleeding, covered in mud with ink trailing through his hair.
He'd never looked more stunning.

"You all right?" I said.

He laughed, and it turned into a cough. "I've felt better.
You?"

"I'm fine," I said. "Let's get you home."

"You going to carry me?" He attempted a grin. "I can't
exactly bike right now."

"I'll ask Ikeda. We can come get your bike later."

I turned my head to look toward the pools. Jun was sitting
upright, coughing up ink as Ikeda dunked her handkerchief
in cold water.

I went to sit with her, watching the ripples as she swirled
the handkerchief around.

"Are you okay?" I said quietly.

Ikeda didn't look up. "Jun called for you," she said.

I knew I should be quiet, but her suffering felt like my own.
I didn't want to hurt anyone anymore. "After all this, you're
still by his side. You deserve better, Ikeda. Why do you stay?"

She shook her head. "You don't understand. Jun has always
been there for me. My parents worked all the time, and I had
no siblings. Without Jun, the world was lonely, empty. Mean-

ingless." She pulled the towel from the water and squeezed the droplets out. "I was terrified when my drawings started to move. Jun stayed with me through my first nightmares. He showed me how to survive." She looked at me, her eyes piercing and strong. "I owe him everything, Katie. I won't leave his side, no matter what."

I could understand. It was how I felt clinging to Tomo, when he'd gotten me through the storm of losing Mom and living adrift in Japan. "Ikeda, let's get them home."

"Katie," Jun called out, and Ikeda's eyes went flat and lifeless. The friendship I'd seen sparking suddenly dulled.

"No," she said.

I blinked. No?

"I'm sick of you and your shit, Katie. Shiori was right— you've messed up everyone's lives."

What was I supposed to do? Jun didn't feel the way she felt.

"I couldn't care less if you make it home," Ikeda spat. "Do you know what Jun's been through? His whole life fell apart with a single mistake." She pointed an accusatory finger at Tomo. "Jun tries to help *him,* to give him control of the ink and a chance to rule the world—and he slaps him in the face. *Mou ii wa yo.* I've had enough of your crap."

"Ikeda, enough," Jun said.

Tomo sat hunched over, covered in bruises, blood and dirt. "It's over, Jun. Go home."

Jun tucked his legs under himself. "You're wrong. This won't end here, Yuu. Whether it's me who does it or not, you need to be stopped. You are dangerous; that hasn't changed."

"You're right," Tomo said. "But you're worse. You don't even try to fight the darkness in you. You've accepted your fate. That's something I'll never do."

"There's only death ahead for both of us," Jun said. "You know that."

Tomo paused a minute, looking down at his sketchbook and then across the bay to Mount Fuji. The snow was perfectly white again, like it had never happened.

"I know," Tomo said. "But that's all any of us have in the end, isn't it? There is death ahead of all of us. And so we live."

I returned to Tomo's side and he wrapped his arm around me for support, leaning down to collect his notebook and blazer.

We limped away from them slowly, one small step at a time.

20

We managed to make our way to Tomo's with me pedaling and him seated and slumped over my back. Nihondaira was a mountain, so we mostly coasted down, but I worked up a sweat as we cycled through Otamachi toward his house.

"This is great," Tomo mumbled into my shoulder as I pulled up his front walkway. "Can you bike me home every day?"

I shoved him off and leaned the bike against the side of the wall around his house. "Maybe if you lose some weight," I puffed.

"Hey," Tomo said, flexing his arm. "This is all muscle." But as he pulled his arm back, the bite wound pressed against his skin and he winced, dropping his arm quickly.

"Let's get you inside," I said. He fumbled in his pocket for the house key and I turned it in the lock, the two of us entering the warm house from the outside cold.

He stumbled toward the couch, but stopped as he looked down at the floor. He'd left a trail of ink. "I better shower," he said.

"Can you handle it?" I asked. He was hunched over and didn't look too steady on his feet.

He tried to grin, but it came out pained. "You better come help me."

I turned all shades of red. "Shut up," I stammered. I couldn't believe he could still joke after the video he'd seen of Jun and me. Maybe between that, the fight and the info that he was descended from two *kami* that hated each other, he was still processing it all.

He tugged at the knot of his school-uniform tie, twisting it back and forth to loosen it from his neck. I followed him carefully as he limped toward the bathroom, in case he collapsed.

"How are you feeling?"

"I'll be okay," he said, dropping the tie to the floor. "But I don't think that's what you meant."

It wasn't. Instead I said, "You went through a lot today."

He fumbled with the buttons on his shirt, his tired fingers struggling to undo them. "I bet the teachers had a fit when they saw the change room."

It felt like ages since those threatening kanji and ink faucets at school. "I told them it was part of the prank played on you."

"So I'll probably only be suspended for about…oh, fifty years, then."

"Give or take," I said.

He still fumbled with the same button. *"Kuse-yo,"* he swore, pretending to laugh. "Can't stop shaking." His eyes blurred with moisture, the tears he was forcing back. I wanted to hold him to me tightly, to protect him from all of this.

So I made excuses for him. "You're just tired. Here." I reached for the button myself, slipping it neatly through the hole. He watched me intensely as I tried to force the blush off my cheeks. *I'm just helping him.*

You're undressing him, Katie. But points for trying.

I moved on to the next button. "So...two *kami*, huh? Does that make you royalty or something?" It was a lame joke, but I was flailing. I needed to talk about it, to put it out there in the open instead of just in our own thoughts.

Tomo leaned his head back, his palms flat against the wall. "I guess it's nice to shrug off the connection with Yomi, at least."

I couldn't imagine being descended from the World of Darkness. The idea had crushed Tomo, sent him spiraling out of control.

He sighed. "I'm tired and a little beat-up, but I feel better than I have in a month. Actually, I feel better than I have since you..." He trailed off.

"Since I came to Japan," I said, my mouth dry.

"That's not what I meant."

"Can we really be together?" I asked. I unbuttoned the last of the buttons and dropped my hands away. "It sounds like Tsukiyomi hates Amaterasu's guts."

"I'm not Tsukiyomi," he said. "And you're not Amaterasu. We'll build our own lives." He shrugged his shirt off and it dropped in a mound on the floor. I tried to pretend I was okay with the fact that he was half-naked, but I felt queasy and awkward, like my cheeks were on fire. I looked away.

"Katie," he said, and the velvet of it turned my head. The scars crisscrossed down his arm, broken up by the *inugami* bite marks. Deep blue bruises bloomed on his tan skin, on his shoulder and below his ribs. I stared a little more intensely than I meant to.

Tomo laughed, resting his hand on the waistband of his pants. "I could keep going." He grinned and leaned in to kiss me.

Fire ran through my veins again, sharp and raw, but this kind I didn't mind. This kind was nice. I wanted more.

I wrapped my arms around him, his bare skin like fire under my fingertips. He winced as my hands slid across the bruises he was covered with.

"Takahashi made a mess of me," he sighed as I accidentally pressed against another bruise.

"I think it was the fall from the sky," I said, giving him more excuses. "In which case, it's my fault for writing in your notebook."

He cupped my neck with his hands, resting his forehead against mine.

"How dare you save my life?" he whispered and pressed a kiss on my jawline.

He pulled away and staggered into the bathroom, closing the door behind him.

I breathed out a sigh and turned my back to the door, sliding down it until I sat at the bottom. Why did I have to get so nervous around him? I could handle him flying around on inky wings and drawing sketches of me that came to life, but I couldn't make out with him when he was shirtless? I needed serious help.

From the other side of the door I heard the sound of his zipper and him shrugging off his pants.

Other thoughts, other thoughts...

"Tomo," I said, looking up at the ceiling.

"Hmm?"

"The thing with Ju—Takahashi. I'm so sorry I hurt you. I wish I could go back and change what I did. You know that, right?"

Pause. "I know."

"He kissed me. And I knew it was wrong. It was a huge mistake. I did pull away, but—"

"Katie," he said, his voice smooth and velvet. "I care about you. But I can't expect you to stay beside me. What I am is not going to change. It's going to get worse until…until it's over."

I shuddered. "I know. But I want to be there, until the end."

"I want you to be," he said. His voice was gentle, and I knew he was pressed against the door. This was our life; always something in our way.

I heard his footsteps as he padded toward the shower and turned on the spray.

"I will," I said quietly to myself. "I'll find a way."

My phone buzzed, and the sound of it made me jump. I flipped it open, the little bell on the *omamori* charm tinkling as the *keitai* snapped into place.

"Yuki," I said with relief and hit Answer, putting the phone to my ear.

"Katie!" Yuki said. "Tan-kun and I were worried. Are you okay?"

"I'm fine," I said. My brain cycled back a few hours. She was calling because we'd bolted from the school.

"And Yuu?"

"Doing okay," I said, leaning back. I liked the soothing sound of the shower behind me. It was nice that I was part of something so intimate, even if I was on the other side of the door. "It was a nasty prank."

"So he didn't do it?"

More lies, more deception. My life couldn't be straightforward, not with Tomo. "Of course not. You saw us arrive at school this morning. Why would he do something like that?"

"I know," Yuki said, a hint of apology in her voice. "I just heard the boys' change room was a mess. They all think he did it, you know."

I wanted to care, but it just didn't seem important anymore. Ink on the chalkboards—big deal. It was the *kami* we had to worry about now.

"Let me know if you need anything, okay?" she said. "I'll bring you my notes tomorrow."

"Thanks," I said, and then I hung up the phone. I had the best friends in the world, I really did. They worried about me, watched out for me. So did Diane.

Who did Tomo have?

Me. His dad, sort of. Ishikawa. And that was about it.

I got to my feet and wandered upstairs into Tomo's bedroom. His blue-checked comforter was a tangled mess on the bed and he'd left a couple dark T-shirts and jeans littered across the floor. He still had all the creepy *sumi-e* ink drawings up, and the Renaissance paintings of angels trampling demons.

I sat down at his desk, where he'd left an open notebook and a pile of textbooks meant for the entrance exams. I wondered if he'd ever had time to study for them.

His handwriting was elegant and practiced, and you could see the flair for calligraphy in the kanji. But even then, you could see the careful control he'd written his notes with. Any kanji with the character *sword* in them were given blunt edges, ones that stopped short instead of trailing off in a slice of a line.

I lifted his pen, twisting it between my fingers. His room smelled faintly of his vanilla hair gel; it was nice being in here, when you avoided looking at the creepy paintings on the walls.

I pressed the pen to the paper and drew a tiny heart in the margin of his notebook. Maybe he'd notice it there later when he was studying.

I lifted the pen and felt ill suddenly, like motion sickness.

The heart flashed once with a golden shimmer, and then the pen ink trailed down the center in a jagged line, breaking the heart in two.

I stared at it, stunned. Downstairs I heard the shower shut off.

My drawing had moved. It had come to life and moved.

The ink in me had awoken when Jun ripped that drawing. I was connected to the paper Katie; like a channel between river and lake, she'd made the connection between Tomo's ink and mine.

"Oh my god," I whispered. Maybe it was Tomohiro's closeness in the house that made it move, like how my doodles had come at me that day in school.

But it felt different. I felt different.

Outside a crow cawed loudly, making me think of the rush of black feathers on Tomo's back.

I stared at the heart with its jagged break down the center. We could never be happy; we could never be together.

I wished the ink had never woken in me. I wished it would just go back to sleep.

I blinked, considering what I'd just thought.

The ink in Tomo took control sometimes, but it always

subsided. Jun said one day it would get so bad that it wouldn't reverse again. But for now, it did. It went back to sleep.

I looked at the broken heart again. Two halves. Two *kami*.

Tomo's door creaked open and he stood there in a pair of track pants and a blue T-shirt, his copper hair dripping wet in odd spikes as he rubbed it with a towel.

He saw my face and his arms lowered. *"Doushita?"* He padded across the room to his desk, leaning over my shoulder. His skin radiated warmth from the shower, and he smelled of milky soap. "My drawing moved, Tomo."

"Just now?"

I nodded, pointing at the broken heart with the pen. "I drew a heart, and the ink broke it in two."

He reached over my shoulder to press his fingers against the heart. He'd left his kendo wristband off and I could see the deep gash where the kanji for *sword* had cut him all those years ago, the old wound the dragon had bitten open in Toro Iseki.

"Harsh," he said, tracing the jagged break in the heart. "The ink's cruel."

"That's what I thought, too. But what if it means something else?" I took a deep breath, my whole body buzzing. "Before I came to Japan, the ink in me was asleep, even past the age it should've awakened. And if I'd gone to Canada to live with Nan and Gramps, that would've been a temporary fix because the ink in you would calm down. Like, go to sleep kind of."

Tomo's face darkened. "So we have to be apart."

"No," I said. "That's not the answer. We have to make the ink go dormant, Tomo."

"How?"

I bit my lip. "I'm not sure. But look at this heart. Two sides. Two *kami*. Split them in half. You don't have to worry about Amaterasu. She has lots of descendants and they're living normal lives. It's Tsukiyomi that's the problem. You just have to put his blood to sleep."

Tomo stared with shining eyes, his mind racing with ideas. "Like a disease," he said. "We just have to make the Tsukiyomi cells go dormant."

"There has to be a way, since the ink was asleep inside of me. And you always regain control when it tries to take over. It goes both ways."

"Don't forget Tsukiyomi and Amaterasu used to be in love," Tomo said, hope rising in his voice. "If we can't make it inactive, maybe we can reconcile them somehow. The potential's there. It's not fate, Katie. We can change it. We can fight against it, right?"

I had to believe it. The alternative was too bleak.

"Right," I said, rising to my feet and grinning at him. It was more potential than we'd had in ages. It was a lead—it was a possible cure.

He went to wrap his arms around me, but I stepped back.

"Dirty and gross, remember?" I said, motioning to the ink and mud splattered all over my uniform. He grabbed me anyway, spinning me in a circle as I squealed in surprise. He pulled me close, his chin on my shoulder. His skin was still pink from the shower; the soapy smell was overpowering, but nice.

"We can do this," he said. "There has to be another way."

There had to, because I couldn't imagine life without him.

We clung to each other in his sunlit room with the cheery bedspread and demon paintings.

The crow outside cawed again; the trees in one of the ink paintings swayed in an unseen gust of wind, which plucked the leaves off the branches into the air. The leaves tumbled out of the painting and onto the floor, shriveled blackness collecting around us in a circle on the floor.

You don't scare me, I thought, looking at the inky pile. *Not when Tomo's at my side.*

We will fight you. And we will win.

★ ★ ★ ★ ★

GLOSSARY

of Japanese
Words and Phrases

Ano ne:
"Listen, okay?"

Ano saa:
"Hey, listen"

Ara:
Expression of surprise

Arigatou:
"Thank you"

Atarimae jan:
"That's a given" or "Naturally"

Baka:
"Stupid."

Bentou:
Japanese lunch box

Betsu ni:
"Nothing special" or "Nothing in particular"

Bikkurishita:
"That surprised me!"

Bogu:
> The set of kendo armor

Chan:
> Suffix used for girl friends or those younger than the speaker

Che:
> "Damn it!"

Chichi:
> A humble way to refer to one's own father

Chigau/Chigaimasu:
> Literally "It's different" or "It's not like that," but it's used as a more polite way to say no

Chouzuya:
> An area in a shrine where you wash your hands before praying. Usually bamboo ladles are provided to dip into the basin of water

Daijoubu:
> "Are you all right?" or "I'm/it's all right"

Dame:
> "It's bad." Used to tell someone not to do or say something

De:
> As used in *Rain,* it means "Well?"

Demo:
> "However" or "But"

Domo:
> Based on context, can mean "Hello," "Thank you" or even "Sorry." It's informal and can come across as rough speech

Dou:
> The breastplate of kendo armor

Dou?:

"How is it?"

Doushita?:

"What happened?"

Ee?:

Can be used when one is surprised, impressed or simply listening and processing what someone is saying. Roughly translates to "Is that so?"

Eki:

A train station

Faito:

An encouraging phrase meaning to fight with one's might or do one's best

Furin:

A traditional Japanese wind chime

Furisode:

A more formal kimono with long sleeves, usually for special events like Coming-of-Age Day

Furoshiki:

A cloth used to wrap a Japanese bentou lunch

Gaijin:

A person from a foreign country

Ganbare:

"Do your best," said to encourage one in academics, sports or life

Ganbarimasu/Ganbarimashou:

"I'll do my best" and "Let's do our best."

Genkan:

The foyer or entrance of a Japanese building. Usually the floor of the *genkan* is lower than the rest of the building, to keep shoes and outside things separate from the clean raised floor inside.

Genki dashite:

"Cheer up" or "Feel reenergized"

Genkoyoushi:

A special paper for writing Japanese essays. The paper has separate squares for each kanji or kana written, and text is written up to down, right to left.

Geta:

Traditional Japanese sandals that vaguely resemble flip-flops. Usually worn with a *yukata* or kimono

Gomen:

"Sorry"

Hai:

"Yes," but usually used to let the speaker know you're paying attention

Hakama:

The skirtlike clothing worn by *kendouka*

Hanabi:

Fireworks

Happi:

A special coat worn during festivals

Hara-kiri:

Ritual suicide, also called "seppuku." Part of the samurai code of life in ancient Japan

Heiki:
"It's okay," "I'm fine" or "Don't worry about it"

Hidoi:
Mean or harsh

Hontou ka:
"For real?"

Ii:
"Good" or "Fine," often used in asking permission

Ii kara:
"It's fine (so just do it already)"

Ikuzo:
Guy slang for "Let's go"

Ima deru yo:
"I'm going to hang up now"

Inugami:
A dog demon from Shinto tradition. Known for their uncontrollable wrath and murderous instincts

Itai/I-te:
"Ouch" or "It hurts"

Ittekimasu:
"I'm leaving (and coming back)," said when leaving the home

Itterasshai:
"Go (and come back) safely," said to the one leaving home

Jaa (ne):
"See you later"

Juku:
A type of cram school where students go to prepare for university entrance exams

Kakigori:
Shaved ice with syrup, much like a snow cone

Kakko ii:
"So cool," often used for attractive guys or a guy you look up to

Kawaii:
"So cute!"

Kaze:
Wind

Keiji-san:
Detective

Keitai:
Cell phone

Kendouka:
A kendo participant

Kiai:
A shout made by *kendouka* to intimidate opponents and tighten stomach muscles for self-defense

Kiri-kaeshi:
A kendo exercise drill

Kissaten:
A coffee shop

Konnyaku:
Konjac, a plant-based gelatin commonly served in noodle or slab form in soups or other dishes

Koshi-himo:
The straps used under an obi to tie a *yukata* or kimono in place

Kote:
Gloves worn during kendo

Kowai ka:
"Are you scared?"

Kun:
Suffix generally used for guy friends

Kyu:
Japanese sound effect

Maa, ne:
"Well," but it can be used as a subtle way of affirming or agreeing with something ("Well, yes")

Masaka:
"It can't be" or "No way"

Matcha:
Powdered green tea

Matte:
"Wait"

Mazui:
"Awful," "Gross" or "Bad"

Men:
The helmet worn during kendo

Mirin:
A sweet rice wine used in cooking

Mochiron:
"Of course"

Momiji:
Maple tree

Montsuki:
A formal men's kimono

Moshi mosh(i):
"Hello?" Said when answering the phone

Mou ii:
"That's enough"

Mou ii wa yo:
"That's enough," said in a feminine way

Moushi wake gozaimasen:
Literally "There is no excuse." A very formal apology

Myoji:
Kanji used for writing Japanese names

Nani:
"What?"

Nanimo hanashine zo:
"I didn't say anything," said in guy slang

Naruhodo:
"Is that right?" Often said with a hint of amusement or disbelief

Ne:
"Isn't it?" It can also be used as "Hey" to get someone's attention (like "*Ne*, Tanaka")

Nikujaga:
A meat-and-potato stew

Ochitsuite:
"Calm down"

Ohayo:
"Good morning"

Oi:
   "Hey"

Okaeri:
   "Welcome home," said when one arrives home

Okonomiyaki:
   A Japanese pancake or pizza-type dish where diners choose the ingredients that go into it, such as cabbage or other veggies, noodles, meat or fish

Omamori:
   A protective charm bought at a shrine or temple

Omiyage:
   Souvenirs

Omurice:
   Omelet rice, a popular Japanese dish

Onigiri:
   Rice balls

Ossu:
   "Yes," usually used in martial arts settings. Can also mean "Hi" between two guy friends

(O)tousan:
   A polite term for *father*. It's more polite than *Tousan*

Roumon:
   A large roofed gate, often at the entrance to a shrine or temple

Samui/Sa-me zo:
   "It's cold," the second form being guy slang

San:
   A polite suffix used for people you don't know well or those older than you

Sankyu:
"Thank you"

Sasuga:
"As expected"

Sayonara:
A formal goodbye; not used every day as it has a strong finality to it

Seijin-shiki:
Coming-of-Age Day, a holiday in January where any youth reaching the age of 20 celebrate their adulthood by donning elaborate kimonos and visiting shrines for good luck

Seiza:
A kneeling stance used in kendo

Senpai:
A student older than the speaker

Shabu shabu:
Hot pot, a type of Japanese meal where raw ingredients are cooked in a broth by the participants

Shikashi:
"However"

Shinai:
A sword made of bamboo slats tied together, used for kendo

Shoudo:
Calligraphy

Sou:
"That's right"

Staato:
"Start"

Suki:

"I like you" or "I love you"

Suki da kara:

"Because I like/love you"

Sumanakatta:

A formal apology

Sumi-e:

Ink and wash paintings, a traditional style of Japanese art

Sumimasen:

"Sorry" or "Excuse me." Can also mean "Thank you" in certain contexts

Supa:

A grocery store or supermarket

Tadaima:

"I'm home," said by one arriving home

Takoyaki:

Breaded balls of octopus, often served at festivals

Tatami:

Traditional mat flooring made of woven straw

Tenugui:

A headband tied under the *men* helmet for kendo

Tomodachi kara:

"Because we're friends (that's why)"

Un:

An informal way to say yes

Urusai:

"Be quiet" or "Shut up!" Literally "Noisy"

Uso:

"No way!" Literally "A lie"

Usotsuki:

A liar

Wakatta:

Informal form of "I got it" or "I understand"

Warui:

"It's bad," can be used as an apology (as in "My bad")

Yabai:

"It's bad" or "It's awesome," depending on context (kind of like "It's sick!"). It can also be used to show a situation is dangerous or out of control, as in "We're in trouble" or "We're screwed"

Yamenasai/Yamero:

"Stop right now," said as a command. *Yamenasai* is a little more parental or authoritative

Yatta (ne):

"I did it!" or a general "Yay!" With *ne* it means "You did it, didn't you?" Sort of like "Good job!"

Yo:

A speech particle used for emphasis

Yomi:

The Shinto World of Darkness or the land of the dead. It can be compared to Hell

Yoyo tsuri:

A balloon yo-yo, often part of a festival fishing game

Yukata:

A lightweight summer kimono

Yuzu:
A citrus fruit that tastes like a mix between grapefruit and orange

Zabuton:
A cushion used for sitting on the floor

ACKNOWLEDGMENTS

I am so grateful to everyone who gave their time, energy and encouragement to make *Rain* the story it is. Thank you to the Harlequin TEEN team, who make it possible for me to share Katie and Tomo's story. To my editor, T.S. Ferguson, who understands my characters and world and propels my writing to a higher level so that I am always growing. Natashya Wilson, Annie Stone and all the lovely people in Editorial, thank you for believing in my characters and my stories.

Erin Craig and Kathleen Oudit—you give Tomohiro a voice through your wonderful interpretations of his art. To Mary Sheldon, a rock star and kindred spirit, with gratitude for your encouragement, friendship and keen editorial eye. To Amy Jones, Lisa Wray, Kristin Errico, Kathleen Reed and all the wonderful people who have worked on *Rain,* thank you so much for making it possible for me to tell my story in a beautifully put-together book.

Thank you to my dear agent Melissa Jeglinski, who never fails to believe in and support me. Working with you is a joy.

With gratitude and love to Kevin and Emily, who tirelessly wash dishes, drive me to book events and tiptoe around my office so that I have the time I need to write. I couldn't do it without you, I really couldn't. I'm so grateful.

Thank you to the dear friends who've helped me to shape *Rain*. To Lisa and Ivan Liew for making sure the police procedures in the book were as accurate as possible, and to Kate Larking and her mom for answering my odd questions about wrist fractures. I am grateful to my friends in Japan for giving me a second home I delight in visiting when I write about the Paper Gods. To Mio Matsui, for her expertise in Japanese slang and teen life, and to the Hasegawa and Sugino families for their kindness and generosity.

I am moved by the support and encouragement of all my writer friends and beta readers: Winston Fong, a kindred spirit who allows me to abstract about life, writing and cosplay; Linda van der Pal for our adventures in meeting Neil Gaiman; Leah Peterson and Eve Silver for their incredible cheerleading and inspiration; and Lance Schonberg and Tanya Gough for your friendship as we navigate these publishing waters. Thanks also to the MSFVers and the Lucky 13s, the two writing communities that keep me afloat. And to Nerdfighteria and the cosplay community for being my safe havens of awesomeness and acceptance.

Finally, to my readers: your words and letters have deeply moved me, and I am so grateful to connect with you through my stories. Thank you for allowing me the greatest gift, to share the worlds in my head with you and to give my characters true life through your eyes and ears. I wish you all great possibility.

Now that Katie has discovered the truth about Tomohiro's powers, can she find a way to quell his dark side for good?

And how far will Jun go to achieve his goals?

Look for the thrilling conclusion to
THE PAPER GODS series
coming summer 2015!

Discover one of Harlequin TEEN's most
authentic contemporary voices,

Katie McGarry

Available wherever books are sold!

Praise for Katie McGarry

"A riveting and emotional ride!"
–*New York Times* bestselling author Simone Elkeles
on *Pushing the Limits*

**"Everything–setting, characters, romance–about
this novel works and works well."**
–*Kirkus Reviews* (starred review) on *Dare You To*

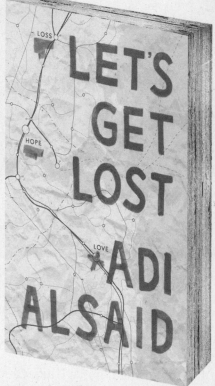